MURDER IN MIDSUMMER

MURDER IN MIDSUMMER

Edited by Cecily Gayford

Ruth Rendell · Arthur Conan Doyle
Dorothy L. Sayers · Margery Allingham
R. Austin Freeman · John Dickson Carr
G. K. Chesterton · Michael Innes
Julian Symons · Ellis Peters

P

PROFILE BOOKS

First published in Great Britain in 2019 by
PROFILE BOOKS LTD
3 Holford Yard
Bevin Way
London WC1X 9HD
www.profilebooks.com

See p. 281 for individual stories copyright information

5 7 9 10 8 6 4

Typeset in Fournier by MacGuru Ltd
Printed and bound by CPI Group (UK) Ltd, Croydon, CR0 4YY

A CIP catalogue record for this book is available from the British Library.

ISBN 978 1 78816 153 4
eISBN 978 1 78283 492 2

Contents

Achilles Heel

Ruth Rendell

The walls of the city afforded on one side a view of the blue Adriatic, on the other, massed roofs, tiled in weathered terra cotta, and cataracts of stone streets descending to the cathedral and the Stradun Placa. It was very hot on the walls, the sun hard and the air dry and clear. Among the red-brown roofs and the complexities of ramparts and stairs, different colours shimmered, the purple of the bougainvillea, the sky-blue of the plumbago, and the flame flash of the orange trumpet flower.

'Lovely,' said Dora Wexford. 'Breathtaking. Aren't you glad now I made you come up here?'

'It's all right for you dark-skinned people,' grumbled her husband. 'My nose is beginning to feel like a fried egg.'

'We'll go down at the next lot of steps and you can administer some more sun cream over a glass of beer.'

It was noon, the date Saturday, 18 June. The full heat of

the day had kept the Yugoslavs, but not the tourists, off the walls. Germans went by with cameras or stood murmuring '*Wunderschön*!' Vivacious Italians chattered, unaffected by the midsummer sun. But some of the snatches of talk which reached Wexford were in languages not only incomprehensible but unidentifiable. It was a surprise to hear English spoken.

'Don't keep on about it, Iris!'

At first they couldn't see the speaker. But now, as they came out of the narrow defile and emerged on to one of the broad jutting courts made by a buttress top, they came face to face with the Englishman. A tall, fair young man, he was standing in the furthest angle of the court, and with him was a dark-haired girl. Her back was to the Wexfords. She was staring out to sea. From her clothes, she looked as if she would have been more at home in the South of France than on the walls of Dubrovnik. She wore a jade-green halter top that left her deeply tanned midriff bare, and a calf-length silk skirt in green and blue with parabolas on it of flamingo pink. Her sandals were pink, the strings criss-crossed up her legs, the wedge heels high. But perhaps the most striking thing about her was her hair. Raven-black and very short, it was cut at the nape in three sharp Vs.

She must have replied to her companion, though Wexford hadn't heard the words. But now, without turning round, she stamped her foot and the man said:

'How can you go to the bloody place, Iris, when we can't find anyone to take us? There's nowhere to land. I wish to God you'd give it a rest.'

Dora took her husband's arm, hastening him along. He

could read her thoughts, not to eavesdrop on someone else's quarrel.

'You're so nosy, darling,' she said when they had reached the steps and were out of earshot. 'I suppose it's what comes of being a policeman.'

Wexford laughed. 'I'm glad you realise that's the reason. Any other man's wife would accuse him of looking at that girl.'

'She *was* beautiful, wasn't she?' said Dora wistfully, conscious of her age. 'Of course we couldn't see her face, but you could tell she had a perfect figure.'

'Except for the legs. Pity she hasn't got the sense to wear trousers.'

'Oh, Reg, what was wrong with her legs? And she was so beautifully tanned. When I see a girl like that it makes me feel such an old has-been.'

'Don't be so daft,' said Wexford crossly. 'You look fine.' He meant it. He was proud of his handsome wife, so young-looking for her late fifties, elegant and decorous in navy skirt and crisp white blouse, her skin already golden after only two days of holiday. 'And I'll tell you one thing,' he added. 'You'd beat her hollow in any ankle competition.'

Dora smiled at him, comforted. They sat down at a table in a pavement café where the shade was deep and a cool breeze blew. Just time for a beer and an orange juice, and then to catch the water taxi back down the coast to Mirna.

In Serbo-Croat *mirna* means peaceful. And so Wexford found the resort after a gruelling winter and spring in Kingsmarkham, after petty crime and serious crime, and finally a squalid murder case which had been solved, not by him in spite of his work and research, but by a young expert from Scotland Yard. It was Mike Burden who had advised him to get right away for his holiday. Not Wales or Cornwall this time, but the Dalmatian coast of Yugoslavia where he, Burden, had taken his children the previous year.

'Mirna,' said Burden. 'There are three good hotels but the village is quite unspoilt. You can go everywhere by water. Two or three old chaps run taxi boats. It never rained once while we were there. And you're into all this nature stuff, this ecology. The marine life's amazing and so are the flowers and butterflies.'

It was the marine life with which Wexford was getting acquainted two mornings after the trip to Dubrovnik. He had left Dora prone on an air bed by the hotel swimming pool, knowing full well that sunbathing was impossible for his Anglo-Saxon skin. Already his nose was peeling. So he had anointed his face, put on a long-sleeved shirt, and walked round the wooded point to Mirna harbour. The little port had a harbour wall built of the same stone as the city of Dubrovnik, and kneeling down to peer over, he saw that beneath the water line the rocks and masonry were thickly covered by a tapestry of sea anemones and tiny shells and flowering weed and starfishes. The water was perfectly clear and unpolluted. He could clearly see the bottom, fifteen feet down, and now a shoal of silvery-brown fish glided out from a sea-bed bush. Fascinated, he leaned over, understanding why so many swimmers out there were equipped with goggles and schnorkels. A scarlet fish darted out from a rock, then a broad silver one, banded with black.

Behind him, a voice said, 'You like it?'

Wexford got up on to his haunches. The man who had spoken was older than he, skinny and wrinkled and tough-looking. He had a walnut face, a dry smile and surprisingly good teeth. He wore a sailor's cap and a blue and white striped tee-shirt, and Wexford recognised him as one of the taxi boatmen.

He replied slowly and carefully, 'I like it very much. It is pretty, beautiful.'

'The shores of your country were like this once. But in the nineteenth century a man called Gosse, a marine biologist, wrote a book about them and within a few years collectors had come and divested the rocks of everything.'

Wexford couldn't help laughing. 'Good God,' he said. 'I beg your pardon, but I thought …?'

'That an old boatman can say "please" and "zank you" and "ten dinara"?'

'Something like that.' Wexford got up to stand inches taller than the other man. 'You speak remarkable English.'

A broad smile. 'No, it is too pedantic. I have only once been to England and that many years ago.' He put out his hand. 'How do you do, *gospodine*? Ivo Racic at your service.'

'Reginald Wexford.'

The hand was iron-hard but the grip gentle. Racic said, 'I do not wish to intrude. I spoke to you because it is rare to find a tourist interested in nature. With most it is only the sunbathing and the food and drink, eh? Or to catch the fish and take the shells.'

'Come and have a drink,' said Wexford, 'or are you working?'

'Josip and Mirko and I, we have a little syndicate, and they will not mind if I have a half an hour off. But I buy the drinks. This is my country and you are my guest.'

They walked towards the avenue of stout palm trees. 'I was born here in Mirna,' said Racic. 'At eighteen I left for the university and when I retired and came back here after forty years and more, those palm trees were just the same, no bigger, no different. Nothing was changed till they built the hotels.'

'What did you do in those forty years? Not run a boat service?'

'I was professor of Anglo-Saxon studies at the University of Beograd, Gospodin Wexford.'

'Ah,' said Wexford, 'all is made plain. And when you retired you took up with Josip and Mirko to run the water taxis. Perhaps they were childhood friends?'

'They were. I see you have perspicacity. And may I enquire in return what is your occupation?'

Wexford said what he always said on holiday, 'I'm a civil servant.'

Racic smiled. 'Here in Yugoslavia we are all civil servants. But let us go for our drinks. *Hajdemo, drug*!'

They chose a cluster of tables set under a vine-covered canopy, through which the sun made a gentle dappling on cobbles. Racic drank *slivovic*. The fiery brandy with its hinted undertaste of plums was forbidden to Wexford who had to watch his blood pressure. He even felt guilty when the white wine called Posip which Racic ordered for him arrived in a tumbler filled to the brim.

'You live here in Mirna?'

'Here alone in my *kucica* that was once my father's house. My wife died in Beograd. But it is a good and pleasant life. I have my pension and my boat and the grapes I grow and the figs, and sometimes a guest like yourself, Gospodin Wexford, on whom to practise my English.'

Wexford would have liked to question him about the political regime, but he felt that this might be unwise and perhaps discourteous. So instead he remarked on the stately appearance of a woman in national costume, white coif, heavily embroidered stiff black dress, who had emerged with a full basket from the grocer's shop. Racic nodded, then pointed a brown thumb to a table outside the shadow of the vines.

'That is better, I think. Healthier, eh? And freer.'

She was sitting in the full sun, a young woman with short black hair geometrically cut, who wore only a pair of white shorts and jade-green halter top. A man came out of the currency exchange bureau, she got up to meet him, and Wexford recognised them as the couple he had seen on the walls of Dubrovnik. They went off hand in hand and got into a white Lancia Gamma parked under the palms.

'Last time I saw them they were quarrelling.'

'They are staying at the Hotel Bosnia,' said Racic. 'On Sunday evening they drove here from Dubrovnik and they are going to remain for a week. Her name I cannot tell you, but his is Philip.'

'May I ask how you come to be such a mine of information, Mr Racic?'

'They came out in my boat this morning.' Racic's dark bright eyes twinkled. 'Just the two of them, to be ferried across to Vrt and back. But let me tell you a little story. Once, about a year ago, a young English couple hired my boat. They were, I think, on their wedding journey, their honeymoon, as you say, and it was evident they were much in love. They had no eyes but for each other and certainly no inclination to speak to the boatman. We were coming into the shore here, perhaps a hundred metres out, when the young husband began telling his wife how much he loved her and how he could hardly wait to get back to the hotel to make love to her. Oh, very frank and explicit he was – and why not with only the old Yugoslav there who speaks nothing but his own outlandish tongue?

'I said nothing. I betrayed nothing in my face. We pulled in, he paid me twenty dinars and they walked off up the quay. Then I saw the young lady had left her bag behind and I called to her. She came back, took it and thanked me. Gospodin Wexford, I could not resist it. "You have a charming husband, madame," I said, "but no more than you deserve." Oh, how she blushed, but I think she was not displeased, though they never came in my boat again.'

Laughing, Wexford said, 'It was hardly a similar conversation you overheard between Philip and his wife, though?'

'No.' Racic looked thoughtful. 'I think I will not tell you what I overheard. It is no business of ours. And now I must make my excuses, but we shall meet again.'

'In your boat, certainly. I must take my wife over to Vrt for the bathing.'

'Better than that. Bring your wife and I will take you for a trip round the islands. On Wednesday? No, I'm not touting for custom. This will be a trip – now for a good colloquial expression – on the house! You and me and Gospoda Wexford.'

'Those very nice Germans,' said Dora, 'have asked us to go with them in their car to Cetinje on Wednesday.'

'Mm,' said Wexford absently. 'Good idea.'

It was nine o'clock but very dark beyond the range of the waterside lights. They had walked into Mirna after dinner, it being too late for the taxi boats, and were having coffee on the terrace of a restaurant at the harbour edge. The nearly tideless Adriatic lapped the stones at their feet with soft gulping sounds.

Suddenly he remembered. 'Oh, God, I can't. I promised that Yugoslav I told you about to go on a trip round the islands with him. It'd look discourteous to let him down. But you go to Cetinje.'

'Well, I should like to. I may never get another chance to see Montenegro. Oh, look, darling, there are those people we saw in Dubrovnik!'

For the first time Wexford saw the girl full-face. Her haircut from the front was as spectacular as from the back, a fringe having been cut into a sharp peak in the centre of her forehead. It looked less like hair, he thought, than a black cap painted on. In spite of the hour, she wore large tinted glasses. Her coloured skirt was the same one she had been wearing that first time.

She and her companion had come on to the terrace from the harbour walk. They walked slowly, she somehow reluctantly, the man called Philip looking about him as if for friends they had arranged to meet here. It couldn't have been for a vacant table, for the terrace was half-empty. Dora kicked her husband's foot under the table, a warning against overt curiosity, and started to talk about her German friends, Werner and Trudi. Out of the corner of his eye,

Wexford saw the man and the girl hesitate, then sit down at a neighbouring table. He made some sort of reply to Dora, conscious that it was he now who was being stared at. A voice he had heard once before said:

'Excuse me, we don't seem to have an ashtray. Would you mind if we had yours?'

Dora handed it to him. 'Please do.'

She hardly looked up. He insisted, smiling. 'You're sure you won't need it?'

'Quite sure. We don't smoke.'

He wasn't the kind to give up easily, thought Wexford, and now, very intrigued by something he had noticed, he didn't want to. Another prod from Dora's foot merely made him withdraw his own under his chair. He turned towards the other table, and to the next question, 'Are you staying long in Mirna?' replied pleasantly, 'A fortnight. We've been here four days.'

The effect of this simple rejoinder was startling. The man couldn't have expressed more satisfaction – and, yes, relief – if Wexford had brought him news of some great inheritance or that a close friend, presumed in danger, was safe.

'Oh, fantastic! That's really great. It's such a change to meet some English people. We must try and get together. This is my wife. We're called Philip and Iris Nyman. Are you Londoners too?'

Wexford introduced himself and Dora and said that they were from Kingsmarkham in Sussex. It was lovely to meet them, said Philip Nyman. They must let him buy them a drink. No? More coffee, then? At last Wexford accepted a cup of coffee, wondering what was so upsetting Iris Nyman that she had responded to the introduction only with a nod and now seemed almost paralysed. Her husband's extrovert behaviour? Certainly his effusive manner would have embarrassed all but the most insensitive. As soon as they had settled the question of the drinks, he launched into a long account of their trip from England, how they had come down through France and Italy, the people they had met, the weather, their delight at their first sight of the Dalmatian coast which they had never previously visited. Iris Nyman showed no delight. She simply stared out to sea, gulping down *slivovic* as if it were lemonade.

'We absolutely adored it. They say it's the least spoilt of the Mediterranean resorts, and that I can believe. We all loved Dubrovnik. That is, I mean, we brought a cousin of my wife's along with us. She was going on to holiday with some people she knows in Greece, so she flew to Athens from Dubrovnik on Sunday and left us to come on here.'

Dora said, 'We saw you in Dubrovnik. On the walls.'

Iris Nyman's glass made a little clinking sound against her teeth. Her husband said, 'You saw us on the walls? D'you know, I think I remember that.' He seemed just slightly taken aback. But not deterred. 'In fact, I seem to remember we were having a bit of a row at the time.'

Dora made a deprecating movement with her hands. 'We just walked past you. It was terribly hot, wasn't it?'

'You're being very charmingly discreet, Mrs Wexford – or may I call you Dora? The point was, Dora, my wife wanted to climb one of the local mountains and I was telling her just how impractical this was. I mean, in that heat, and for what? To get the same view you get from the walls.'

'So you managed to dissuade her?' Wexford said quietly.

'Indeed I did, but you came along rather at the height of the ding-dong. Another drink, darling? And how about you, Dora? Won't you change your mind?'

They replied simultaneously, 'Another *slivovic*,' and 'Thank you so much, but we must go.' It was a long time since Wexford had seen his wife so huffy and so thoroughly out of countenance. He marvelled at Nyman's continuing efforts, his fixed smile.

'Let me guess, you're staying at the Adriatic?' He took silence for assent. 'We're at the Bosnia. Wait a minute, how about making a date for, say, Wednesday? We could all have a trip somewhere in my car.'

The Wexfords, having previous engagements, were able to refuse with clear consciences. They said good night, Wexford nodding non-committally at Nyman's insistence that they must meet again, mustn't lose touch after having been so lucky as to encounter each other. His eyes followed them. Wexford looked back once to see.

'Well!' said Dora when they were out of earshot, 'what an insufferably rude woman!'

'Just very nervous, I think,' said Wexford thoughtfully. He gave her his arm and they began the walk back along the waterside path. It was very dark, the sea inky and calm, the island invisible. 'When you come to think of it, that was all very odd.'

'Was it? She was rude and he was effusive to the point of impertinence, if you call that odd. He forced himself on us, got us to tell him our names – you could see she just didn't want to know. I was amazed when he called me Dora.'

'That part wasn't so odd. After all, that's how one does

make holiday acquaintances. Presumably it was much the same with Werner and Trudi.'

'No, it wasn't, Reg, not at all. For one thing, we're much of an age and we're staying at the same hotel. Trudi speaks quite good English, and we were watching the children in the paddling pool and she happened to mention her grandsons who are just the same age as ours, and that started it. You must see that's quite different from a man of thirty walking into a café and latching on to a couple old enough to be his parents. I call it pushy.'

Wexford reacted impatiently. 'That's as may be. Perhaps you didn't notice there was a perfectly clean ashtray in the middle of that table before they sat down at it.'

'*What?*' Dora halted, staring at him in the dark.

'There was. He must have put it in his pocket to give him an excuse for speaking to us. Now that was odd. And giving us all that gratuitous information was odd. And telling a deliberate lie was very odd indeed. Come along, my dear. Don't stand there gawping at me.'

'What do you mean, a deliberate lie?'

'When you told them we'd seen them on the walls, he said he remembered it and we must have overheard the quarrel between himself and his wife. Now that was odd in itself. Why mention it at all? Why should we care about his domestic – or maybe I should say mural – rows? He said the quarrel had been over climbing a mountain, but no one climbs the mountains here in summer. Besides, I remember precisely what he did say up on the walls. He said, "We can't find anyone to take us." OK, so he might have meant they couldn't get a guide. But "there's nowhere to land"? That's what he said, no doubt about it. You don't land on mountains, Dora, unless you assault them by helicopter.'

'I wonder why, though. I wonder what he's up to.'

'So do I,' said Wexford, 'but I'm pretty sure it's not pinching ashtrays from waterside cafés.'

They rounded the point and came within sight of the lights of the Hotel Adriatic. A little further and they could see each other's faces. Dora saw his and read there much to disquiet her.

'You're not going to start detecting, Reg!'

'Can't help it, it's in my bones. But I won't let it interfere with your holiday, that's a promise.'

On Tuesday morning Racic's taxi boat was waiting at the landing stage outside the hotel.

'Gospoda Wexford, it is a great pleasure to meet you.'

Courteously he handed Dora into the boat. Its awning of green canvas, now furled, gave it somewhat the look of a gondola. As the engines started, Dora made her excuses for the following day.

'You will like Cetinje,' said Racic. 'Have a good time. Gospodin Wexford and I will have a bachelor day out. All boys together, eh? Are you quite comfortable? A little more suitable than that one for a lady, I hope.'

He pointed across the bay to where a man was paddling a yellow and blue inflatable dinghy. The girl with him wore a very brief bikini. The Nymans.

'If you could manage to avoid passing those people, Mr Racic,' said Dora, 'that would make me very comfortable indeed.'

Racic glanced at Wexford. 'You have met them? They have annoyed you?'

'Not that. They spoke to us last night in Mirna and the man was rather pushing.'

'I will keep close to the shore and cross to Vrt from the small peninsula there.'

For most of the morning there was no one else on the little shingly beach of Vrt, which Racic had told them meant a garden. The huddle of cottages behind were overhung with the blue trumpet flowers of the morning glory, and among the walls rose the slender spires of cypress trees. Wexford sat in the shade reading while Dora sunbathed. The dinghy came close only once, but the Wexfords went unrecognised, perhaps because they were in swimming costumes. Iris Nyman stood up briefly before jumping with an explosive splash into the deep water.

'Rude she may be,' said Dora, 'but I'll grant she's got a lovely figure. And you were wrong about her legs, Reg. Her legs are perfect.'

'Didn't notice,' said Wexford.

Josip took them back. He was a thin smiling brown man, not unlike Racic, but he had no English beyond 'thank you' and 'good-bye'. They hired him again in the afternoon to take them into Mirna, and they spent a quiet, pleasant evening drinking coffee with Werner and Trudi Muller on the Germans' balcony.

Wednesday came in with a storm at sunrise, and Wexford, watching the lightning and the choppy sea, wondered if Burden had been over-optimistic with his guarantee of fine weather. But by nine the sun was out and the sky clear. He saw Dora off in the Mullers' Mercedes, then walked down to the landing stage. Racic's boat glided in.

'I have brought bread and sausage for our lunch, and Posip in a flask to keep it cool.'

'Then we must eat it for our elevenses because I'm taking you out to lunch.'

This they ate in Dubrovnik after Racic had taken him to the island of Lokrum. Wexford listened with deepening interest to the boatman–professor's stories. How the ease and wealth of the city merchants had led to a literary renascence, how Dubrovnik-built ships had taken part in the Spanish Armada, how an earthquake had devastated the city and almost destroyed the state. They set off again for Lopud, Sipan and Kolocep, returning across the broad calm waters as the sun began to dip towards the sea.

'Does that little island have a name?' Wexford asked.

'It is called Vrapci, which is to say "sparrows". There are thousands of sparrows, so they say, and only sparrows, for no one goes there. One cannot land a boat.'

'You mean you can't get off a boat because the rocks are too sheer? What about the other side?'

'I will pull in close and you shall see. There is a beach but no one would wish to use it. Wait.'

The island was very small, perhaps no more than half a mile in circumference, and totally overgrown with stunted pines. At their roots the grey rock fell sheer to the water from a height of about ten feet. Racic brought the boat about and they came to the Adriatic side of Vrapci. No sparrows were to be seen, no life of any kind. Between ramparts of rock was a small and forbidding beach of shingle over which an overhanging pine cast deep shade. Looking up at the sky and then down at this dark and stony cove, Wexford could see that, no matter what its altitude, the sun would never penetrate to this beach. Where the shingle narrowed, at the apex, was a cleft in the rock just wide enough to allow the passage of a man's body.

'Not very attractive,' he said. 'Why should people want to come here?'

'They don't, as far as I know. Except perhaps – well, there is a new fashion, Gospodin Wexford, or Mister as I should call you.'

'Call me Reg.'

Racic inclined his head. 'Reg, yes, thank you. I like the name, though I have not previously encountered it. There is a fashion, as I mentioned, for nude bathing. Here in Yugoslavia we do not allow it, for it is not proper, not decorous. No doubt you have seen painted on some of the rocks the words – in, I fear, lamentable English – "No Nudist". But there are some who would defy this rule, especially on the small islands. Vrapci might take their fancy if they could find a boat and a boatman to bring them.'

'A boat could land on the beach and its occupants swim off the rocks on the other side in the sun.'

'If they were good swimmers. But we will not try it, Reg, not at our age being inclined to strip ourselves naked and risk our necks, eh?'

Once more they were off across the wide sea. Wexford looked back to the city walls, those man-made defensive cliffs, and brought himself hesitantly to ask:

'Would you tell me what you overheard of the conversation

between that English couple, Philip and Iris Nyman, when you took them out in your boat?'

'So that is their name? Nyman?' He was stalling.

'I have a good reason for asking.'

'May I know it?'

Wexford sighed. 'I'm a policeman.'

Racic's face went very still and tight. 'I don't much like that. You were sent here to watch these people? You should have told me before.'

'No, Ivo, no.' Wexford brought out the unfamiliar name a little self-consciously. 'No, you've got me wrong. I never saw or heard of them till last Saturday. But now I've seen them and spoken to them I believe they're doing something illegal. If that's so it's my duty to do something about it. They're my countrymen.'

'Reg,' said Racic more gently, 'what I overheard can have nothing to do with this matter of an illegality. It was personal and private.'

'You won't tell me?'

'No. We are not old housewives to spend our time in gossip over the garden walls of our *kucice*, eh?'

Wexford grinned. 'Then will you do something for me? Will you contrive to let these people know – subtly, of course – that you understand the English language?'

'You are sure that what they are doing is against the law?'

'I am sure. It's drugs or some kind of confidence trick.'

There was silence, during which Racic seemed to commune with his sea. Then he said quietly, 'I trust you, Reg. Yes, I will do this if I can.'

'Then go into Mirna. They're very likely having a drink on the waterfront.'

Mirko's boat passed them as they came in and Mirko waved, calling, '*Dobro vece!*'

On the jetty stood a queue of tourists, waiting to be ferried back to the Adriatic or to the hotel at Vrt. There were perhaps a dozen people, and Philip and Iris Nyman brought up the end of the line. It worked out better than Wexford could have hoped. The first four got into Josip's boat, bound for Vrt, the next group into Mirko's which, with its capacity of only eight, was inadequate to take the Nymans.

'Hotel Adriatic,' said Philip Nyman. Then he recognised Wexford. 'Well, well, we meet again. Had a good day?'

Wexford replied that he had been to Dubrovnik. He helped the girl into the boat. She thanked him, seeming less nervous, and even gave him a diffident smile. The motor started and they were off, Racic the anonymous taxi-man, the piece of equipment without which the vehicle won't go.

'I saw you out in your dinghy yesterday,' said Wexford.

'Did you?' Philip Nyman seemed gratified. 'We can't use it tonight, though. It's not safe after dark and you've really got to be in swimming costumes. We're dining at your hotel with another English couple that we met yesterday and we thought we'd have a romantic walk back along the path.'

They were rather more dressed up than usual. Nyman wore a cream-coloured safari suit, his wife a yellow and black dress and high-heeled black sandals. Wexford was on the alert for an invitation to join them for dinner and was surprised when none came.

Both the Nymans lit cigarettes. Wexford noticed Racic

stiffen. He had learned enough about the man's principles and shibboleths to be aware of his feelings on pollution. Those cigarette butts would certainly end up in the sea. Anger with his passengers might make him all the more willing to fulfil his promise. But for the moment he remained silent. They rounded the point on to a sea where the sun seemed to have laid a skin of gold.

'So beautiful!' said Iris Nyman. 'A pity you have to go so soon.'

'We're staying till Saturday,' said Nyman, though without renewing his suggestion that they and the Wexfords should meet again. The girl took a last draw on her cigarette and threw it overboard.

'Oh, well,' said Nyman, 'there's so much muck in there already, a bit more won't do any harm,' and he cast his still-lighted butt into the ripples of melted gold.

They were approaching the hotel landing stage and Racic cut the motor. Nyman felt in his pocket for change. It was Wexford who got up first. He said to Racic as the Yugoslav made the boat fast:

'I've had a splendid day. Thanks very much indeed.'

He wasn't looking at them but he fancied the amused glance Nyman would have given his wife at this display of the Englishman's well-known assumption that all but cretins speak his language. Racic drew himself up to his not very great height. What accent he had, what stiltedness and syntactical awkwardness, seemed to be lost. He spoke as if he had been born in Kensington and educated at Oxford.

'I'm glad you enjoyed it, I certainly did. Give my regards to your wife and tell her I hope to see her soon.'

There was no sound from the Nymans. They got out of the boat, Racic saying, 'Let me give you a hand, madame.' Nyman's voice sounded stifled when he produced his twenty dinars and muttered his thanks. Neither said a word to Wexford. They didn't look back. They walked away and his eyes followed them.

'Did I do all right, Reg? I was moved by the foul contamination of my sea.'

Absently, still staring, Wexford said, 'You did fine.'

'What do you look at with such concentration?'

'Legs,' said Wexford. 'Thanks again. I'll see you tomorrow.'

He walked up towards the hotel, looking for them, but they were nowhere in sight. On the terrace he turned and looked back and there they were, walking hurriedly along the waterfront path back to Mirna, their new friends and their dinner engagement forgotten. Wexford went into the hotel and took the lift up to his room. Dora wasn't back yet. Feeling rather shaken, he lay down on one of the twin beds. This latest development or discovery was, at any rate, far from what he had expected. And what now? Somehow get hold of the Dubrovnik police? He reached for the phone to call reception but dropped it again when Dora walked in.

She came up to him in consternation. 'Are you all right, darling?'

His blood pressure, his heart, too much sun – he could tell what she was thinking. It was rare for him to take a rest in the daytime. 'Of course I am. I'm fine.' He sat up. 'Dora, something most peculiar …'

'You're detecting again! I knew it.' She kicked off her

shoes and threw open the doors to the balcony. 'You haven't even asked me if I've had a nice day.'

'I can see you have. Come in, my dear, don't be difficult. I always like to think you're the only woman I know who isn't difficult.' She looked at him warily. 'Listen,' he said. 'Do something for me. Describe the woman we saw on the walls.'

'Iris Nyman? What do you mean?'

'Just do as I ask, there's a good girl.'

'You're mad. You *have* had a touch of the sun. Well, I suppose if it humours you … Medium height, good figure, very tanned, about thirty, geometric haircut. She was wearing a jade green halter top and a blue and green and pink skirt.'

'Now describe the woman we saw with Nyman on Monday.'

'There's no difference except for a black top and a stole.'

Wexford nodded. He got off the bed, walked past her on to the balcony and said:

'They're not the same woman.'

'What on earth are you suggesting?'

'I wish I knew,' said Wexford, 'but I do know the Iris Nyman we saw on the walls is not the Iris Nyman I saw in Mirna on Monday morning and we saw that night and we saw yesterday and I saw this evening.'

'You're letting your imagination run away with you. You are, Reg. That hair, for instance, it was striking, and those clothes, and being with Philip Nyman.'

'Don't you see you've named the very things that would be used to make anyone think they're the same woman? Neither of us saw her face that first time. Neither of us heard her voice. We only noticed the striking things about her.'

'What makes you think they're not the same?'

'Her legs. The legs are different. You drew my attention to them. One might say you set me off on this.'

Dora leaned over the balcony rail. Her shoulders sagged. 'Then I wish I hadn't. Reg, you never discuss cases with me at home. Why do it here?'

'There's no one else.'

'Thanks very much. All this about their not being the same woman, it's nonsense, you've dreamed it up. Why would anyone try and fake a thing like that? Come to that, how could anyone?'

'Easily. All you need is a female accomplice of similar build and age. On Saturday or Sunday this accomplice had her hair cut and dyed and assumed Iris Nyman's clothes. I mean to find out why.'

Dora turned her back on the sunset and fixed him with a cold and stony look. 'No, Reg, no. I'm not being difficult. I'm just behaving like any normal woman would when she goes on holiday and finds her husband can't leave his job at home for just two weeks. This is the first foreign holiday I've had in ten years. If you'd been sent here to watch these people, if it was work, I wouldn't say a word. But it's just something you've dreamed up because you can't relax and enjoy the sun and the sea like other people.'

'OK,' said her husband, 'look at it that way.' He was very fond of his wife, he valued her and quickly felt guilt over his frequent enforced neglect of her. This time any neglect would be as if by design, the result of that bone-deep need of his to unravel mysteries. 'Don't give me that Gorgon face. I've said I won't let this spoil your holiday and I won't.' He touched her cheek, gently rubbing it. 'And now I'm going to have my bath.'

Not much more than twelve hours later he was walking the path to Mirna. The sun was already hot and there was a speedboat out in the bay. Carpet sellers had spread their wares in the market place, and the cafés were open for those who wanted coffee or – even at this hour – plum brandy.

The Bosnia, most of it mercifully concealed by pines and ranks of cypresses, looked from close to, with its floors in plate-like layers and its concrete flying buttresses, more like an Unidentified Flying Object come to rest in the woods than a holiday hotel. Wexford crossed a forecourt as big as a football pitch and entered a foyer that wouldn't have disgraced some capital city's palace of justice.

The receptionist spoke good English. 'Mr and Mrs Nyman checked out last evening, sir.'

'Surely they expected to stay another three days?'

'I cannot tell you, sir. They left last evening before dinner. I cannot help you more.'

So that was that.

'What are you going to do now?' said Dora over a late breakfast. 'Have a hilarious cops-and-robbers car chase up the Dalmatian coast?'

'I'm going to wait and see. And in the meantime I'm going to enjoy my holiday and see that you enjoy yours.' He watched her relax and smile for the first time since the previous evening.

The Nymans were at the back of his mind all the time, but he did manage to enjoy the rest of his holiday. Werner and Trudi took them to Mostar to see the Turkish bridge. They went on a coach to Budva, and the members of the taxi boat syndicate ferried them from Mirna to Vrt and out to Lokrum. It was in secret that Wexford daily bought a London newspaper, a day old and three times its normal price. He wasn't sure why he did so, what he hoped or feared. On their last morning he nearly didn't bother. After all, he would be home in not much more than twenty-four hours and then he would have to take some action. But as he passed the reception desk, Dora having already entered the dining room for breakfast, the clerk held out the newspaper to him as a matter of course.

Wexford thanked him – and there it was on the front page. *Disappearance of Tycoon's Daughter*, said the headline. *Beachwear King Fears Kidnap Plot.*

The text beneath read: 'Mrs Iris Nyman, 32, failed to return to her North London home from a shopping expedition yesterday. Her father, Mr James Woodhouse, Chairman of Sunsports Ltd, a leading manufacturer of beachwear, fears his daughter may have been kidnapped and expects a ransom demand. Police are taking a serious view.

'Mrs Nyman's husband, 33-year-old Philip Nyman, said at the couple's home in Flask Walk, Hampstead, today, "My wife and I had just got back from a motoring holiday in Italy and Yugoslavia. On the following morning Iris went out shopping and never returned. I am frantic with worry. She seemed to be happy and relaxed."

'Mr Woodhouse's company, of which Mrs Nyman is a director, was this year involved in a vast takeover bid as a result of which two other major clothing firms were absorbed into Sunsports Ltd. The company's turnover last year was in the region of £100,000,000.'

There was a photograph of Iris Nyman in black glasses. Wexford would have been hard put to it to say whether this was of the woman on the walls or the woman in Mirna.

That night they gave Racic a farewell dinner at the Dubrovacka restaurant.

'Don't say what they all say, Reg, that you will come back next year. Dalmatia is beautiful to you and Gospoda Wexford now, but a few days and the memory will fade. Someone will say, San Marino for you next time, or Ibiza, and there you will go. Is it not so?'

'I said I shall be back,' said Wexford, 'and I meant it.' He raised his glass of Posip. 'But not in a year's time. It'll be sooner than that.'

Three hundred and sixty-two days sooner, as Racic pointed out.

'And here I am, sitting in the *vrt* of your *kucica*!'

'Reg, we shall have you fluent in Serbo-Croat yet.'

'Alas, no. I must be back in London again tomorrow night.'

They were in Racic's garden, halfway up the terraced hill behind Mirna, sitting in wicker chairs under his vine and his fig tree. Pink and white and red oleanders shimmered in the dusk, and above their heads bunches of small green grapes hung between the slats of a canopy. On the table was a bottle of Posip and the remains of a dinner of king prawns and Dalmatian buttered potatoes, salad and bread and big ripe peaches.

'And now we have eaten,' said Racic, 'you will please tell me the tale of the important business that brought you back to Mirna so pleasantly soon. It concerns Mr and Mrs Nyman?'

'Ivo, we shall have you a policeman yet.'

Racic laughed and refilled Wexford's glass. Then he looked serious. 'Not a laughing matter, I think, not pleasant.'

'Far from it. Iris Nyman is dead, murdered, unless I am much mistaken. This afternoon I accompanied the Dubrovnik police out into the bay and we took her body out of the cave on Vrapci.'

'*Zaboga*! You cannot mean it! That girl who was at the Bosnia and who came out with her husband in my boat?'

'Well, no, not that one. She's alive and in Athens from where, I imagine, she'll be extradited.'

'I don't understand. Tell me the tale from the beginning.'

Wexford leaned back in his chair and looked up through the vines at the violet sky where the first stars had begun to show. 'I'll have to start with the background,' he said, and after a pause, 'Iris Nyman was the daughter and only child of James Woodhouse, the chairman of a company called Sunsports Ltd which makes sports- and beachwear and has a large export trade. She married when she was very young, less than twenty, a junior salesman in her father's firm. After the marriage Woodhouse made a director of her, settled a lot of money on her, bought her a house and gave her a company car. To justify her company fees and expenses, she was in the habit of annually making a trip to holiday resorts in Europe with her husband, ostensibly to wear Sunsports clothes and note who else was wearing them, and also to study the success of rival markets. Probably, she simply holidayed.

'The marriage was not a happy one. At any rate, Philip Nyman wasn't happy. Iris was a typically arrogant rich girl who expected always to have her own way. Besides, the money and the house and the car were all hers. He remained a salesman. Then, a year or so ago, he fell in love with a cousin of Iris, a girl called Anna Ashby.

'Apparently, Iris knew nothing about this, and her father certainly didn't.'

'Then how can you ...?' Racic interrupted.

'These affairs are always known to someone, Ivo. One of Anna's friends has made a statement to Scotland Yard.' Wexford paused and drank some of his wine. 'That's the background,' he said. 'Now for what happened a month or so ago.

'The Nymans had arranged to motor down as usual to the south of France, but this time to cross northern Italy and spend a week or ten days here on the Dalmatian coast. Anna Ashby had planned to spend part of the summer with friends in Greece so, *at Iris's invitation*, she was to accompany the Nymans as far as Dubrovnik where she would stay a few days with them, then go on by air to Athens.

'In Dubrovnik, after the three of them had been there a few days, Iris got hold of the idea of bathing off Vrapci. Perhaps she wanted to bathe in the nude, perhaps she had already been on the "topless" beach at St Tropez. I don't know. Philip Nyman has admitted nothing of this. Up until the time I left, he was still insisting that his wife had returned to England with him.'

'It was your idea, then,' put in Racic, 'that this poor woman's body was concealed on the isle of sparrows?'

'It was a guess,' said Wexford. 'I overheard some words,

I was later told a lie. I'm a policeman. Whether they went to Vrapci on Saturday, June 18th, or Sunday, June 19th, I can't tell you. Suffice that they did go – in that inflatable dinghy of theirs. The three of them went but only two came back, Nyman and Anna Ashby.'

'They killed Mrs Nyman?'

Wexford looked thoughtful. 'I think so, certainly. Of course there's a possibility that she drowned, that it was an accident. But in that case wouldn't any normal husband have immediately informed the proper authority? If he had recovered the body, wouldn't he have brought it back with him? We're awaiting the results of the post-mortem, but even if that shows no wounds or bruises on the body, even if the lungs are full of water, I should be very surprised to learn that Nyman and, or, Anna hadn't hastened her death or watched her drown.'

Both were silent for a moment, Racic nodding slowly as he digested what Wexford had told him. Then he got up and fetched from the house a candelabrum, but thinking better of it, switched on an electric lamp attached to the wall.

'Any light will attract the insects, but there at least they will not trouble us. So it was this Anna Ashby who came to Mirna, posing as Mrs Nyman?'

'According to the manager of the hotel in Dubrovnik where the three of them had been staying, Nyman checked out and paid his bill early on the evening of the 19th. Neither of the women was with him. Iris was dead and Anna was at the hairdresser's, having her hair cut and dyed to the same style and colour as her cousin's. The police have already found the hairdresser who did the job.'

'They came here next,' said Racic. 'Why didn't they go straight back to England? And now I must ask, surely they did not intend to play this game in England? Even if the two women, as cousins, to a degree resembled each other, this Anna could not hope to deceive a father, close friends, Mrs Nyman's neighbours.'

'The answer to your first question is that to have returned to England a week earlier than expected would have looked odd. Why go back? The weather was perfect. Nyman wanted to give the impression they had both been well and happy during their holiday. No, his idea was to make sufficient people here in Yugoslavia believe that Iris was alive after June 19th. That's why he latched on to us and got our name and home town out of us. He wanted to be sure of witnesses if need be. Anna was less bold, she was frightened to death. But Philip actually found himself two more English witnesses, though, thanks to your intervention, he never kept the appointment to dine with them.'

'My intervention?'

'Your excellent English. And now perhaps you'll tell me what you overheard in the boat.'

Racic laughed. His strong white teeth gleamed in the lamplight. 'I knew she was not Mrs Nyman, Reg, but that knowledge would not have helped you then, eh? You had seen the lady on the walls but not, I presume, her marriage document. I thought to myself, why should I tell this busybody of a policeman the secrets of my passengers? But now, to use an idiom, here goes. Reg, the lady said, "I feel so guilty, it is terrible what we have done," and he replied, "Everyone here thinks you are my wife, and no one at home will suspect a thing. One day you will be and we shall forget all this." Now, would you have supposed they were talking of murder or of illicit passion?'

Wexford smiled. 'Nyman must have thought we'd confer, you and I, and jump to the former conclusion. Or else he'd forgotten what he'd said. He has rather a way of doing that.'

'And after they left?'

'Anna was to travel on Iris's passport in the hope it would be stamped at at least one frontier. In fact, it was stamped at two, between Yugoslavia and Italy and again at Calais. At Dover Anna presumably left him and caught the first plane to Athens she could get. Nyman went home, reaching there in the night of the 28th, the precise date on which he and Iris had planned to return. On the following afternoon he told his father-in-law and the police that Iris was missing.'

'He hoped the search for her or her body,' said Racic, 'would be confined to England because he had incontrovertible proof she had stayed with him in Mirna and had travelled back with him to England. No one would think of looking for her here, for it was known to many witnesses that she left here alive. But what did he hope to gain? Surely, if your laws are like ours, and I believe all laws are alike in this, without her body it would be years before he could inherit her money or marry again?'

'You have to remember this wasn't a premeditated murder. It must have happened on the spur of the moment. So conceal the body where it may never be found or not found until it's beyond identification, announce that his wife has gone missing in England, and he gets the sympathy of his powerful father-in-law and certainly Iris's house to live in and Iris's car to drive. He keeps his job which he would have lost had he divorced Iris, and very likely gets all or some of her allowance transferred to him. Anna gets her hair back to its natural colour – brown, incidentally – lets it grow out, returns home and they resume their friendship. One day Iris will be presumed dead and they can marry.'

Racic cut himself a slice of bread and nibbled at an olive. 'I see it all or nearly all. I see that, but for your presence here in Mirna, the conspiracy had every chance of success. What I don't see is, if this woman made herself look so much like this woman you saw on the walls, if she had the same hair and clothes – but I am a fool! You saw her face.'

'I didn't see her face and I didn't hear her voice. Dora and I saw her very briefly and then only from the back.'

'It is beyond my comprehension.'

'The legs,' said Wexford. 'The legs were different.'

'But, my dear Reg, my dear policeman, surely the leg of one brown-skinned slender young woman is much like the leg of such another? Or was there a mole perhaps or a protruding vein?'

'Not as far as I know. The only time I saw the true Iris Nyman she wore a skirt that covered her legs to mid-calf. In fact, I could see very little of her legs.'

'Then I am flummoxed.'

'Ankles,' said Wexford. 'There are two types of normal ankle in this world, and the difference between them can only be seen from the back. In one type the calf seems to join the heel with a narrowing but no distinct shaft. In the other, the type of beauty, the Achilles tendon makes a long slender shaft with deep indentations on either side of it beneath the ankle bones. I saw Iris Nyman's legs only from behind and in her the Achilles tendon was not apparent. It was a flaw in her appearance. When I first noticed Anna Ashby's legs from behind as she was getting off your boat, I observed the long shaft of the tendon leading up into the muscle of a shapely calf. She had no flaw in her legs, but you might call that perfection her Achilles Heel.'

'*Zaboga!* Beauty, eh? Only two types in the world?' Racic extended one foot and rolled up his trouser leg. Wexford's was already rucked up. In the lamplight they peered down at each other's calves from behind. 'Yours are all right,' said Racic. 'In fact, they are fine. In the beauty class.'

'So are yours, you old professor and boatman.'

Racic burst out laughing. '*Tesko meni!* Two elderly gentlemen who should know better, airing their limbs in an ankle competition! Whatever next?'

'Well, I shouldn't,' said Wexford, 'but next let's finish up the Posip.'

The Adventure of the Lion's Mane

Arthur Conan Doyle

It is a most singular thing that a problem which was certainly as abstruse and unusual as any which I have faced in my long professional career should have come to me after my retirement, and be brought, as it were, to my very door. It occurred after my withdrawal to my little Sussex home, when I had given myself up entirely to that soothing life of Nature for which I had so often yearned during the long years spent amid the gloom of London. At this period of my life the good Watson had passed almost beyond my ken. An occasional weekend visit was the most that I ever saw of him. Thus I must act as my own chronicler. Ah! had he but been with me, how much he might have made of so wonderful a happening and of my eventual triumph against every difficulty! As it is, however, I must needs tell my tale in my own plain way, showing by my words each step upon the difficult road which lay before me as I searched for the mystery of the Lion's Mane.

My villa is situated upon the southern slope of the downs, commanding a great view of the Channel. At this point the coast-line is entirely of chalk cliffs, which can only be descended by a single, long, tortuous path, which is steep and slippery. At the bottom of the path lie a hundred yards of pebbles and shingle, even when the tide is at full. Here and there, however, there are curves and hollows which make splendid swimming-pools filled afresh with each flow. This admirable beach extends for some miles in each direction, save only at one point where the little cove and village of Fulworth break the line.

My house is lonely. I, my old housekeeper, and my bees have the estate all to ourselves. Half a mile off, however, is Harold Stackhurst's well-known coaching establishment, The Gables, quite a large place, which contains some score of young fellows preparing for various professions, with a staff of several masters. Stackhurst himself was a well-known rowing Blue in his day, and an excellent all-round scholar. He and I were always friendly from the day I came to the coast, and he was the one man who was on such terms with me that we could drop in on each other in the evenings without an invitation.

Towards the end of July, 1907, there was a severe gale, the wind blowing up-channel, heaping the seas to the base of the cliffs and leaving a lagoon at the turn of the tide. On the morning of which I speak the wind had abated, and all Nature was newly washed and fresh. It was impossible to work upon so delightful a day, and I strolled out before breakfast to enjoy the exquisite air. I walked along the cliff path which led to the steep descent to the beach. As I walked I heard a shout behind me, and there was Harold Stackhurst waving his hand in cheery greeting.

'What a morning, Mr Holmes! I thought I should see you out.'

'Going for a swim, I see.'

'At your old tricks again,' he laughed, patting his bulging pocket. 'Yes. McPherson started early, and I expect I may find him there.'

Fitzroy McPherson was the science master, a fine upstanding young fellow whose life had been crippled by heart trouble following rheumatic fever. He was a natural athlete, however, and excelled in every game which did not throw too great a strain upon him. Summer and winter he went for his swim, and, as I am a swimmer myself, I have often joined him.

At this moment we saw the man himself. His head showed above the edge of the cliff where the path ends. Then his whole figure appeared at the top, staggering like a drunken man. The next instant he threw up his hands and, with a terrible cry, fell upon his face. Stackhurst and I rushed forward – it may have been fifty yards – and turned him on his back. He was obviously dying. Those glazed sunken eyes and dreadful livid cheeks could mean nothing else. One glimmer of life came into his face for an instant, and he uttered two or three words with an eager air of warning. They were slurred and indistinct, but to my ear the last of them, which burst in a shriek from his lips, were 'the Lion's Mane.' It was utterly irrelevant and unintelligible, and yet I could twist the sound into no other sense. Then he half raised himself from the ground, threw his arms into the air, and fell forward on his side. He was dead.

My companion was paralysed by the sudden horror of it, but I, as may well be imagined, had every sense on the alert. And I had need, for it was speedily evident that we were in the presence of an extraordinary case. The man was dressed only in his Burberry overcoat, his trousers, and an unlaced pair of canvas shoes. As he fell over, his Burberry, which had been simply thrown round his shoulders, slipped off, exposing his trunk. We stared at it in amazement. His back was covered with dark red lines as though he had been terribly flogged by a thin wire scourge. The instrument with which this punishment had been inflicted was clearly flexible, for the long, angry weals curved round his shoulders and ribs. There was blood dripping down his chin, for he had bitten through his lower lip in the paroxysm of his agony. His drawn and distorted face told how terrible that agony had been.

I was kneeling and Stackhurst standing by the body when a shadow fell across us, and we found that Ian Murdoch was by our side. Murdoch was the mathematical coach at the establishment, a tall, dark, thin man, so taciturn and aloof that none can be said to have been his friend. He seemed to live in some high abstract region of surds and conic sections, with little to connect him with ordinary life. He was looked upon as an oddity by the students, and would have been their butt, but there was some strange outlandish blood in the man, which showed itself not only in his coal-black eyes and swarthy face but also in occasional outbreaks of temper, which could only be described as ferocious. On one occasion, being plagued by a little dog belonging to McPherson, he had caught the creature up and hurled it through the plate-glass window, an action for which Stackhurst would certainly have given him his dismissal had he not been a very valuable teacher. Such was the strange complex man who now appeared beside us. He seemed to be honestly shocked at the sight before him, though the incident of the dog may show that there was no great sympathy between the dead man and himself.

'Poor fellow! Poor fellow! What can I do? How can I help?'

'Were you with him? Can you tell us what has happened?'

'No, no, I was late this morning. I was not on the beach at all. I have come straight from The Gables. What can I do?'

'You can hurry to the police-station at Fulworth. Report the matter at once.'

Without a word he made off at top speed, and I proceeded to take the matter in hand, while Stackhurst, dazed at this tragedy, remained by the body. My first task naturally was to note who was on the beach. From the top of the path I could see the whole sweep of it, and it was absolutely deserted save that two or three dark figures could be seen far away moving towards the village of Fulworth. Having satisfied myself upon this point, I walked slowly down the path. There was clay or soft marl mixed with the chalk, and every here and there I saw the same footstep, both ascending and descending. No one else had gone down to the beach by this track that morning. At one place I observed the print of an open hand with the fingers towards the incline. This could only mean that poor McPherson had fallen as he ascended. There were rounded depressions, too, which suggested that he had come down upon his knees more than once. At the bottom of the path was the considerable lagoon left by the retreating tide. At the side of it McPherson had undressed, for there lay his towel on a rock. It was folded and dry, so that it would seem that, after all, he had never entered the water. Once or twice as I hunted round amid the hard shingle I came on little patches of sand where the print of his canvas shoe, and also of his naked foot, could be seen. The latter fact proved that he had made all ready to bathe, though the towel indicated that he had not actually done so.

And here was the problem clearly defined – as strange a one as had ever confronted me. The man had not been on the beach more than a quarter of an hour at the most. Stackhurst had followed him from The Gables, so there could be no doubt about that. He had gone to bathe and had stripped, as the naked footsteps showed. Then he had suddenly huddled on his clothes again – they were all dishevelled and unfastened – and he had returned without bathing, or at any rate without drying himself. And the reason for his change of purpose had been that he had been scourged in some savage, inhuman fashion, tortured until he bit his lip through in his agony, and was left with only strength enough to crawl away and to die. Who had done this barbarous deed? There were, it is true, small grottos and caves in the base of the cliffs, but the low sun shone directly into them, and there was no place for concealment. Then, again, there were those distant figures on the beach. They seemed too far away to have been connected with the crime, and the broad lagoon in which McPherson had intended to bathe lay between him and them, lapping up to the rocks. On the sea two or three fishing-boats were at no great distance. Their occupants might be examined at our leisure. There were several roads for inquiry, but none which led to any very obvious goal.

When I at last returned to the body I found that a little group of wondering folk had gathered round it. Stackhurst was, of course, still there, and Ian Murdoch had just arrived with Anderson, the village constable, a big, ginger-moustached man of the slow, solid Sussex breed – a breed which covers much good sense under a heavy, silent exterior. He listened to everything, took note of all we said, and finally drew me aside.

'I'd be glad of your advice, Mr Holmes. This is a big thing for me to handle, and I'll hear of it from Lewes if I go wrong.'

I advised him to send for his immediate superior, and for a doctor; also to allow nothing to be moved, and as few fresh footmarks as possible to be made, until they came. In the meantime I searched the dead man's pockets. There were his handkerchief, a large knife, and a small folding card-case. From this projected a slip of paper, which I unfolded and handed to the constable. There was written on it in a scrawling, feminine hand:

I will be there, you may be sure.
MAUDIE.

It read like a love affair, an assignation, though when and

where were a blank. The constable replaced it in the card-case and returned it with the other things to the pockets of the Burberry. Then, as nothing more suggested itself, I walked back to my house for breakfast, having first arranged that the base of the cliffs should be thoroughly searched.

Stackhurst was round in an hour or two to tell me that the body had been removed to The Gables, where the inquest would be held. He brought with him some serious and definite news. As I expected, nothing had been found in the small caves below the cliff, but he had examined the papers in McPherson's desk and there were several which showed an intimate correspondence with a certain Miss Maud Bellamy, of Fulworth. We had then established the identity of the writer of the note.

'The police have the letters,' he explained. 'I could not bring them. But there is no doubt that it was a serious love affair. I see no reason, however, to connect it with that horrible happening save, indeed, that the lady had made an appointment with him.'

'But hardly at a bathing-pool which all of you were in the habit of using,' I remarked.

'It is mere chance,' said he, 'that several of the students were not with McPherson.'

'*Was* it mere chance?'

Stackhurst knit his brows in thought.

'Ian Murdoch held them back,' said he. 'He would insist upon some algebraic demonstration before breakfast. Poor chap, he is dreadfully cut up about it all.'

'And yet I gather that they were not friends.'

'At one time they were not. But for a year or more Murdoch

has been as near to McPherson as he ever could be to anyone. He is not of a very sympathetic disposition by nature.'

'So I understand. I seem to remember your telling me once about a quarrel over the ill-usage of a dog.'

'That blew over all right.'

'But left some vindictive feeling, perhaps.'

'No, no, I am sure they were real friends.'

'Well, then, we must explore the matter of the girl. Do you know her?'

'Everyone knows her. She is the beauty of the neighbourhood – a real beauty, Holmes, who would draw attention everywhere. I knew that McPherson was attracted by her, but I had no notion that it had gone so far as these letters would seem to indicate.'

'But who is she?'

'She is the daughter of old Tom Bellamy, who owns all the boats and bathing-cots at Fulworth. He was a fisherman to start with, but is now a man of some substance. He and his son William run the business.'

'Shall we walk into Fulworth and see them?'

'On what pretext?'

'Oh, we can easily find a pretext. After all, this poor man did not ill-use himself in this outrageous way. Some human hand was on the handle of that scourge, if indeed it was a scourge which inflicted the injuries. His circle of acquaintances in this lonely place was surely limited. Let us follow it up in every direction and we can hardly fail to come upon the motive, which in turn should lead us to the criminal.'

It would have been a pleasant walk across the thyme-scented downs had our minds not been poisoned by the tragedy we had witnessed. The village of Fulworth lies in a hollow curving in a semicircle round the bay. Behind the old-fashioned hamlet several modern houses have been built upon the rising ground. It was to one of these that Stackhurst guided me.

'That's The Haven, as Bellamy called it. The one with the corner tower and slate roof. Not bad for a man who started with nothing but – By Jove, look at that!'

The garden gate of The Haven had opened and a man had emerged. There was no mistaking that tall, angular, straggling figure. It was Ian Murdoch, the mathematician. A moment later we confronted him upon the road.

'Hullo!' said Stackhurst. The man nodded, gave us a sideways glance from his curious dark eyes, and would have passed us, but his principal pulled him up.

'What were you doing there?' he asked.

Murdoch's face flushed with anger. 'I am your subordinate, sir, under your roof. I am not aware that I owe you any account of my private actions.'

Stackhurst's nerves were near the surface after all he had endured. Otherwise, perhaps, he would have waited. Now he lost his temper completely.

'In the circumstances your answer is pure impertinence, Mr Murdoch.'

'Your own question might perhaps come under the same heading.'

'This is not the first time that I have had to overlook your insubordinate ways. It will certainly be the last. You will kindly make fresh arrangements for your future as speedily as you can.'

'I had intended to do so. I have lost today the only person who made The Gables habitable.'

He strode off upon his way, while Stackhurst, with angry eyes, stood glaring after him. 'Is he not an impossible, intolerable man?' he cried.

The one thing that impressed itself forcibly upon my mind was that Mr Ian Murdoch was taking the first chance to open a path of escape from the scene of the crime. Suspicion, vague and nebulous, was now beginning to take outline in my mind. Perhaps the visit to the Bellamys might throw some further light upon the matter. Stackhurst pulled himself together, and we went forward to the house.

Mr Bellamy proved to be a middle-aged man with a flaming red beard. He seemed to be in a very angry mood, and his face was soon as florid as his hair.

'No, sir, I do not desire any particulars. My son here' – indicating a powerful young man, with a heavy, sullen face, in the corner of the sitting-room – 'is of one mind with me that Mr McPherson's attentions to Maud were insulting. Yes, sir, the word "marriage" was never mentioned, and yet there were letters and meetings, and a great deal more of which neither of us could approve. She has no mother, and we are her only guardians. We are determined—'

But the words were taken from his mouth by the appearance of the lady herself. There was no gainsaying that she would have graced any assembly in the world. Who could have imagined that so rare a flower would grow from such a root and in such an atmosphere? Women have seldom been an attraction to me, for my brain has always governed my heart, but I could not look upon her perfect clear-cut face, with all the soft freshness of the downlands in her delicate colouring, without realising that no young man would cross her path unscathed. Such was the girl who had pushed open the door and stood now, wide-eyed and intense, in front of Harold Stackhurst.

'I know already that Fitzroy is dead,' she said. 'Do not be afraid to tell me the particulars.'

'This other gentleman of yours let us know the news,' explained the father.

'There is no reason why my sister should be brought into the matter,' growled the younger man.

The sister turned a sharp, fierce look upon him. 'This is my business, William. Kindly leave me to manage it in my own way. By all accounts there has been a crime committed. If I can help to show who did it, it is the least I can do for him who is gone.'

She listened to a short account from my companion, with a composed concentration which showed me that she possessed strong character as well as great beauty. Maud Bellamy will always remain in my memory as a most complete and remarkable woman. It seems that she already knew me by sight, for she turned to me at the end.

'Bring them to justice, Mr Holmes. You have my sympathy and my help, whoever they may be.' It seemed to me that she glanced defiantly at her father and brother as she spoke.

'Thank you,' said I. 'I value a woman's instinct in such matters. You use the word "they". You think that more than one was concerned?'

'I knew Mr McPherson well enough to be aware that he was a brave and a strong man. No single person could ever have inflicted such an outrage upon him.'

'Might I have one word with you alone?'

'I tell you, Maud, not to mix yourself up in the matter,' cried her father angrily.

She looked at me helplessly. 'What can I do?'

'The whole world will know the facts presently, so there can be no harm if I discuss them here,' said I. 'I should have preferred privacy, but if your father will not allow it he must share the deliberations.' Then I spoke of the note which had been found in the dead man's pocket. 'It is sure to be produced at the inquest. May I ask you to throw any light upon it that you can?'

'I see no reason for mystery,' she answered. 'We were engaged to be married, and we only kept it secret because Fitzroy's uncle, who is very old and said to be dying, might have disinherited him if he had married against his wish. There was no other reason.'

'You could have told us,' growled Mr Bellamy.

'So I would, father, if you had ever shown sympathy.'

'I object to my girl picking up with men outside her own station.'

'It was your prejudice against him which prevented us from telling you. As to this appointment' – she fumbled in her dress and produced a crumpled note – 'it was in answer to this.'

DEAREST [ran the message]:
The old place on the beach just after sunset on Tuesday. It is the only time I can get away.
F.M.

'Tuesday was today, and I had meant to meet him tonight.'

I turned over the paper. 'This never came by post. How did you get it?'

'I would rather not answer that question. It has really nothing to do with the matter which you are investigating. But anything which bears upon that I will most freely answer.'

She was as good as her word, but there was nothing which was helpful in our investigation. She had no reason to think that her fiancé had any hidden enemy, but she admitted that she had had several warm admirers.

'May I ask if Mr Ian Murdoch was one of them?'

She blushed and seemed confused.

'There was a time when I thought he was. But that was all changed when he understood the relations between Fitzroy and myself.'

Again the shadow round this strange man seemed to me to be taking more definite shape. His record must be examined. His rooms must be privately searched. Stackhurst was a willing collaborator, for in his mind also suspicions were forming. We returned from our visit to The Haven with the hope that one free end of this tangled skein was already in our hands.

A week passed. The inquest had thrown no light upon the matter and had been adjourned for further evidence. Stackhurst had made discreet inquiry about his subordinate, and there had been a superficial search of his room, but without result. Personally, I had gone over the whole ground again, both physically and mentally, but with no new conclusions. In all my chronicles the reader will find no case which brought me so completely to the limit of my powers. Even my imagination could conceive no solution to the mystery. And then there came the incident of the dog.

It was my old housekeeper who heard of it first by that strange wireless by which such people collect the news of the countryside.

'Sad story this, sir, about Mr McPherson's dog,' said she one evening.

I do not encourage such conversations, but the words arrested my attention.

'What of Mr McPherson's dog?'

'Dead, sir. Died of grief for its master.'

'Who told you this?'

'Why, sir, everyone is talking of it. It took on terrible, and has eaten nothing for a week. Then today two of the young gentlemen from The Gables found it dead – down on the beach, sir, at the very place where its master met his end.'

'At the very place.' The words stood out clear in my memory. Some dim perception that the matter was vital rose in my mind. That the dog should die was after the beautiful, faithful nature of dogs. But 'in the very place'! Why should this lonely beach be fatal to it? Was it possible that it also had been sacrificed to some revengeful feud? Was it possible—? Yes, the perception was dim, but already something was building up in my mind. In a few minutes I was on my way to The Gables, where I found Stackhurst in his study. At my request he sent for Sudbury and Blount, the two students who had found the dog.

'Yes, it lay on the very edge of the pool,' said one of them. 'It must have followed the trail of its dead master.'

I saw the faithful little creature, an Airedale terrier, laid out upon the mat in the hall. The body was stiff and rigid, the eyes projecting, and the limbs contorted. There was agony in every line of it.

From The Gables I walked down to the bathing-pool. The sun had sunk and the shadow of the great cliff lay black across the water, which glimmered dully like a sheet of lead. The place was deserted and there was no sign of life save for two sea-birds circling and screaming overhead. In the fading light I could dimly make out the little dog's spoor upon the sand round the very rock on which his master's towel had been laid. For a long time I stood in deep meditation while the shadows grew darker around me. My mind was filled with racing thoughts. You have known what it was to be in a nightmare in which you feel that there is some all-important thing for which you search and which you know is there, though it remains forever just beyond your reach. That was how I felt that evening as I stood alone by that place of death. Then at last I turned and walked slowly homeward.

I had just reached the top of the path when it came to me. Like a flash, I remembered the thing for which I had so eagerly and vainly grasped. You will know, or Watson has written in vain, that I hold a vast store of out-of-the-way knowledge without scientific system, but very available for the needs of my work. My mind is like a crowded box-room with packets of all sorts stowed away therein – so many that I may well have but a vague perception of what was there. I had known that there was something which might bear upon this matter. It was still vague, but at least I knew how I could make it clear. It was monstrous, incredible, and yet it was always a possibility. I would test it to the full.

There is a great garret in my little house which is stuffed with books. It was into this that I plunged and rummaged for an hour. At the end of that time I emerged with a little chocolate and silver volume. Eagerly I turned up the chapter of which I had a dim remembrance. Yes, it was indeed a far-fetched and unlikely proposition, and yet I could not be at rest until I had made sure if it might, indeed, be so. It was late when I retired, with my mind eagerly awaiting the work of the morrow.

But that work met with an annoying interruption. I had hardly swallowed my early cup of tea and was starting for the beach when I had a call from Inspector Bardle of the Sussex Constabulary – a steady, solid, bovine man with thoughtful eyes, which looked at me now with a very troubled expression.

'I know your immense experience, sir,' said he. 'This is quite unofficial, of course, and need go no farther. But I am fairly up against it in this McPherson case. The question is, shall I make an arrest, or shall I not?'

'Meaning Mr Ian Murdoch?'

'Yes, sir. There is really no one else when you come to think of it. That's the advantage of this solitude. We narrow it down to a very small compass. If he did not do it, then who did?'

'What have you against him?'

He had gleaned along the same furrows as I had. There was Murdoch's character and the mystery which seemed to hang round the man. His furious bursts of temper, as shown in the incident of the dog. The fact that he had quarrelled with McPherson in the past, and that there was some reason to think that he might have resented his attentions to Miss Bellamy. He had all my points, but no fresh ones, save that Murdoch seemed to be making every preparation for departure.

'What would my position be if I let him slip away with all this evidence against him?' The burly, phlegmatic man was sorely troubled in his mind.

'Consider,' I said, 'all the essential gaps in your case. On the morning of the crime he can surely prove an alibi. He had been with his scholars till the last moment, and within a few minutes of McPherson's appearance he came upon us from behind. Then bear in mind the absolute impossibility that he could single-handed have inflicted this outrage upon a man quite as strong as himself. Finally, there is this question of the instrument with which these injuries were inflicted.'

'What could it be but a scourge or flexible whip of some sort?'

'Have you examined the marks?' I asked.

'I have seen them. So has the doctor.'

'But I have examined them very carefully with a lens. They have peculiarities.'

'What are they, Mr Holmes?'

I stepped to my bureau and brought out an enlarged photograph. 'This is my method in such cases,' I explained.

'You certainly do things thoroughly, Mr Holmes.'

'I should hardly be what I am if I did not. Now let us consider this weal which extends round the right shoulder. Do you observe nothing remarkable?'

'I can't say I do.'

'Surely it is evident that it is unequal in its intensity. There is a dot of extravasated blood here, and another there. There are similar indications in this other weal down here. What can that mean?'

'I have no idea. Have you?'

'Perhaps I have. Perhaps I haven't. I may be able to say more soon. Anything which will define what made that mark will bring us a long way towards the criminal.'

'It is, of course, an absurd idea,' said the policeman, 'but if a red-hot net of wire had been laid across the back, then these better-marked points would represent where the meshes crossed each other.'

'A most ingenious comparison. Or shall we say a very stiff cat-o'-nine-tails with small hard knots upon it?'

'By Jove, Mr Holmes, I think you have hit it.'

'Or there may be some very different cause, Mr Bardle. But your case is far too weak for an arrest. Besides, we have those last words – "the Lion's Mane".'

'I have wondered whether Ian—'

'Yes, I have considered that. If the second word had borne any resemblance to Murdoch – but it did not. He gave it almost in a shriek. I am sure that it was "Mane".'

'Have you no alternative, Mr Holmes?'

'Perhaps I have. But I do not care to discuss it until there is something more solid to discuss.'

'And when will that be?'

'In an hour – possibly less.'

The inspector rubbed his chin and looked at me with dubious eyes.

'I wish I could see what was in your mind, Mr Holmes. Perhaps it's those fishing-boats.'

'No, no, they were too far out.'

'Well, then, is it Bellamy and that big son of his? They were not too sweet upon Mr McPherson. Could they have done him a mischief?'

'No, no, you won't draw me until I am ready,' said I with a smile. 'Now, Inspector, we each have our own work to do. Perhaps if you were to meet me here at midday—'

So far we had got when there came the tremendous interruption which was the beginning of the end.

My outer door was flung open, there were blundering footsteps in the passage, and Ian Murdoch staggered into the room, pallid, dishevelled, his clothes in wild disorder, clawing with his bony hands at the furniture to hold himself erect. 'Brandy! Brandy!' he gasped, and fell groaning upon the sofa.

He was not alone. Behind him came Stackhurst, hatless and panting, almost as distrait as his companion.

'Yes, yes, brandy!' he cried. 'The man is at his last gasp. It was all I could do to bring him here. He fainted twice upon the way.'

Half a tumbler of the raw spirit brought about a wondrous change. He pushed himself up on one arm and swung his coat from his shoulders. 'For God's sake oil, opium, morphia!' he cried. 'Anything to ease this infernal agony!'

The inspector and I cried out at the sight. There, criss-crossed upon the man's naked shoulder, was the same strange reticulated pattern of red, inflamed lines which had been the death-mark of Fitzroy McPherson.

The pain was evidently terrible and was more than local,

for the sufferer's breathing would stop for a time, his face would turn black, and then with loud gasps he would clap his hand to his heart, while his brow dropped beads of sweat. At any moment he might die. More and more brandy was poured down his throat, each fresh dose bringing him back to life. Pads of cotton-wool soaked in salad-oil seemed to take the agony from the strange wounds. At last his head fell heavily upon the cushion. Exhausted Nature had taken refuge in its last storehouse of vitality. It was half a sleep and half a faint, but at least it was ease from pain.

To question him had been impossible, but the moment we were assured of his condition Stackhurst turned upon me.

'My God!' he cried, 'what is it, Holmes? What is it?'

'Where did you find him?'

'Down on the beach. Exactly where poor McPherson met his end. If this man's heart had been weak as McPherson's was, he would not be here now. More than once I thought he was gone as I brought him up. It was too far to The Gables, so I made for you.'

'Did you see him on the beach?'

'I was walking on the cliff when I heard his cry. He was at the edge of the water, reeling about like a drunken man. I ran down, threw some clothes about him, and brought him up. For heaven's sake, Holmes, use all the powers you have and spare no pains to lift the curse from this place, for life is becoming unendurable. Can you, with all your world-wide reputation, do nothing for us?'

'I think I can, Stackhurst. Come with me now! And you, Inspector, come along! We will see if we cannot deliver this murderer into your hands.'

Leaving the unconscious man in the charge of my housekeeper, we all three went down to the deadly lagoon. On the shingle there was piled a little heap of towels and clothes left by the stricken man. Slowly I walked round the edge of the water, my comrades in Indian file behind me. Most of the pool was quite shallow, but under the cliff where the beach was hollowed out it was four or five feet deep. It was to this part that a swimmer would naturally go, for it formed a beautiful pellucid green pool as clear as crystal. A line of rocks lay above it at the base of the cliff, and along this I led the way, peering eagerly into the depths beneath me. I had reached the deepest and stillest pool when my eyes caught that for which they were searching, and I burst into a shout of triumph.

'*Cyanea*!' I cried. '*Cyanea*! Behold the Lion's Mane!'

The strange object at which I pointed did indeed look like a tangled mass torn from the mane of a lion. It lay upon a rocky shelf some three feet under the water, a curious waving, vibrating, hairy creature with streaks of silver among its yellow tresses. It pulsated with a slow, heavy dilation and contraction.

'It has done mischief enough. Its day is over!' I cried. 'Help me, Stackhurst! Let us end the murderer for ever.'

There was a big boulder just above the ledge, and we pushed it until it fell with a tremendous splash into the water. When the ripples had cleared we saw that it had settled upon the ledge below. One flapping edge of yellow membrane showed that our victim was beneath it. A thick oily scum oozed out from below the stone and stained the water round, rising slowly to the surface.

'Well, this gets me!' cried the inspector. 'What was it, Mr

Holmes? I'm born and bred in these parts, but I never saw such a thing. It don't belong to Sussex.'

'Just as well for Sussex,' I remarked. 'It may have been the southwest gale that brought it up. Come back to my house, both of you, and I will give you the terrible experience of one who has good reason to remember his own meeting with the same peril of the seas.'

When we reached my study we found that Murdoch was so far recovered that he could sit up. He was dazed in mind, and every now and then was shaken by a paroxysm of pain. In broken words he explained that he had no notion what had occurred to him, save that terrific pangs had suddenly shot through him, and that it had taken all his fortitude to reach the bank.

'Here is a book,' I said, taking up the little volume, 'which first brought light into what might have been forever dark. It is *Out of Doors*, by the famous observer J.G. Wood. Wood himself very nearly perished from contact with this vile creature, so he wrote with a very full knowledge. *Cyanea capillata* is the miscreant's full name, and he can be as dangerous to life as, and far more painful than, the bite of the cobra. Let me briefly give this extract.

> 'If the bather should see a loose roundish mass of tawny membranes and fibres, something like very large handfuls of lion's mane and silver paper, let him beware, for this is the fearful stinger, *Cyanea capillata*.

'Could our sinister acquaintance be more clearly described?

'He goes on to tell of his own encounter with one when swimming off the coast of Kent. He found that the creature radiated almost invisible filaments to the distance of fifty feet, and that anyone within that circumference from the deadly centre was in danger of death. Even at a distance the effect upon Wood was almost fatal.

> 'The multitudinous threads caused light scarlet lines upon the skin which on closer examination resolved into minute dots or pustules, each dot charged as it were with a red-hot needle making its way through the nerves.

'The local pain was, as he explains, the least part of the exquisite torment.

> 'Pangs shot through the chest, causing me to fall as if struck by a bullet. The pulsation would cease, and then the heart would give six or seven leaps as if it would force its way through the chest.

'It nearly killed him, although he had only been exposed to it in the disturbed ocean and not in the narrow calm waters of a bathing-pool. He says that he could hardly recognise himself afterwards, so white, wrinkled and shrivelled was his face. He gulped down brandy, a whole bottleful, and it seems to have saved his life. There is the book, Inspector. I leave it with you, and you cannot doubt that it contains a full explanation of the tragedy of poor McPherson.'

'And incidentally exonerates me,' remarked Ian Murdoch with a wry smile. 'I do not blame you, Inspector, nor you, Mr Holmes, for your suspicions were natural. I feel that on the very eve of my arrest I have only cleared myself by sharing the fate of my poor friend.'

'No, Mr Murdoch. I was already upon the track, and had I been out as early as I intended I might well have saved you from this terrific experience.'

'But how did you know, Mr Holmes?'

'I am an omnivorous reader with a strangely retentive memory for trifles. That phrase "the Lion's Mane" haunted my mind. I knew that I had seen it somewhere in an unexpected context. You have seen that it does describe the creature. I have no doubt that it was floating on the water when McPherson saw it, and that this phrase was the only one by which he could convey to us a warning as to the creature which had been his death.'

'Then I, at least, am cleared,' said Murdoch, rising slowly to his feet. 'There are one or two words of explanation which I should give, for I know the direction in which your inquiries have run. It is true that I loved this lady, but from the day when she chose my friend McPherson my one desire was to help her to happiness. I was well content to stand aside and act as their go-between. Often I carried their messages, and it was because I was in their confidence and because she was so dear to me that I hastened to tell her of my friend's death, lest someone should forestall me in a more sudden and heartless manner. She would not tell you, sir, of our relations lest you should disapprove and I might suffer. But with your leave I must try to get back to The Gables, for my bed will be very welcome.'

Stackhurst held out his hand. 'Our nerves have all been at concert-pitch,' said he. 'Forgive what is past, Murdoch. We shall understand each other better in the future.' They passed out together with their arms linked in friendly fashion. The inspector remained, staring at me in silence with his ox-like eyes.

'Well, you've done it!' he cried at last. 'I had read of you, but I never believed it. It's wonderful!'

I was forced to shake my head. To accept such praise was to lower one's own standards.

'I was slow at the outset – culpably slow. Had the body been found in the water I could hardly have missed it. It was the towel which misled me. The poor fellow had never thought to dry himself, and so I in turn was led to believe that he had never been in the water. Why, then, should the attack of any water creature suggest itself to me? That was where I went astray. Well, well, Inspector, I often ventured to chaff you gentlemen of the police force, but *Cyanea capillata* very nearly avenged Scotland Yard.'

The Unsolved Puzzle of the Man with No Face

Dorothy L. Sayers

'And what would *you* say, sir,' said the stout man, 'to this here business of the bloke what's been found down on the beach at East Felpham?'

The rush of travellers after the Bank Holiday had caused an overflow of third-class passengers into the firsts, and the stout man was anxious to seem at ease in his surroundings. The youngish gentleman whom he addressed had obviously paid full fare for a seclusion which he was fated to forgo. He took the matter amiably enough, however, and replied in a courteous tone:

'I'm afraid I haven't read more than the headlines. Murdered, I suppose, wasn't he?'

'It's murder, right enough,' said the stout man, with relish. 'Cut about he was, something shocking.'

'More like as if a wild beast had done it,' chimed in the

thin, elderly man opposite. 'No face at all he hadn't got, by what my paper says. It'll be one of these maniacs, I shouldn't be surprised, what goes about killing children.'

'I wish you wouldn't talk about such things,' said his wife, with a shudder. 'I lays awake at nights thinking what might 'appen to Lizzie's girls, till my head feels regular in a fever, and I has such a sinking in my inside I has to get up and eat biscuits. They didn't ought to put such dreadful things in the papers.'

'It's better they should, ma'am,' said the stout man, 'then we're warned, so to speak, and can take our measures accordingly. Now, from what I can make out, this unfortunate gentleman had gone bathing all by himself in a lonely spot. Now, quite apart from cramps, as is a thing that might 'appen to the best of us, that's a very foolish thing to do.'

'Just what I'm always telling my husband,' said the young wife. The young husband frowned and fidgeted. 'Well, dear, it really isn't safe, and you with your heart not strong—' Her hand sought his under the newspaper. He drew away, self-consciously, saying: 'That'll do, Kitty.'

'The way I look at it is this,' pursued the stout man. 'Here we've been and had a war, what has left 'undreds o' men in what you might call a state of unstable ekilibrium. They've seen all their friends blown up or shot to pieces. They've been through five years of 'orrors and bloodshed, and it's given 'em what you might call a twist in the mind towards 'orrors. They may seem to forget it and go along as peaceable as anybody to all outward appearance, but it's all artificial, if you get my meaning. Then, one day something 'appens to upset them –they 'as words with the wife, or the weather's extra hot, as it is today – and something goes pop inside their brains and makes raving monsters of them. It's all in the books. I do a good bit of reading myself of an evening, being a bachelor without encumbrances.'

'That's all very true,' said a prim little man, looking up from his magazine, 'very true indeed – too true. But do you think it applies in the present case? I've studied the literature of crime a good deal – I may say I make it my hobby – and it's my opinion there's more in this than meets the eye. If you will compare this murder with some of the most mysterious crimes of late years – crimes which, mind you, have never been solved, and, in my opinion, never will be – what do you find?' He paused and looked round. 'You will find many features in common with this case. But especially you will find that the face – and the face only, mark you – has been disfigured, as though to prevent recognition. As though to blot out the victim's personality from the world. And you will find that, in spite of the most thorough investigation, the criminal is never discovered. Now what does all that point to? To organisation. Organisation. To an immensely powerful influence at work behind the scenes. In this very magazine that I'm reading now—' he tapped the page impressively – 'there's an account – not a faked-up story, but an account extracted from the annals of the police of the organisation of one of these secret societies, which mark down men against whom they bear a grudge, and destroy them. And, when they do this, they disfigure their faces with the mark of the Secret Society, and they cover up the track of the assassin so completely – having money and resources at their disposal – that nobody is ever able to get at them.'

'I've read of such things, of course,' admitted the stout

man, 'but I thought as they mostly belonged to the medeevial days. They had a thing like that in Italy once. What did they call it now? A Gomorrah, was it? Are there any Gomorrahs nowadays?'

'You spoke a true word, sir, when you said Italy,' replied the prim man. 'The Italian mind is made for intrigue. There's the Fascisti. That's come to the surface now, of course, but it started by being a secret society. And, if you were to look below the surface, you would be amazed at the way in which that country is honeycombed with hidden organisations of all sorts. Don't you agree with me, sir?' he added, addressing the first-class passenger.

'Ah!' said the stout man, 'no doubt this gentleman has been in Italy and knows all about it. Should you say this murder was the work of a Gomorrah, sir?'

'I hope not, I'm sure,' said the first-class passenger. 'I mean, it rather destroys the interest, don't you think? I like a nice, quiet, domestic murder myself, with the millionaire found dead in the library. The minute I open a detective story and find a Camorra in it, my interest seems to dry up and turn to dust and ashes – a sort of Sodom and Camorra, as you might say.'

'I agree with you there,' said the young husband, 'from what you might call the artistic standpoint. But in this particular case I think there may be something to be said for this gentleman's point of view.'

'Well,' admitted the first-class passenger, 'not having read the details—'

'The details are clear enough,' said the prim man. 'This poor creature was found lying dead on the beach at East Felpham early this morning, with his face cut about in the most dreadful manner. He had nothing on him but his bathing-dress.'

'Stop a minute. Who was he, to begin with?'

'They haven't identified him yet. His clothes had been taken—'

'That looks more like robbery, doesn't it?' suggested Kitty.

'If it was just robbery,' retorted the prim man, 'why should his face have been cut up in that way? No – the clothes were taken away, as I said, to prevent identification. That's what these societies always try to do.'

'Was he stabbed?' demanded the first-class passenger.

'No,' said the stout man. 'He wasn't. He was strangled.'

'Not a characteristically Italian method of killing,' observed the first-class passenger.

'No more it is,' said the stout man. The prim man seemed a little disconcerted.

'And if he went down there to bathe,' said the thin, elderly man, 'how did he get there? Surely somebody must have missed him before now, if he was staying at Felpham. It's a busy spot for visitors in the holiday season.'

'No,' said the stout man, 'not East Felpham. You're thinking of West Felpham, where the yacht-club is. East Felpham is one of the loneliest spots on the coast. There's no house near except a little pub all by itself at the end of a long road, and after that you have to go through three fields to get to the sea. There's no real road, only a cart track, but you can take a car through. I've been there.'

'He came in a car,' said the prim man. 'They found the track of the wheels. But it had been driven away again.'

'It looks as though the two men had come there together,' suggested Kitty.

'I think they did,' said the prim man. 'The victim was probably gagged and bound and taken along in the car to the place, and then he was taken out and strangled and—'

'But why should they have troubled to put on his bathing-dress?' said the first-class passenger.

'Because,' said the prim man, 'as I said, they didn't want to leave any clothes to reveal his identity.'

'Quite; but why not leave him naked? A bathing-dress seems to indicate an almost excessive regard for decorum, under the circumstances.'

'Yes, yes,' said the stout man impatiently, 'but you 'aven't read the paper carefully. The two men couldn't have come there in company, and for why? There was only one set of footprints found, and they belonged to the murdered man.'

He looked round triumphantly.

'Only one set of footprints, eh?' said the first-class passenger quickly. 'This looks interesting. Are you sure?'

'It says so in the paper. A single set of footprints, it says, made by bare feet, which by a careful comparison 'ave been shown to be those of the murdered man, lead from the position occupied by the car to the place where the body was found. What do you make of that?'

'Why,' said the first-class passenger, 'that tells one quite a lot, don't you know. It gives one a sort of a bird's-eye view of the place, and it tells one the time of the murder, besides castin' quite a good bit of light on the character and circumstances of the murderer – or murderers.'

'How do you make that out, sir?' demanded the elderly man.

'Well, to begin with – though I've never been near the place, there is obviously a sandy beach from which one can bathe.'

'That's right,' said the stout man.

'There is also, I fancy, in the neighbourhood, a spur of rock running out into the sea, quite possibly with a handy diving-pool. It must run out pretty far; at any rate, one can bathe there before it is high water on the beach.'

'I don't know how you know that, sir, but it's a fact. There's rocks and a bathing-pool, exactly as you describe, about a hundred yards farther along. Many's the time I've had a dip off the end of them.'

'And the rocks run right back inland, where they are covered with short grass.'

'That's right.'

'The murder took place shortly before high tide, I fancy, and the body lay just about at high-tide mark.'

'Why so?'

'Well, you say there were footsteps leading right up to the body. That means that the water hadn't been up beyond the body. But there were no other marks. Therefore the murderer's footprints must have been washed away by the tide. The only explanation is that the two men were standing together just below the tide-mark. The murderer came up out of the sea. He attacked the other man – maybe he forced him back a little on his own tracks – and there he killed him. Then the water came up and washed out any marks the murderer may have left. One can imagine him squatting there, wondering if the sea was going to come up high enough.'

'Ow!' said Kitty. 'You make me creep all over.'

'Now, as to these marks on the face,' pursued the first-class passenger. 'The murderer, according to the idea I get of the thing, was already in the sea when the victim came along. You see the idea?'

'I get you,' said the stout man. 'You think as he went in off them rocks what we was speaking of, and came up through the water, and that's why there weren't no footprints.'

'Exactly. And since the water is deep round those rocks, as you say, he was presumably in a bathing-dress too.'

'Looks like it.'

'Quite so. Well, now – what was the face-slashing done with? People don't usually take knives out with them when they go for a morning dip.'

'That's a puzzle,' said the stout man.

'Not altogether. Let's say, either the murderer had a knife with him or he had not. If he had—'

'If he had,' put in the prim man eagerly, 'he must have laid wait for the deceased on purpose. And, to my mind, that bears out my idea of a deep and cunning plot.'

'Yes. But, if he was waiting there with the knife, why didn't he stab the man and have done with it? Why strangle him, when he had a perfectly good weapon there to hand? No – I think he came unprovided, and, when he saw his enemy there, he made for him with his hands in the characteristic British way.'

'But the slashing?'

'Well, I think that when he had got his man down, dead before him, he was filled with a pretty grim sort of fury and wanted to do more damage. He caught up something that was lying near him on the sand – it might be a bit of old iron, or even one of those sharp shells you sometimes see about, or a bit of glass – and he went for him with that in a desperate rage of jealousy or hatred.'

'Dreadful, dreadful!' said the elderly woman.

'Of course, one can only guess in the dark, not having seen the wounds. It's quite possible that the murderer dropped his knife in the struggle, and had to do the actual killing with his hands, picking the knife up afterwards. If the wounds were clean knife-wounds, that is probably what happened, and the murder was premeditated. But if they were rough, jagged gashes, made by an impromptu weapon, then I should say it was a chance encounter, and that the murderer was either mad or—'

'Or?'

'Or had suddenly come upon somebody whom he hated very much.'

'What do you think happened afterwards?'

'That's pretty clear. The murderer, having waited, as I said, to see that all his footprints were cleaned up by the tide, waded or swam back to the rock where he had left his clothes, taking the weapon with him. The sea would wash away any blood from his bathing-dress or body. He then climbed out upon the rocks, walked, with bare feet, so as to leave no tracks on any seaweed or anything, to the grass of the shore, dressed, went along to the murdered man's car, and drove it away.'

'Why did he do that?'

'Yes, why? He may have wanted to get somewhere in a hurry. Or he may have been afraid that if the murdered man were identified too soon it would cast suspicion on him. Or it may have been a mixture of motives. The point is, where did he come from? How did he come to be bathing at that remote spot, early in the morning? He didn't get there by car, or there would be a second car to be accounted for. He may have been camping near the spot; but it would have taken him a long time to strike camp and pack all his belongings into the car, and he might have been seen. I am rather inclined to think he had bicycled there, and that he hoisted the bicycle into the back of the car, and took it away with him.'

'But, in that case, why take the car?'

'Because he had been down at East Felpham longer than he expected, and he was afraid of being late. Either he had to get back to breakfast at some house, where his absence would be noticed, or else he lived some distance off, and had only just time enough for the journey home. I think, though, he had to be back to breakfast.'

'Why?'

'Because, if it was merely a question of making up time on the road, all he had to do was to put himself and his bicycle on the train for part of the way. No; I fancy he was staying in a smallish hotel somewhere. Not a large hotel, because there nobody would notice whether he came in or not. And not, I think, in lodgings, or somebody would have mentioned before now that they had had a lodger who went bathing at East Felpham. Either he lives in the neighbourhood, in which case he should be easy to trace, or was staying with friends who have an interest in concealing his movements. Or else – which I think is more likely – he was in a smallish hotel, where he would be missed from the breakfast-table, but where his favourite bathing-place was not a matter of common knowledge.'

'That seems feasible,' said the stout man.

'In any case,' went on the first-class passenger, 'he must have been staying within easy bicycling distance of East Felpham, so it shouldn't be too hard to trace him. And then there is the car.'

'Yes. Where is the car, on your theory?' demanded the prim man, who obviously still had hankerings after the Camorra theory.

'In a garage, waiting to be called for,' said the first-class passenger promptly.

'Where?' persisted the prim man.

'Oh, somewhere on the other side of wherever it was the murderer was staying. If you have a particular reason for not wanting it to be known that you were in a certain place at a specified time, it's not a bad idea to come back from the opposite direction. I rather think I should look for the car at West Felpham, and the hotel in the nearest town on the main road beyond where the two roads to East and West Felpham join. When you've found the car, you've found the name of the victim, naturally. As for the murderer, you will have to look for an active man, a good swimmer, and ardent cyclist – probably not very well off, since he cannot afford to have a car – who has been taking a holiday in the neighbourhood of the Felphams, and who has a good reason for disliking the victim, whoever he may be.'

'Well, I never,' said the elderly woman admiringly. 'How beautiful you do put it all together. Like Sherlock Holmes, I do declare.'

'It's a very pretty theory,' said the prim man, 'but, all the same, you'll find it's a secret society. Mark my words. Dear me! We're just running in. Only twenty minutes late. I call that very good for holiday time. Will you excuse me? My bag is just under your feet.'

There was an eighth person in the compartment, who had remained throughout the conversation apparently buried in a newspaper. As the passengers decanted themselves upon the platform, this man touched the first-class passenger upon the arm.

'Excuse me, sir,' he said. 'That was a very interesting suggestion of yours. My name is Winterbottom, and I am investigating this case. Do you mind giving me your name? I might wish to communicate with you later on.'

'Certainly,' said the first-class passenger. 'Always delighted to have a finger in any pie, don't you know. Here is my card. Look me up any time you like.'

Detective-Inspector Winterbottom took the card, and read the name:

LORD PETER WIMSEY
110A PICCADILLY.

The *Evening Views* vendor outside Piccadilly Tube Station arranged his placard with some care. It looked very well, he thought.

MAN WITH
NO FACE
IDENTIFIED

It was, in his opinion, considerably more striking than that displayed by a rival organ, which announced, unimaginatively:

BEACH MURDER
VICTIM
IDENTIFIED

A youngish gentleman in a grey suit who emerged at that moment from the Criterion Bar appeared to think so too, for he exchanged a copper for the *Evening Views*, and at once plunged into its perusal with such concentrated interest that he bumped into a hurried man outside the station, and had to apologise.

The *Evening Views*, grateful to murderer and victim alike for providing so useful a sensation in the dead days after the Bank Holiday, had torn Messrs Negretti & Zambra's rocketing thermometrical statistics from the 'banner' position which they had occupied in the lunch edition, and substituted:

FACELESS VICTIM OF BEACH OUTRAGE IDENTIFIED

MURDER OF PROMINENT
PUBLICITY ARTIST

POLICE CLUES

The body of a middle-aged man who was discovered, attired only in a bathing costume, and with his face horribly disfigured by some jagged instrument, on the beach at East Felpham last Monday morning, has been identified as that of Mr Coreggio Plant, studio manager of Messrs Crichton, Ltd, the well-known publicity experts of Holborn.

Mr Plant, who was forty-five years of age and a bachelor, was spending his annual holiday in making a motoring tour along the West Coast. He had no companion with him, and had left no address for the forwarding of letters, so that, without the smart work of Detective-Inspector Winterbottom of the Westshire Police, his disappearance might not in the ordinary way have been noticed until he became due to return to his place of business in three weeks' time. The murderer had no doubt counted on this, and had removed the motor-car, containing the belongings of his victim, in the hope of covering up all traces of this dastardly outrage so as to gain time for escape.

A rigorous search for the missing car, however, eventuated in its discovery in a garage at West Felpham, where it had been left for decarbonisation and repairs to the magneto. Mr Spiller, the garage proprietor, himself saw the man who left the car, and has furnished a description of him to the police. He is said to be a small, dark man of foreign appearance. The police hold a clue to his identity, and an arrest is confidently expected in the near future.

Mr Plant was for fifteen years in the employment of Messrs Crichton, being appointed Studio Manager in the latter years of the war. He was greatly liked by all his colleagues, and his skill in the lay-out and designing of advertisements did much to justify the truth of Messrs Crichton's well-known slogan: 'Crichton's for Admirable Advertising.'

The funeral of the victim will take place tomorrow at Golders Green Cemetery.

(Pictures on Back Page.)

Lord Peter Wimsey turned to the back page. The portrait of the victim did not detain him long; it was one of those characterless studio photographs which establish nothing except that the sitter has a tolerable set of features. He noted that Mr Plant had been thin rather than fat, commercial in appearance rather than artistic, and that the photographer had chosen to show him serious rather than smiling. A picture of East Felpham beach, marked with a cross where the body was found, seemed to arouse in him rather more than a casual interest. He studied it intently for some time, making little surprised noises. There was no obvious reason why he should have been surprised, for the photograph bore out in every detail the deductions he had made in the train. There was the curved line of sand, with a long spur of rock stretching out behind it into deep water, and running back till it mingled with the short, dry turf. Nevertheless, he looked at it for several minutes with close attention before folding the newspaper and hailing a taxi; and when he was in the taxi he unfolded the paper and looked at it again.

'Your lordship having been kind enough,' said Inspector Winterbottom, emptying his glass rather too rapidly for true connoisseurship, 'to suggest I should look you up in Town, I made so bold to give you a call in passing. Thank you, I won't say no. Well, as you've seen in the papers by now, we found that car, all right.'

Wimsey expressed his gratification at this result:

'And very much obliged I was to your lordship for the hint,' went on the Inspector generously, 'not but what I wouldn't say but I should have come to the same conclusion myself, given a little more time. And, what's more, we're on the track of the man.'

'I see he's supposed to be foreign-looking. Don't say he's going to turn out to be a Camorrist, after all!'

'No, my lord.' The Inspector winked. 'Our friend in the corner had got his magazine stories a bit on the brain, if you ask me. And you were a bit out, too, my lord, with your bicyclist idea.'

'Was I? That's a blow.'

'Well, my lord, these here theories *sound* all right, but half the time they're too fine-spun altogether. Go for the facts – that's our motto in the Force – facts and motive, and you won't go far wrong.'

'Oh, you've discovered the motive, then?'

The Inspector winked again.

'There's not many motives for doing a man in,' said he. 'Women or money – or women *and* money – it mostly comes down to one or the other. This fellow Plant went in for being a bit of a lad, you see. He kept a little cottage down Felpham way, with a nice little skirt to furnish it and keep the love-nest warm for him – see?'

'Oh! I thought he was doing a motor tour.'

'Motor tour your foot!' said the Inspector, with more energy than politeness. 'That's what the old (epithet) told 'em at the office. Handy reason, don't you see, for leaving no address behind him. No, no. There was a lady in it all right. I've seen her. A very taking piece, too, if you like 'em skinny, which I don't. I prefer 'em better upholstered, myself.'

'That chair is really more comfortable with a cushion,' put in Wimsey, with anxious solicitude. 'Allow me.'

'Thanks, my lord, thanks. I'm doing very well. It seems that this woman – by the way, we're speaking in confidence, you understand. I don't want this to go further till I've got my man under lock and key.'

Wimsey promised discretion.

'That's all right, my lord, that's all right. I know I can rely on you. Well, the long and the short is, this young woman had another fancy man – a sort of an Italiano, whom she'd chucked for Plant, and this same dago got wind of the business, and came down to East Felpham on the Sunday night looking for her. He's one of these professional partners in a Palais de Dance up Cricklewood way, and that's where the girl comes from, too. I suppose she thought Plant was a cut above him. Anyway, down he comes, and busts in upon them Sunday night when they were having a bit of supper – and that's when the row started.'

'Didn't you know about this cottage and the goings-on there?'

'Well, you know, there's such a lot of these weekenders nowadays. We can't keep tabs on all of them, so long as they behave themselves and don't make a disturbance. The woman's been there – so they tell me – since last June, with him coming down Saturday to Monday; but it's a lonely spot, and the constable didn't take much notice. He came in the evenings, so there wasn't anybody much to recognise him, except the old girl who did the slops and things, and she's half-blind. And of course, when they found him, he hadn't any face to recognise. It'd be thought he'd just gone off in the ordinary way. I dare say the dago fellow reckoned on that. As I was saying, there was a big row, and the dago was kicked out. He must have lain in wait for Plant down by the bathing-place, and done him in.'

'By strangling?'

'Well, he was strangled.'

'Was his face cut up with a knife, then?'

'Well, no – I don't think it was a knife. More like a broken bottle, I should say, if you ask me. There's plenty of them come in with the tide.'

'But then we're brought back to our old problem. If this Italian was lying in wait to murder Plant, why didn't he take a weapon with him, instead of trusting to the chance of his hands and a broken bottle?'

The Inspector shook his head.

'Flighty,' he said. 'All these foreigners are flighty. No headpiece. But there's our man, and there's our motive, plain as a pikestaff. You don't want more.'

'And where is the Italian fellow now?'

'Run away. That's pretty good proof of guilt in itself. But we'll have him before long. That's what I've come to Town about. He can't get out of the country. I've had an all-stations call sent out to stop him. The dance-hall people were able to supply us with a photo and a good description. I'm expecting a report in now any minute. In fact, I'd best be getting along. Thank you very much for your hospitality, my lord.'

'The pleasure is mine,' said Wimsey, ringing the bell to have the visitor shown out. 'I have enjoyed our little chat immensely.'

Sauntering into the Falstaff at twelve o'clock the following morning, Wimsey, as he had expected, found Salcombe

Hardy supporting his rather plump contours against the bar. The reporter greeted his arrival with a heartiness amounting almost to enthusiasm, and called for two large Scotches immediately. When the usual skirmish as to who should pay had been honourably settled by the prompt disposal of the drinks and the standing of two more, Wimsey pulled from his pocket the copy of last night's *Evening Views*.

'I wish you'd ask the people over at your place to get hold of a decent print of this for me,' he said, indicating the picture of East Felpham beach.

Salcombe Hardy gazed limpid inquiry at him from eyes like drowned violets.

'See here, you old sleuth,' he said, 'does this mean you've got a theory about the thing? I'm wanting a story badly. Must keep up the excitement, you know. The police don't seem to have got any further since last night.'

'No; I'm interested in this from another point of view altogether. I did have a theory – of sorts – but it seems it's all wrong. Bally old Homer nodding, I suppose. But I'd like a copy of the thing.'

'I'll get Warren to get you one when we come back. I'm just taking him down with me to Crichton's. We're going to have a look at a picture. I say, I wish you'd come, too. Tell me what to say about the damned thing.'

'Good God! I don't know anything about commercial art.'

''Tisn't commercial art. It's supposed to be a portrait of this blighter Plant. Done by one of the chaps in his studio or something. Kid who told me about it says it's clever. I don't know. Don't suppose she knows, either. You go in for being artistic, don't you?'

'I wish you wouldn't use such filthy expressions, Sally. Artistic! Who is this girl?'

'Typist in the copy department.'

'Oh, Sally!'

'Nothing of that sort. I've never met her. Name's Gladys Twitterton. I'm sure that's beastly enough to put anybody off. Rang us up last night and told us there was a bloke there who'd done old Plant in oils, and was it any use to us? Drummer thought it might be worth looking into. Make a change from that everlasting syndicated photograph.'

'I see. If you haven't got an exclusive story, an exclusive picture's better than nothing. The girl seems to have her wits about her. Friend of the artist's?'

'No – said he'd probably be frightfully annoyed at her having told me. But I can wangle that. Only I wish you'd come and have a look at it. Tell me whether I ought to say it's an unknown masterpiece or merely a striking likeness.'

'How the devil can I say if it's a striking likeness of a bloke I've never seen?'

'I'll say it's that, in any case. But I want to know if it's well painted.'

'Curse it, Sally, what's it matter whether it is or not? I've got other things to do. Who's the artist, by the way? Anybody one's ever heard of?'

'Dunno. I've got the name here somewhere.' Sally rooted in his hip-pocket, and produced a mass of dirty correspondence, its angles blunted by constant attrition. 'Some comic name like Buggle or Snagtooth – wait a bit here it is. Crowder. Thomas Crowder. I knew it was something out of the way.'

'Singularly like Buggle or Snagtooth. All right, Sally. I'll make a martyr of myself. Lead me to it.'

'We'll have another quick one. Here's Warren. This is Lord Peter Wimsey. This is on me.'

'On me,' corrected the photographer, a jaded young man with a disillusioned manner. 'Three large White Labels, please. Well, here's all the best. Are you fit, Sally? Because we'd better make tracks. I've got to be up at Golders Green by two for the funeral.'

Mr Crowder of Crichton's appeared to have had the news broken to him already by Miss Twitterton, for he received the embassy in a spirit of gloomy acquiescence.

'The directors won't like it,' he said, 'but they've had to put up with such a lot that I suppose one irregularity more or less won't give 'em apoplexy.' He had a small, anxious, yellow face like a monkey. Wimsey put him down as being in the late thirties. He noticed his fine, capable hands, one of which was disfigured by a strip of sticking plaster.

'Damaged yourself?' said Wimsey pleasantly, as they made their way upstairs to the studio. 'Mustn't make a practice of that, what? An artist's hands are his livelihood – except, of course for Armless Wonders, and people of that kind! Awkward job, painting with your toes.'

'Oh, it's nothing much,' said Crowder, 'but it's best to keep the paint out of surface scratches. There's such a thing as lead-poisoning. Well, here's this dud portrait, such as it is. I don't mind telling you that it didn't please the sitter. In fact, he wouldn't have it at any price.'

'Not flattering enough?' asked Hardy.

'As you say.' The painter pulled out a four by three canvas

from its hiding-place behind a stack of poster cartoons, and heaved it up on to the easel.

'Oh!' said Hardy, a little surprised. Not that there was any reason for surprise as far as the painting itself was concerned. It was a straightforward handling enough; the skill and originality of the brushwork being of the kind that interests the painter without shocking the ignorant.

'Oh!' said Hardy. 'Was he really like that?'

He moved closer to the canvas, peering into it as he might have peered into the face of the living man, hoping to get something out of him. Under this microscopic scrutiny, the portrait, as is the way of portraits, dislimned, and became no more than a conglomeration of painted spots and streaks. He made the discovery that, to the painter's eye, the human face is full of green and purple patches.

He moved back again, and altered the form of his question:

'So that's what he was like, was he?'

He pulled out the photograph of Plant from his pocket, and compared it with the portrait. The portrait seemed to sneer at his surprise.

'Of course, they touch these things up at these fashionable photographers,' he said. 'Anyway, that's not my business. This thing will make a jolly good eye-catcher, don't you think so, Wimsey? Wonder if they'd give us a two-column spread on the front page. Well, Warren, you'd better get down to it.'

The photographer, bleakly unmoved by artistic or journalistic considerations, took silent charge of the canvas, mentally resolving it into a question of panchromatic plates and coloured screens. Crowder gave him a hand in shifting the easel into a better light. Two or three people from other departments, passing through the studio on their lawful occasions, stopped, and lingered in the neighbourhood of the disturbance, as though it were a street accident. A melancholy, grey-haired man, temporary head of the studio, *vice* Coreggio Plant, deceased, took Crowder aside, with a muttered apology, to give him some instructions about adapting a whole quad to an eleven-inch treble. Hardy turned to Lord Peter.

'It's damned ugly,' he said. 'Is it good?'

'Brilliant,' said Wimsey. 'You can go all out. Say what you like about it.'

'Oh, splendid! Could we discover one of our neglected British masters?'

'Yes; why not? You'll probably make the man the fashion, and ruin him as an artist, but that's his pigeon.'

'But, I say – do you think it's a good likeness? He's made him look a most sinister sort of fellow. After all, Plant thought it was so bad he wouldn't have it.'

'The more fool he. Ever heard of the portrait of a certain statesman that was so revealing of his inner emptiness that he hurriedly bought it up and hid it to prevent people like you from getting hold of it?'

Crowder came back.

'I say,' said Wimsey, 'whom does that picture belong to? You? Or the heirs of the deceased, or what?'

'I suppose it's back on my hands,' said the painter. 'Plant – well, he more or less commissioned it, you see, but—'

'How more or less?'

'Well, he kept on hinting, don't you know, that he would

like me to do him, and, as he was my boss, I thought I'd better. No price actually mentioned. When he saw it, he didn't like it, and told me to alter it.'

'But you didn't.'

'Oh – well, I put it aside, and said I'd see what I could do with it. I thought he'd perhaps forget about it.'

'I see. Then presumably it's yours to dispose of.'

'I should think so. Why?'

'You have a very individual technique, haven't you?' pursued Wimsey. 'Do you exhibit much?'

'Here and there. I've never had a show in London.'

'I fancy I once saw a couple of small seascapes of yours somewhere. Manchester, was it? Or Liverpool? I wasn't sure of your name, but I recognised the technique immediately.'

'I dare say. I did send a few things to Manchester about two years ago.'

'Yes – I felt sure I couldn't be mistaken. I want to buy the portrait. Here's my card, by the way. I'm not a journalist; I collect things.'

Crowder looked from the card to Wimsey, and from Wimsey to the card a little reluctantly.

'If you want to exhibit it, of course,' said Lord Peter, 'I should be delighted to leave it with you as long as you liked.'

'Oh, it's not that,' said Crowder. 'The fact is, I'm not altogether keen on the thing. I should like to – that is to say, it's not really finished.'

'My dear man, it's a bally masterpiece.'

'Oh, the painting's all right. But it's not altogether satisfactory as a likeness.'

'What the devil does the likeness matter? I don't know

what the late Plant looked like, and I don't care. As I look at the thing it's a damn fine bit of brushwork, and if you tinker about with it you'll spoil it. You know that as well as I do. What's biting you? It isn't the price, is it? You know I shan't boggle about that. I can afford my modest pleasures, even in these thin and piping times. You don't want me to have it? Come, now – what's the real reason?'

'There's no reason at all why you shouldn't have it if you really want it, I suppose,' said the painter, still a little sullenly. 'If it's really the painting that interests you.'

'What do you suppose it is? The notoriety? I can have all I want of that commodity, you know, for the asking or even without asking. Well, anyhow, think it over, and when you've decided, send me a line and name your price.'

Crowder nodded without speaking, and the photographer having by this time finished his job, the party took their leave.

As they left the building, they became involved in the stream of Crichton's staff going out to lunch. A girl, who seemed to have been loitering in a semi-intentional way in the lower hall, caught them as the lift descended.

'Are you the *Evening Views* people? Did you get your picture all right?'

'Miss Twitterton?' said Hardy interrogatively. 'Yes, rather – thank you so much for giving us the tip. You'll see it on the front page this evening.'

'Oh, that's splendid! I'm frightfully thrilled. It has made an excitement here – all this business. Do they know anything yet about who murdered Mr Plant? Or am I being horribly indiscreet?'

'We're expecting news of an arrest any minute now,' said Hardy. 'As a matter of fact, I shall have to buzz back to the office as fast as I can to sit with one ear glued to the telephone. You will excuse me, won't you? And, look here – will you let me come round another day, when things aren't so busy, and take you out to lunch?'

'Of course. I should love to.' Miss Twitterton giggled. 'I do so want to hear about all the murder cases.'

'Then here's the man to tell you about them, Miss Twitterton,' said Hardy, with mischief in his eye. 'Allow me to introduce Lord Peter Wimsey.'

Miss Twitterton offered her hand in an ecstasy of excitement which almost robbed her of speech.

'How do you do?' said Wimsey. 'As this blighter is in such a hurry to get back to his gossip-shop, what do you say to having a spot of lunch with me?'

'Well, really—' began Miss Twitterton.

'He's all right,' said Hardy; 'he won't lure you into any gilded dens of infamy. If you look at him you will see he has a kind, innocent face.'

'I'm sure I never thought of such a thing,' said Miss Twitterton. 'But, you know – really – I've only got my old things on. It's no good wearing anything decent in this dusty old place.'

'Oh, nonsense!' said Wimsey. 'You couldn't possibly look nicer. It isn't the frock that matters – it's the person who wears it. *That's* all right, then. See you later, Sally! Taxi! Where shall we go? What time do you have to be back, by the way?'

'Two o'clock,' said Miss Twitterton regretfully.

'Then we'll make the Savoy do,' said Wimsey; 'it's reasonably handy.'

Miss Twitterton hopped into the waiting taxi with a little squeak of agitation.

'Did you see Mr Crichton?' she said. 'He went by just as we were talking. However, I dare say he doesn't really know me by sight. I hope not – or he'll think I'm getting too grand to need a salary.' She rooted in her handbag. 'I'm sure my face is getting all shiny with excitement. What a silly taxi. It hasn't got a mirror – and I've bust mine.'

Wimsey solemnly produced a small looking-glass from his pocket.

'How wonderfully competent of you!' exclaimed Miss Twitterton. 'I'm afraid, Lord Peter, you are used to taking girls about.'

'Moderately so,' said Wimsey. He did not think it necessary to mention that the last time he had used that mirror it had been to examine the back teeth of a murdered man.

'Of course,' said Miss Twitterton, 'they had to say he was popular with his colleagues. Haven't you noticed that murdered people are always well dressed and popular?'

'They have to be,' said Wimsey. 'It makes it more mysterious and pathetic. Just as girls who disappear are always bright and home-loving, and have no men friends.'

'Silly, isn't it?' said Miss Twitterton, with her mouth full of roast duck and green peas. 'I should think everybody was only too glad to get rid of Plant – nasty, rude creature. So mean, too, always taking credit for other people's work. All those poor things in the studio, with all the spirit squashed out of them. I always say, Lord Peter, you can tell if a head of a department's fitted for his job by noticing the atmosphere of the place as you go into it. Take the copy-room, now. We're all as cheerful and friendly as you like, though I must say the language that goes on there is something awful, but these writing fellows are like that, and they don't mean anything by it. But then, Mr Ormerod is a real gentleman – that's our copy-chief, you know – and he makes them all take an interest in the work, for all they grumble about the cheese-bills and the department-store bilge they have to turn out. But it's quite different in the studio. A sort of dead-and-alive feeling about it, if you understand what I mean. We girls notice things like that more than some of the high-up people think. Of course, I'm very sensitive to these feelings – almost psychic, I've been told.'

Lord Peter said there was nobody like a woman for sizing up character at a glance. Women, he thought, were remarkably intuitive.

'That's a fact,' said Miss Twitterton. 'I've often said, if I could have a few frank words with Mr Crichton, I could tell him a thing or two. There are wheels within wheels beneath the surface of a place like this that these brass-hats have no idea of.'

Lord Peter said he felt sure of it.

'The way Mr Plant treated people he thought were beneath him,' went on Miss Twitterton, 'I'm sure it was enough to make your blood boil. I'm sure, if Mr Ormerod sent me with a message to him, I was glad to get out of the room again. Humiliating, it was, the way he'd speak to you. I don't care if he's dead or not; being dead doesn't make a person's past behaviour any better, Lord Peter. It wasn't so much the rude things he said. There's Mr Birkett, for example; *he's* rude enough, but nobody minds him. He's just like a big, blundering puppy – rather a lamb, really. It was Mr Plant's nasty sneering way we all hated so. And he was always running people down.'

'How about this portrait?' asked Wimsey. 'Was it like him at all?'

'It was a lot too like him,' said Miss Twitterton emphatically. 'That's why he hated it so. He didn't like Crowder, either. But, of course, he knew he could paint, and he made him do it because he thought he'd be getting a valuable thing cheap. And Crowder couldn't very well refuse or Plant would have got him sacked.'

'I shouldn't have thought that would have mattered much to a man of Crowder's ability.'

'Poor Mr Crowder! I don't think he's ever had much luck. Good artists don't always seem able to sell their pictures. And I know he wanted to get married – otherwise he'd never have taken up this commercial work. He's told me a good bit about himself. I don't know why – but I'm one of the people men seem to tell things to.'

Lord Peter filled Miss Twitterton's glass.

'Oh, please! No, really! Not a drop more! I'm talking a lot too much as it is. I don't know what Mr Ormerod will say when I go in to take his letters. I shall be writing down all kinds of funny things. Ooh! I really must be getting back. Just look at the time!'

'It's not really late. Have a black coffee – just as a corrective.' Wimsey smiled. 'You haven't been talking at all too much. I've enjoyed your picture of office life enormously. You have a very vivid way of putting things, you know. I see now why Mr Plant was not altogether a popular character.'

'Not in the office, anyway – whatever he may have been elsewhere,' said Miss Twitterton darkly.

'Oh?'

'Oh, he was a one!' said Miss Twitterton. 'He certainly was a one. Some friends of mine met him one evening up in the West End, and they came back with some nice stories. It was quite a joke in the office – old Plant and his rosebuds, you know. Mr Cowley – he's the Cowley, you know, who rides in the motor-cycle races – he always said he knew what to think of Mr Plant and his motor tours. That time Mr Plant pretended he'd gone touring in Wales, Mr Cowley was asking him about the roads, and he didn't know a thing about them. Because Mr Cowley really had been touring there, and he knew quite well Mr Plant hadn't been where he said he had; and, as a matter of fact, Mr Cowley knew he'd been staying the whole time in a hotel at Aberystwyth, in very attractive company.'

Miss Twitterton finished her coffee, and slapped the cup down defiantly.

'And now I really *must* run away, or I shall be most dreadfully late. And thank you ever so much.'

'Hullo!' said Inspector Winterbottom. 'You've bought that portrait, then?'

'Yes', said Wimsey: 'It's a fine bit of work.' He gazed thoughtfully at the canvas. 'Sit down, Inspector; I want to tell you a story.'

'And I want to tell *you* a story,' replied the Inspector.

'Let's have yours first,' said Wimsey, with an air of flattering eagerness.

'No, no, my lord. You take precedence. Go ahead.' He snuggled down with a chuckle into his armchair.

'Well,' said Wimsey. 'Mine's a sort of a fairy-story. And, mind you, I haven't verified it.'

'Go ahead, my lord, go ahead.'

'Once upon a time,' said Wimsey sighing.

'That's the good old-fashioned way to begin a fairy-story,' said Inspector Winterbottom.

'Once upon a time,' repeated Wimsey, 'there was a painter. He was a good painter, but the bad fairy of Financial Success had not been asked to his christening – what?'

'That's often the way with painters,' agreed the Inspector.

'So he had to take up a job as a commercial artist, because nobody would buy his pictures and, like so many people in fairy-tales, he wanted to marry a goose-girl.'

'There's many people want to do the same,' said the Inspector.

'The head of his department,' went on Wimsey, 'was a man with a mean, sneering soul. He wasn't even really good at his job, but he had been pushed into authority during the war, when better men went to the Front. Mind you, I'm rather sorry for the man. He suffered from an inferiority complex' – the Inspector snorted – 'and he thought the only way to keep his end up was to keep other people's end down. So he became a little tin tyrant and a bully. He took all the credit for the work of the men under his charge, and he sneered and harassed them till they got inferiority complexes even worse than his own.'

'I've known that sort,' said the Inspector, 'and the marvel to me is how they get away with it.'

'Just so,' said Wimsey. 'Well, I dare say this man would have gone on getting away with it all right if he hadn't thought of getting this painter to paint his portrait.'

'Damn silly thing to do,' said the Inspector. 'It was only making the painter fellow conceited with himself.'

'True. But, you see, this tin tyrant person had a fascinating female in tow, and he wanted the portrait for the lady. He thought that, by making the painter do it, he would get a good portrait at starvation price. But unhappily he'd forgotten that, however much an artist will put up with in the ordinary way, he is bound to be sincere with his art. That's the one thing a genuine artist won't muck about with.'

'I dare say,' said the Inspector. 'I don't know much about artists.'

'Well, you can take it from me. So the painter painted the portrait as he saw it, and he put the man's whole creeping, sneering, paltry soul on the canvas for everybody to see.'

Inspector Winterbottom stared at the portrait, and the portrait sneered back at him.

'It's not what you'd call a flattering picture, certainly,' he admitted.

'Now, when a painter paints a portrait of anybody,' went on Wimsey, 'that person's face is never the same to him again. It's like – what shall I say? Well, it's like the way a gunner, say, looks at a landscape where he happens to be posted. He doesn't see it as a landscape. He doesn't see it as a thing of magic beauty, full of sweeping lines and lovely colour. He sees it as so much cover, so many landmarks to aim by, so many gun-emplacements. And when the war is over and he goes back to it, he will still see it as cover and landmarks and gun-emplacements. It isn't a landscape any more. It's a war map.'

'I know that,' said Inspector Winterbottom. 'I was a gunner myself.'

'A painter gets just the same feeling of deadly familiarity with every line of a face he's once painted,' pursued Wimsey. 'And, if it's a face he hates, he hates it with a new and more irritable hatred. It's like a defective barrel organ, everlastingly grinding out the same old maddening tune, and making the same damned awful wrong note every time the barrel goes round.'

'Lord, how you can talk!' ejaculated the Inspector.

'That was the way the painter felt about this man's hateful face. All day and every day he had to see it. He couldn't get away because he was tied to his job, you see.'

'He ought to have cut loose,' said the Inspector. 'It's no good going on like that, trying to work with uncongenial people.'

'Well, anyway, he said to himself, he could escape for a bit during his holidays. There was a beautiful little quiet spot he knew on the West Coast where nobody ever came. He'd been there before and painted it. Oh, by the way, that reminds me – I've got another picture to show you.'

He went to a bureau and extracted a small panel in oils from a drawer.

'I saw that two years ago at a show in Manchester, and I happened to remember the name of the dealer who bought it.'

Inspector Winterbottom gaped at the panel. 'But that's East Felpham!' he exclaimed.

'Yes. It's only signed T.C., but the technique is rather unmistakable, don't you think?'

The Inspector knew little about technique, but initials he understood. He looked from the portrait to the panel, and back at Lord Peter.

'The painter—'

'Crowder?'

'If it's all the same to you, I'd rather go on calling him the painter. He packed up his traps on his push-bike carrier, and took his tormented nerves down to this beloved and secret spot for a quiet weekend. He stayed at a quiet little hotel in the neighbourhood, and each morning he cycled off to this lovely little beach to bathe. He never told anybody at the hotel where he went, because it was *his* place, and he didn't want other people to find it out.'

Inspector Winterbottom set the panel down on the table, and helped himself to whisky.

'One morning – it happened to be the Monday morning' – Wimsey's voice became slower and more reluctant – 'he went down as usual. The tide was not yet fully in, but he ran out over the rocks to where he knew there was a deep bathing pool. He plunged in and swam about, and let the small noise of his jangling troubles be swallowed up in the innumerable laughter of the sea.'

'Eh?'

'κυμάτων ανήριθμον γέλασμα – quotation from the classics. Some people say it means the dimpled surface of the waves in the sunlight – but how could Prometheus, bound upon his rock, have seen it? Surely it was the chuckle of the incoming tide among the stones that came up to his ears on the lonely peak where the vulture fretted at his heart. I remember arguing about it with old Philpotts in class, and getting rapped over the knuckles for contradicting him. I didn't know at the time that he was engaged in producing a translation on his own account, or doubtless I should have contradicted him more rudely, and been told to take my trousers down. Dear old Philpotts!'

'I don't know anything about that,' said the Inspector.

'I beg your pardon. Shocking way I have of wandering. The painter – well, he swam round the end of the rocks, for the tide was nearly in by that time; and, as he came up from the sea he saw a man standing on the beach – that beloved beach, remember, which he thought was his own sacred haven of peace. He came wading towards it, cursing the Bank Holiday rabble who must needs swarm about everywhere with their cigarette-packets and their kodaks and their gramophones – and then he saw that it was a face he knew. He knew every hated line in it, on that clear, sunny morning. And, early as it was, the heat was coming up over the sea like a haze.'

'It was a hot weekend,' said the Inspector.

'And then the man hailed him, in his smug, mincing voice. "Hullo!" he said. "You here? How did you find my little bathing-place?" And that was too much for the painter. He felt as if his last sanctuary had been invaded. He leapt at the lean throat – it's rather a stringy one, you may notice, with a prominent Adam's apple – an irritating throat. The water chuckled round their feet as they swayed to and fro. He felt his thumbs sink into the flesh he had painted. He saw, and laughed to see, the hateful familiarity of the features change and swell into an unrecognisable purple. He watched the sunken eyes bulge out, and the thin mouth distort itself as the blackened tongue thrust through it – I am not unnerving you, I hope?'

The Inspector laughed.

'Not a bit. It's wonderful, the way you describe things. You ought to write a book.'

'I sing but as the throstle sings, Amid the branches dwelling,' replied his lordship negligently, and went on without further comment.

'The painter throttled him. He flung him back on the sand. He looked at him, and his heart crowed within him. He stretched out his hand, and found a broken bottle, with a good jagged edge. He went to work with a will, stamping and tearing away every trace of the face he knew and loathed. He blotted it out, and destroyed it utterly.

'He sat beside the thing he had made. He began to be frightened. They had staggered back beyond the edge of the water, and there were the marks of his feet on the sand. He had blood on his face and on his bathing-suit, and he had cut his hand with the bottle. But the blessed sea was still coming in. He watched it pass over the bloodstains and the footprints, and wipe the story of his madness away. He remembered that this man had gone from his place, leaving no address behind him. He went back, step by step, into the water, and as it came up to his breast, he saw the red stains smoke away like a faint mist in the brown-blueness of the tide. He went – wading and swimming and plunging his face and arms deep in the water, looking back from time to time to see what he had left behind him. I think that when he got back to the point and drew himself out, clean and cool, upon the rocks, he remembered that he ought to have taken the body back with him, and let the tide carry it away, but it was too late. He was clean, and he could not bear to go back for the thing. Besides, he was late, and they would wonder at the hotel if he was not back in time for breakfast. He ran lightly over the bare rocks and the grass that showed no footprint. He dressed himself, taking care to leave no trace of his presence. He took the car, which would have told a story. He put his bicycle in the back seat, under the rugs, and he went – but you know as well as I do where he went.'

Lord Peter got up with an impatient movement, and went over to the picture, rubbing his thumb meditatively over the texture of the painting.

'You may say, if he hated the face so much, why didn't he destroy the picture? He couldn't. It was the best thing he'd ever done. He took a hundred guineas for it. It was cheap at a hundred guineas. But then I think he was afraid to refuse me. My name is rather well known. It was a sort of blackmail, I suppose. But I wanted that picture.'

Inspector Winterbottom laughed again.

'Did you take any steps, my lord, to find out if Crowder has really been staying at East Felpham?'

'No.' Wimsey swung round abruptly. 'I have taken no steps at all. That's your business. I have told you the story, and, on my soul, I'd rather have stood by and said nothing.'

'You needn't worry.' The Inspector laughed for the third time. 'It's a good story, my lord, and you told it well. But you're right when you say it's a fairy-story. We've found this Italian fellow – Francesco, he called himself, and he's the man, all right.'

'How do you know? Has he confessed?'

'Practically. He's dead. Killed himself. He left a letter to the woman, begging for forgiveness, and saying that when he saw her with Plant he felt murder come into his heart. "I have revenged myself," he says, "on him who dared to love you." I suppose he got the wind up when he saw we were after him – I wish these newspapers wouldn't be always putting these criminals on their guard – so he did away with himself to cheat the gallows. I may say it's been a disappointment to me.'

'It must have been,' said Wimsey. 'Very unsatisfactory, of course. But I'm glad my story turned out to be only a fairy-tale, after all. You're not going?'

'Got to get back to my duty,' said the Inspector, heaving himself to his feet. 'Very pleased to have met you, my lord. And I mean what I say – you ought to take to literature.'

Wimsey remained after he had gone, still looking at the portrait.

'"What is Truth?" said jesting Pilate. No wonder, since it is so completely unbelievable ... I could prove it ... if I liked ... but the man had a villainous face, and there are few good painters in the world.'

The Villa *Marie Celeste*

Margery Allingham

The newspapers were calling the McGill house in Chestnut Grove 'the villa *Marie Celeste*' before Chief Inspector Charles Luke noticed the similarity between the two mysteries, and that so shook him that he telephoned Albert Campion and asked him to come over.

They met in the Sun, a discreet pub in the suburban High Street, and stood talking in the small bar-parlour which was deserted at that time of day just after opening in the evening.

'The two stories *are* alike,' Luke said, picking up his drink. He was at the height of his career then, a dark, muscular cockney, high-cheekboned and packed with energy, and as usual he talked nineteen to the dozen, forcing home his points with characteristic gestures of his long hands. 'I read the rehash of the *Marie Celeste* in the *Courier* this morning and it took me to the fair. Except that she was a ship and twenty-nine Chestnut Grove is a semi-detached suburban house, the two desertion stories are virtually the same, even to the half-eaten breakfast left on the table in each case. It's uncanny, Campion.'

The quiet, fair man in the horn rims stood listening affably as was his habit. As usual he looked vague and probably ineffectual: in the shadier corners of Europe it was said of him that no one ever took him seriously until just about two hours too late. At the moment he appeared faintly amused. The thumping force of Luke's enthusiasm always tickled him.

'You think you know what has happened to the McGill couple, then?' he ventured.

'The hell I do!' The policeman opened his small black eyes to their widest extent. 'I tell you it's the same tale as the classic mystery of the *Marie Celeste*. They've gone like a stain under a bleach. One minute they were having breakfast together, like every other married couple for miles, and the next they were gone, sunk without trace.'

Mr Campion hesitated. He looked a trifle embarrassed. 'As I recall the story of the *Marie Celeste* it had the simple charm of the utterly incredible,' he said at last. 'Let's see, she was a brig brought into Gib by a prize crew of innocent sailor-men, who had a wonderful tale to tell. According to them she was sighted in mid-ocean with all her sails set, her decks clean, her lockers tidy but not a soul on board. The details were fascinating. There were three cups of tea on the captain's table still warm to the touch, in his cabin. There was a cat asleep in the galley and a chicken ready for stewing in a pot on the stove.' He sighed gently. 'Quite beautiful,' he said, 'but witnesses also swore that with no one at the wheel she was still dead on course, and that seemed a little much to the court of inquiry, who after kicking it about as long as they could, finally made the absolute minimum award.'

Luke glanced at him sharply.

'That wasn't the *Courier's* angle last night,' he said. 'They called it "the world's favourite unsolved mystery".'

'So they did!' Mr Campion was laughing. 'Because nobody wants a prosaic explanation of fraud and greed. The mystery of the *Marie Celeste* is just the prime example of the story which really is a bit too good to spoil, don't you think?'

'I don't know. It's not an idea which occurred to me.' Luke sounded slightly irritated. 'I was merely quoting the main outlines of the two tales: eighteen seventy-two and the *Marie Celeste* is a bit before my time. On the other hand, twenty-nine Chestnut Grove is definitely my business, and you can take it from me no witness is being allowed to use his imagination in this inquiry. Just give your mind to the details, Campion ...' He set his tumbler down on the bar and began ticking off each item on his fingers.

'Consider the couple,' he said. 'They sound normal enough. Peter McGill was twenty-eight and his wife Maureen a year younger. They'd been married three years and got on well together. For the first two years they had to board with his mother while they were waiting for a house. That didn't work out too well so they rented a couple of rooms from Maureen's married sister. That lasted for six months and they got the offer of this house in Chestnut Grove.'

'Any money troubles?' Mr Campion inquired.

'No.' The Chief clearly thought the fact remarkable. 'Peter seems to be the one lad in the family who had nothing to grumble about. His firm – they're locksmiths in Aldgate;

he's in the office – are very pleased with him. His reputation is that he keeps within his income and he's recently had a raise. I saw the senior partner this morning and he's genuinely worried, poor old boy. He liked the young man and had nothing but praise for him.'

'What about the girl?'

'She's another good type. Steady, reliable, kept on at her job as a typist until a few months ago when her husband decided she should retire to enjoy the new house and maybe raise a family. She certainly did her housework. The place is like a new pin now and they've been gone six days.'

For the first time Mr Campion's eyes darkened with interest.

'Forgive me,' he said, 'but the police seem to have come into this disappearance very quickly. Surely six days is no time for a couple to be missing. What are you looking for, Charles? A body?'

Luke shrugged. 'Not officially,' he said, 'but one doesn't have to have a nasty mind to wonder. We came into the inquiry quickly because the alarm was given quickly. The circumstances were extraordinary and the family got the wind up. That's the explanation of that.' He paused and stood for a moment hesitating. 'Come along and have a look,' he said, and his restless personality was a live thing in the confined space. 'We'll come back and have the other half of this drink after you've seen the set-up – I've got something really recherché here. I want you in on it.'

Mr Campion, as obliging as ever, followed him out into the network of trim little streets lined with bandbox villas each set in a nest of flower garden. Luke was still talking.

'It's just down the end here and along to the right,' he said, nodding towards the end of the avenue. 'I'll give you the outline as we go. On the twelfth of June last Bertram Heskith, a somewhat overbright specimen who is the husband of Maureen's elder sister – the one they lodged with two doors down the road before number twenty-nine became available – dropped round to see them as he usually did just before eight in the morning. He came in at the back door which was standing open and found a half-eaten breakfast for two on the table in the smart new kitchen. No one was about so he pulled up a chair and sat down to wait.' Luke's long hands were busy as he talked and Mr Campion could almost see the bright little room with the built-in furniture and the pot of flowers on the window ledge.

'Bertram is a toy salesman and one of a large family,' Luke went on. 'He's out of a job at the moment but is not despondent. He's a talkative man, a fraction too big for his clothes now and he likes his noggin, but he's sharp enough. He'd have noticed at once if there had been anything at all unusual to see. As it was he poured himself a cup of tea out of the pot under the cosy and sat there waiting, reading the newspaper which he found lying open on the floor by Peter McGill's chair. Finally it occurred to him that the house was very quiet and he put his head round the door and shouted up the stairs. When he got no reply he went up and found the bed unmade, the bathroom still warm and wet with steam and Maureen's everyday hat and coat lying on a chair with her familiar brown handbag upon it. Bertram came down, examined the rest of the house and went on out into the garden. Maureen had been doing the laundry before breakfast. There was linen, almost dry, on the line and a basket lying on the green under it but that was all. The little rectangle of land was quite empty.'

As his deep voice ceased he gave Campion a sidelong glance.

'And that my lad is that,' he said. 'Neither Peter nor Maureen have been seen since. When they didn't show up Bertram consulted the rest of the family and after waiting for two days they went to the police.'

'Really?' Mr Campion was fascinated despite himself. 'Is that all you've got?'

'Not quite, but the rest is hardly helpful,' Luke sounded almost gratified. 'Wherever they are they're not in the house or garden. If they walked out they did it without being seen, which is more of a feat than you'd expect because they had interested relatives and friends all round them and the only things that anyone is sure they took with them are a couple of clean linen sheets. "Fine winding sheets" one lady called them.'

Mr Campion's brows rose behind his big spectacles.

'That's a delicate touch,' he said. 'I take it there is no suggestion of foul play? It's always possible, of course.'

'Foul play is becoming positively common in London, I don't know what the old town is up to,' Luke said gloomily, 'but this set-up sounds healthy and happy enough. The McGills seem to have been pleasant normal young people and yet there are one or two little items which make you wonder. As far as we can find out Peter was not on his usual train to the city that morning, but we have one witness, a third cousin of his, who says she followed him up the street from his house to the corner just as she often did on weekday mornings. At the top she went one way and she assumed that he went the other as usual but no one else seems to have seen him and she's probably mistaken. Well now, here we are. Stand here for a minute.'

He had paused on the pavement of a narrow residential street, shady with plane trees and lined with pairs of pleasant little houses, stone-dashed and bay-windowed, in a style which is now a little out of fashion.

'The next gate along here belongs to the Heskiths,' he went on, lowering his voice a tone or so. 'We'll walk rather quickly past there because we don't want any more help from Bertram at the moment. He's a good enough chap but he sees himself as the watchdog of his sister-in-law's property and the way he follows me round makes me self-conscious. His house is number twenty-five – the odd numbers are on this side – twenty-nine is two doors along. Now number thirty-one – which is actually adjoined to twenty-nine on the other side – is closed. The old lady who owns it is in hospital; but in thirty-three there live two sisters, who are aunts of Peter's. They moved there soon after the young couple. One is a widow' – Luke sketched a portly juglike silhouette with his hands – 'and the other is a spinster who looks like two yards of pump-water. Both are very interested in their nephew and his wife, but whereas the widow is prepared to take a more or less benevolent view of her young relations, the spinster, Miss Dove, is apt to be critical. She told me Maureen didn't know how to lay out the money and I think that from time to time she'd had a few words with the girl on the subject. I heard about the "fine linen sheets" from her. Apparently she'd told Maureen off about buying anything so expensive, but the young bride had saved up for them and she'd got them.' He sighed. 'Women are like that,' he said. 'They get a yen for something and they want it and that's all there is to it. Miss Dove says she watched Maureen hanging them out on the line early in the morning of the day she vanished. There's one upstairs window in her house from which she can just see part of the garden at twenty-nine if she stands on a chair and clings to the sash.' He grinned. 'She happened to be doing just that at about half-past six on the day the McGills disappeared and she insists she saw them hanging there. She recognised them by the crochet on the top edge. They're certainly not in the house now. Miss Dove hints delicately that I should search Bertram's home for them.'

Mr Campion's pale eyes had narrowed and his mouth was smiling.

'It's a peach of a story,' he murmured. 'A sort of circumstantial history of the utterly impossible. The whole thing just can't have happened. How very odd, Charles. Did anyone else see Maureen that morning? Could she have walked out of the front door and come up the street with the linen over her arm unnoticed? I am not asking would she but could she?'

'No.' The Chief made no bones about it. 'Even had she wanted to, which is unlikely, it's virtually impossible. There are the cousins opposite, you see. They live in the house with the red geraniums over there directly in front of number twenty-nine, are some sort of distant relatives of Peter's. A father, mother, five marriageable daughters – it was one of them who says she followed Peter up the road that morning. Also there's an old Irish granny who sits up in bed in the window of the front room all day. She's not very reliable – for instance she can't remember if Peter came out of the house at his usual time that day – but she would have noticed if Maureen had done so. No one saw Maureen that morning except Miss Dove, who, as I told you, watched her hanging linen on the line. The paper comes early; the milkman heard her washing machine from the scullery door when he left his bottles but he did not see her.'

'What about the postman?'

'He's no help. He's a new man on the round and can't even remember if he called at twenty-nine. It's a long street and, as he says, the houses are all alike. He gets to twenty-nine about seven-twenty-five and seldom meets anybody at that door. He wouldn't know the McGills if he saw them, anyhow. Come on in, Campion, take a look round and see what you think.'

Mr Campion followed his friend down the road and up a narrow garden path to where a uniformed man stood on guard before the front door. He was aware of a flutter behind the curtains in the house opposite as they appeared and a tall thin woman with a determinedly blank expression walked down the path of the next house but one and bowed to Luke meaningly as she paused at her gate for an instant before going back.

'Miss Dove,' said Luke unnecessarily, as he opened the door. Number twenty-nine had few surprises for Mr Campion. It was almost exactly as he had imagined it. The furniture in the hall and front room was new and sparse, leaving plenty of room for future acquisitions, but the kitchen-dining-room was well lived in and conveyed a distinct personality. Someone without much money, who had yet liked nice things, had lived there. He or she, and he suspected it was a she, had been generous, too, despite her economies, if the 'charitable' calendars and the packets of gipsy pegs bought at the door were any guide. The breakfast-table had been left as Bertram Heskith had found it and his cup was still there beside a third plate.

The thin man wandered through the house without comment, Luke at his heels. The scene was just as stated. There was no sign of hurried flight, no evidence of packing, no hint of violence. The dwelling was not so much untidy as in the process of being used. There was a pair of man's pyjamas on the stool in the bathroom and a towel hung over the basin to dry. The woman's handbag on the coat on a chair in the bedroom contained the usual miscellany, and two pounds three shillings, some coppers and a set of keys. Mr Campion looked at everything, the clothes hanging neatly in the cupboard, the dead flowers still in the vases, but the only item which appeared to hold his attention was the wedding group which he found in a silver frame on the dressing-table. He stood before it for a long time, apparently fascinated, yet it was not a remarkable picture. As is occasionally the case in such photographs the two central figures were the least dominant characters in the entire group of vigorous, laughing guests. Maureen timid and gentle, with a slender figure and big dark eyes, looked positively scared of her own bridesmaids while Peter, although solid and with a determined chin, had a panic-stricken look about him which contrasted with the cheerful assured grin of the best man.

'That's Heskith,' said Luke. 'You can see the sort of chap he is – not one of nature's great outstanding success types but not the man to go imagining things. When he says he felt the two were there that morning, perfectly normal and happy as usual, I believe him.'

'No Miss Dove here?' said Campion still looking at the group.

'No. That's her sister though, deputising for the bride's mother. And that's the girl from opposite, the one who thinks she saw Peter go up the road.' Luke put a forefinger over the face of the third bridesmaid. 'There's another sister here and the rest are cousins. I understand the pic doesn't do the bride justice. Everybody says she was a good-natured pretty girl …' He corrected himself. 'Is, I mean.'

'The bridegroom looks a reasonable type to me,' murmured Mr Campion. 'A little apprehensive, perhaps.'

'I wonder.' Luke spoke thoughtfully. 'The Heskiths had another photo of him and perhaps it's more marked in that, but don't you think there's a sort of ruthlessness in that face, Campion? It's not quite recklessness, more like decision. I knew a sergeant in the war with a face like that. He was mild enough in the ordinary way but once something shook him he acted fast and pulled no punches whatever. Well, that's neither here nor there. Come and inspect the linen line, and then, Heaven help you, you'll know just about as much as I do.'

He led the way out to the back and stood for a moment on the concrete path which ran under the kitchen window separating the house from the small rectangle of shorn grass which was all there was of a garden.

A high rose hedge, carefully trained on rustic fencing, separated it from the neighbours on the right; at the bottom there was a garden shed and a few fruit trees and, on the left, greenery in the neglected garden of the old lady who was in hospital had grown up high so that a green wall screened the lawn from all but the prying eyes of Miss Dove, who, even at that moment, Mr Campion suspected, was standing on a chair and clinging to a sash to peer at them.

Luke indicated the empty line slung across the green. 'I had the linen brought in,' he said. 'The Heskiths were worrying and there seemed no earthly point in leaving it out to rot.'

'What's in the shed?'

'A spade and fork and a hand-mower,' said the Chief promptly. 'Come and look. The floor is beaten earth and if it's been disturbed in thirty years I'll eat my ticket. I suppose we'll have to fetch it up in the end but we'll be wasting our time.'

Mr Campion went over and glanced into the tarred wooden hut. It was tidy and dusty and the floor was dry and hard. Outside a dilapidated pair of steps leaned against the six-foot brick wall which marked the boundary.

Mr Campion tried them gingerly. They held, but not as it were with any real assurance, and he climbed up to look over the wall to the narrow path which separated it from the tarred fence of the rear garden of a house in the next street.

'That's an odd right of way,' Luke said. 'It leads down between the two residential roads. These suburban places are not very matey, you know. Half the time one street doesn't know the next. Chestnut Grove is classier than Philpott Avenue which runs parallel with it.'

Mr Campion descended, dusting his hands. He was grinning and his eyes were dancing.

'I wonder if anybody there noticed her,' he said. 'She must have been carrying the sheets, you know.'

The chief turned round slowly and stared at him.

'You're not suggesting that she simply walked down here over the wall and out! In the clothes she'd been washing in? It's crazy. Why should she? Did her husband go with her?'

'No. I think he went down Chestnut Grove as usual, doubled back down this path as soon as he came to the other end of it near the station, picked up his wife and went off with her through Philpott Avenue to the bus stop. They'd only got to get to the Broadway to find a cab, you see.'

Luke's dark face still wore an expression of complete incredulity.

'But for Pete's sake *why?*' he demanded. 'Why clear out in the middle of breakfast on a wash-day morning? Why take the sheets? Young couples can do the most unlikely things but there are limits. They didn't take their savings bank books you know. There's not much in them but they're still there in the writing desk in the front room. What are you getting at, Campion?'

The thin man walked slowly back on to the patch of grass.

'I expect the sheets were dry and she'd folded them into the basket before breakfast,' he began slowly. 'As she ran out of the house they were lying there and she couldn't resist taking them with her. The husband must have been irritated with her when he saw her with them but people are like that. When they're running from a fire they save the oddest things.'

'But she wasn't running from a fire.'

'Wasn't she!' Mr Campion laughed. 'There were several devouring flames all round them just then I should have thought. Listen, Charles. If the postman called he reached the house at seven-twenty-five. I think he did call and with an ordinary plain business envelope which was too commonplace for him to remember. It would be the plainest of plain envelopes. Well, who was due at seven-thirty?'

'Bert Heskith. I told you.'

'Exactly. So there were five minutes in which to escape. Five minutes for a determined, resourceful man like Peter McGill to act promptly. His wife was generous and easygoing, remember, and so, thanks to that decision which you yourself noticed in his face, he rose to the occasion. He had only five minutes, Charles, to escape all those powerful personalities with their jolly, avid faces, whom we saw in the wedding group. They were all living remarkably close to him, ringing him round as it were, so that it was a ticklish business to elude them. He went the front way so that the kindly watchful eye would see him as usual and not be alarmed. There wasn't time to take anything at all and it was only because Maureen flying through the back garden to escape the back way saw the sheets in the basket and couldn't resist her treasures that they salvaged them. She wasn't quite so ruthless as Peter. She had to take something from the old life however glistening were the prospects for—' He broke off abruptly. Chief Inspector Luke, with dawning comprehension in his eyes, was already halfway to the gate on the way to the nearest police telephone box.

Mr Campion was in his own sitting-room in Bottle Street,

Piccadilly, later that evening when Luke called. He came in jauntily, his black eyes dancing with amusement.

'It wasn't the Irish Sweep but the Football Pools,' he said. 'I got the details out of the promoters. They've been wondering what to do ever since the story broke. They're in touch with the McGills, of course, but Peter had taken every precaution to ensure secrecy and is insisting on his rights. He must have known his wife's tender heart and have made up his mind what he'd do if ever a really big win came off. The moment he got the letter telling him of his luck he put the plan into practice.' He paused and shook his head admiringly. 'I hand it to him,' he said. 'Seventy-five thousand pounds is like a nice fat chicken, plenty and more for two but only a taste for the whole of a very big family.'

'What will you do?'

'Us? The police? Oh, officially we're baffled. We shall retire gracefully. It's not our business.' He sat down and raised the glass his host handed to him.

'Here's to the mystery of the Villa *Marie Celeste,*' he said. 'I had a blind spot for it. It foxed me completely. Good luck to them, though. You know, Campion, you had a point when you said that the really insoluble mystery is the one which no one can bring himself to spoil. What put you on to it?'

'I suspect the charm of relatives who call at seven-thirty in the morning,' said Mr Campion simply.

The Blue Scarab

R. Austin Freeman

Medico-legal practice is largely concerned with crimes against the person, the details of which are often sordid, gruesome and unpleasant. Hence the curious and romantic case of the Blue Scarab (though really outside our speciality) came as somewhat of a relief. But to me it is of interest principally as illustrating two of the remarkable gifts which made my friend, Thorndyke, unique as an investigator: his uncanny power of picking out the one essential fact at a glance, and his capacity to produce, when required, inexhaustible stores of unexpected knowledge of the most out-of-the-way subjects.

It was late in the afternoon when Mr James Blowgrave arrived, by appointment, at our chambers, accompanied by his daughter, a rather strikingly pretty girl of about twenty-two; and when we had mutually introduced ourselves, the consultation began without preamble.

'I didn't give any details in my letter to you,' said Mr

Blowgrave. 'I thought it better not to, for fear you might decline the case. It is really a matter of a robbery, but not quite an ordinary robbery. There are some unusual and rather mysterious features in the case. And as the police hold out very little hope, I have come to ask if you will give me your opinion on the case and perhaps look into it for me. But first I had better tell you how the affair happened.

'The robbery occurred just a fortnight ago, about half-past nine o'clock in the evening. I was sitting in my study with my daughter, looking over some things that I had taken from a small deed-box, when a servant rushed in to tell us that one of the outbuildings was on fire. Now, my study opens by a French window on the garden at the back, and, as the out-building was in a meadow at the side of the garden, I went out that way, leaving the French window open; but before going I hastily put the things back in the deed-box and locked it.

'The building – which I used partly as a lumber store and partly as a workshop – was well alight and the whole household was already on the spot, the boy working the pump and the two maids carrying the buckets and throwing water on the fire. My daughter and I joined the party and helped to carry the buckets and take out what goods we could reach from the burning building. But it was nearly half an hour before we got the fire completely extinguished, and then my daughter and I went to our rooms to wash and tidy ourselves up. We returned to the study together, and when I had shut the French window my daughter proposed that we should resume our interrupted occupation. Thereupon I took out of my pocket the key of the deed-box and turned to the cabinet on which the box always stood.

'But there was no deed-box there.

'For a moment I thought I must have moved it, and cast my eyes round the room in search of it. But it was nowhere to be seen, and a moment's reflection reminded me that I had left it in its usual place. The only possible conclusion was that during our absence at the fire, somebody must have come in by the window and taken it. And it looked as if that somebody had deliberately set fire to the outbuilding for the express purpose of luring us all out of the house.'

'That is what the appearances suggest,' Thorndyke agreed. 'Is the study window furnished with a blind, or curtains?'

'Curtains,' replied Mr Blowgrave. 'But they were not drawn. Anyone in the garden could have seen into the room; and the garden is easily accessible to an active person who could climb over a low wall.'

'So far, then,' said Thorndyke, 'the robbery might be the work of a casual prowler who had got into the garden and watched you through the window, and assuming that the things you had taken from the box were of value, seized an easy opportunity to make off with them. Were the things of any considerable value?'

'To a thief they were of no value at all. There were a number of share certificates, a lease, one or two agreements, some family photographs and a small box containing an old letter and a scarab. Nothing worth stealing, you see, for the certificates were made out in my name and were therefore unnegotiable.'

'And the scarab?'

'That may have been lapis lazuli, but more probably it was

a blue glass imitation. In any case it was of no considerable value. It was about an inch and a half long. But before you come to any conclusion, I had better finish the story. The robbery was on Tuesday, the 7th of June. I gave information to the police, with a description of the missing property, but nothing happened until Wednesday, the 15th, when I received a registered parcel bearing the Southampton postmark. On opening it I found, to my astonishment, the entire contents of the deed-box, with the exception of the scarab, and this rather mysterious communication.'

He took from his pocket and handed to Thorndyke an ordinary envelope addressed in typewritten characters, and sealed with a large, elliptical seal, the face of which was covered with minute hieroglyphics.

'This,' said Thorndyke, 'I take to be an impression of the scarab; and an excellent impression it is.'

'Yes,' replied Mr Blowgrave, 'I have no doubt that it is the scarab. It is about the same size.'

Thorndyke looked quickly at our client with an expression of surprise. 'But,' he asked, 'don't you recognise the hieroglyphics on it?'

Mr Blowgrave smiled deprecatingly. 'The fact is,' said he, 'I don't know anything about hieroglyphics, but I should say, as far as I can judge, these look the same. What do you think, Nellie?'

Miss Blowgrave looked at the seal vaguely and replied, 'I am in the same position. Hieroglyphics are to me just funny things that don't mean anything. But these look the same to me as those on our scarab, though I expect any other hieroglyphics would, for that matter.'

Thorndyke made no comment on this statement, but examined the seal attentively through his lens. Then he drew out the contents of the envelope, consisting of two letters, one typewritten and the other in a faded brown handwriting. The former he read through and then inspected the paper closely, holding it up to the light to observe the watermark.

'The paper appears to be of Belgian manufacture,' he remarked, passing it to me. I confirmed this observation and then read the letter, which was headed 'Southampton' and ran thus:

> DEAR OLD PAL,
> I am sending you back some trifles removed in error. The ancient document is enclosed with this, but the curio is at present in the custody of my respected uncle. Hope its temporary loss will not inconvenience you, and that I may be able to return it to you later. Meanwhile, believe me,
> Your ever affectionate,
> RUDOLPHO.

'Who is Rudolpho?' I asked.

'The Lord knows,' replied Mr Blowgrave. 'A pseudonym of our absent friend, I presume. He seems to be a facetious sort of person.'

'He does,' agreed Thorndyke. 'This letter and the seal appear to be what the schoolboys would call a leg-pull. But still, this is all quite normal. He has returned you the worthless things and has kept the one thing that has any sort of negotiable value. Are you quite clear that the scarab is not more valuable than you have assumed?'

'Well,' said Mr Blowgrave, 'I have had an expert's opinion on it. I showed it to M. Fouquet, the Egyptologist, when he was over here from Brussels a few months ago, and his opinion was that it was a worthless imitation. Not only was it not a genuine scarab, but the inscription was a sham, too; just a collection of hieroglyphic characters jumbled together without sense or meaning.'

'Then,' said Thorndyke, taking another look at the seal through his lens, 'it would seem that Rudolpho, or Rudolpho's uncle, has got a bad bargain. Which doesn't throw much light on the affair.'

At this point Miss Blowgrave intervened. 'I think, father,' said she, 'you have not given Dr Thorndyke quite all the facts about the scarab. He ought to be told about its connection with Uncle Reuben.'

As the girl spoke Thorndyke looked at her with a curious expression of suddenly awakened interest. Later I understood the meaning of that look, but at the time there seemed to me nothing particularly arresting in her words.

'It is just a family tradition,' Mr Blowgrave said deprecatingly. 'Probably it is all nonsense.'

'Well, let us have it, at any rate,' said Thorndyke. 'We may get some light from it.'

Thus urged, Mr Blowgrave hemmed a little shyly and began:

'The story concerns my great-grandfather Silas Blowgrave, and his doings during the war with France. It seems that he commanded a privateer of which he and his brother Reuben were the joint owners, and that in the course of their last cruise they acquired a very remarkable and valuable collection of jewels. Goodness knows how they got them; not very honestly, I suspect, for they appear to have been a pair of precious rascals. Something has been said about the loot from a South American church or cathedral, but there is really nothing known about the affair. There are no documents. It is mere oral tradition and very vague and sketchy. The story goes that when they had sold off the ship, they came down to live at Shawstead in Hertfordshire, Silas occupying the manor house – in which I live at present – and Reuben a farm adjoining. The bulk of the loot they shared out at the end of the cruise, but the jewels were kept apart to be dealt with later – perhaps when the circumstances under which they had been acquired had been forgotten. However, both men were inveterate gamblers and it seems – according to the testimony of a servant of Reuben's who overheard them – that on a certain night when they had been playing heavily, they decided to finish up by playing for the whole collection of jewels as a single stake. Silas, who had the jewels in his custody, was seen to go to the manor house and return to Reuben's house carrying a small, iron chest.

'Apparently they played late into the night, after everyone else but the servant had gone to bed, and the luck was with Reuben, though it seems probable that he gave luck some assistance. At any rate, when the play was finished and the chest handed over, Silas roundly accused him of cheating, and we may assume that a pretty serious quarrel took place. Exactly what happened is not clear, for when the quarrel began Reuben dismissed the servant, who retired to her bedroom in a distant part of the house. But in the morning it was discovered that Reuben and the chest of jewels had both disappeared, and there were distinct traces of blood in the room in which the two men had been playing. Silas professed to know nothing about the disappearance; but a strong – and probably just – suspicion arose that he had murdered his brother and made away with the jewels. The result was that Silas also disappeared, and for a long time his whereabouts was not known even by his wife.

'Later it transpired that he had taken up his abode under an assumed name, in Egypt, and that he had developed an enthusiastic interest in the then new science of Egyptology – the Rosetta Stone had been deciphered only a few years previously. After a time he resumed communication with his wife, but never made any statement as to the mystery of his brother's disappearance. A few months before his death he visited his home in disguise and he then handed to his wife a little sealed packet which was to be delivered to his only son, William, on his attaining the age of twenty-one. That packet contained the scarab and the letter which you have taken from the envelope.'

'Am I to read it?' asked Thorndyke.

'Certainly, if you think it worth while,' was the reply. Thorndyke opened the yellow sheet of paper and, glancing through the brown and faded writing, read aloud:

> Cairo, 4 March, 1833.
>
> My Dear Son,
>
> I am sending you, as my last gift, a valuable scarab and a few words of counsel on which I would bid you meditate. Believe me, there is much wisdom in the lore of Old Egypt. Make it your own. Treasure the scarab as a precious inheritance. Handle it often but show it to none. Give your

Uncle Reuben Christian burial. It is your duty, and you will have your reward. He robbed your father, but he shall make restitution.

Farewell!

Your affectionate father,

SILAS BLOWGRAVE.

As Thorndyke laid down the letter he looked inquiringly at our client.

'Well,' he said, 'here are some plain instructions. How have they been carried out?'

'They haven't been carried out at all,' replied Mr Blowgrave. 'As to his son William, my grandfather, he was not disposed to meddle in the matter. This seemed to be a frank admission that Silas killed his brother and concealed the body, and William didn't choose to reopen the scandal. Besides, the instructions are not so very plain. It is all very well to say, "Give your Uncle Reuben Christian burial," but where the deuce is Uncle Reuben?'

'It is plainly hinted,' said Thorndyke, 'that whoever gives the body Christian burial will stand to benefit, and the word "restitution" seems to suggest a clue to the whereabouts of the jewels. Has no one thought it worth while to find out where the body is deposited?'

'But how could they?' demanded Blowgrave. 'He doesn't give the faintest clue. He talks as if his son knew where the body was. And then, you know, even supposing Silas did not take the jewels with him, there was the question, whose property were they? To begin with, they were pretty certainly stolen property, though no one knows where they came from. Then Reuben apparently got them from Silas by fraud, and Silas got them back by robbery and murder. If William had discovered them he would have had to give them up to Reuben's sons, and yet they weren't strictly Reuben's property. No one had an undeniable claim to them, even if they could have found them.'

'But that is not the case now,' said Miss Blowgrave.

'No,' said Mr Blowgrave, in answer to Thorndyke's look of inquiry. 'The position is quite clear now. Reuben's grandson, my cousin Arthur, has died recently, and as he had no children, he has dispersed his property. The old farmhouse and the bulk of his estate he has left to a nephew, but he made a small bequest to my daughter and named her as the residuary legatee. So that whatever rights Reuben had to the jewels are now vested in her, and on my death she will be Silas's heir, too. As a matter of fact,' Mr Blowgrave continued, 'we were discussing this very question on the night of the robbery. I may as well tell you that my girl will be left pretty poorly off when I go, for there is a heavy mortgage on our property and mighty little capital. Uncle Reuben's jewels would have made the old home secure for her if we could have laid our hands on them. However, I mustn't take up your time with our domestic affairs.'

'Your domestic affairs are not entirely irrelevant,' said Thorndyke. 'But what is it that you want me to do in the matter?'

'Well,' said Blowgrave, 'my house has been robbed and my premises set fire to. The police can apparently do nothing. They say there is no clue at all unless the robbery was committed by somebody in the house, which is absurd, seeing that the servants were all engaged in putting out the fire. But I want the robber traced and punished, and I want to get the scarab back. It may be intrinsically valueless, as M. Fouquet said, but Silas's testamentary letter seems to indicate that it had some value. At any rate, it is an heirloom, and I am loath to lose it. It seems a presumptuous thing to ask you to investigate a trumpery robbery, but I should take it as a great kindness if you would look into the matter.'

'Cases of robbery pure and simple,' replied Thorndyke, 'are rather alien to my ordinary practice, but in this one there are certain curious features that seem to make an investigation worth while. Yes, Mr Blowgrave, I will look into the case, and I have some hope that we may be able to lay our hands on the robber, in spite of the apparent absence of clues. I will ask you to leave both these letters for me to examine more minutely, and I shall probably want to make an inspection of the premises – perhaps tomorrow.'

'Whenever you like,' said Blowgrave. 'I am delighted that you are willing to undertake the inquiry. I have heard so much about you from my friend Stalker, of the Griffin Life Assurance Company, for whom you have acted on several occasions.'

'Before you go,' said Thorndyke, 'there is one point that we must clear up. Who is there besides yourselves that knows of the existence of the scarab and this letter and the history attaching to them?'

'I really can't say,' replied Blowgrave. 'No one has seen them but my cousin Arthur. I once showed them to him, and he may have talked about them in the family. I didn't treat the matter as a secret.'

When our visitors had gone we discussed the bearings of the case.

'It is quite a romantic story,' said I, 'and the robbery has its points of interest, but I am rather inclined to agree with the police – there is mighty little to go on.'

'There would have been less,' said Thorndyke, 'if our sporting friend hadn't been so pleased with himself. That typewritten letter was a piece of gratuitous impudence. Our gentleman overrated his security and crowed too loud.'

'I don't see that there is much to be gleaned from the letter, all the same,' said I.

'I am sorry to hear you say that, Jervis,' he exclaimed, 'because I was proposing to hand the letter over to you to examine and report on.'

'I was only referring to the superficial appearances,' I said hastily. 'No doubt a detailed examination will bring something more distinctive into view.'

'I have no doubt it will,' he said, 'and as there are reasons for pushing on the investigation as quickly as possible, I suggest that you get to work at once. I will occupy myself with the old letter and the envelope.'

On this I began my examination without delay, and as a preliminary I proceeded to take a facsimile photograph of the letter by putting it in a large printing frame with a sensitive plate and a plate of clear glass. The resulting negative showed not only the typewritten lettering, but also the watermark and wire lines of the paper, and a faint grease spot. Next I turned my attention to the lettering itself, and here I soon began to accumulate quite a number of identifiable peculiarities. The machine was apparently a Corona, fitted with the small 'Elite' type, and the alignment was markedly defective. The 'lower case' – or small – 'a' was well below the line, although the capital 'A' appeared to be correctly placed; the 'u' was slightly above the line, and the small 'm' was partly clogged with dirt.

Up to this point I had been careful to manipulate the letter with forceps (although it had been handled by at least three persons, to my knowledge), and I now proceeded to examine it for fingerprints. As I could detect none by mere inspection, I dusted the back of the paper with finely powdered fuchsin, and distributed the powder by tapping the paper lightly. This brought into view quite a number of fingerprints, especially round the edges of the letter, and though most of them were very faint and shadowy, it was possible to make out the ridge pattern well enough for our purpose. Having blown off the excess of powder, I took the letter to the room where the large copying camera was set up, to photograph it before developing the fingerprints on the front. But here I found our laboratory assistant, Polton, in possession, with the sealed envelope fixed to the copying easel. 'I shan't be a minute, sir,' said he. 'The doctor wants an enlarged photograph of this seal. I've got the plate in.'

I waited while he made his exposure and then proceeded to take the photograph of the letter, or rather of the fingerprints on the back of it. When I had developed the negative I powdered the front of the letter and brought out several more fingerprints – thumbs this time. They were a little difficult to see where they were imposed on the lettering, but, as the latter was bright blue and the fuchsin powder was red, this confusion disappeared in the photograph, in which the lettering was almost invisible while the fingerprints were more distinct than they had appeared to the eye.

This completed my examination, and when I had verified the make of typewriter by reference to our album of specimens of typewriting, I left the negatives for Polton to dry and print and went down to the sitting-room to draw up my little report. I had just finished this and was speculating on what had become of Thorndyke, when I heard his quick step on the stair and a few moments later he entered with a roll of paper in his hand. This he unrolled on the table, fixing it open with one or two lead paper-weights, and I came round to inspect it, when I found it to be a sheet of the Ordnance map on the scale of twenty-five inches to the mile.

'Here is the Blowgraves' place,' said Thorndyke, 'nearly in the middle of the sheet. This is his house – Shawstead Manor – and that will probably be the out-building that was on fire. I take it that the house marked Dingle Farm is the one that Uncle Reuben occupied.'

'Probably,' I agreed. 'But I don't see why you wanted this map if you are going down to the place itself tomorrow.'

'The advantage of a map,' said Thorndyke, 'is that you can see all over it at once and get the lie of the land well into your mind; and you can measure all distances accurately and quickly with a scale and a pair of dividers. When we go down tomorrow, we shall know our way about as well as Blowgrave himself.'

'And what use will that be?' I asked. 'Where does the topography come into the case?

'Well, Jervis,' he replied, 'there is the robber, for instance; he came from somewhere and he went somewhere. A study of the map may give us a hint as to his movements. But here comes Polton "with the documents," as poor Miss Flite would say. What have you got for us, Polton?'

'They aren't quite dry, sir,' said Polton, laying four large bromide prints on the table. 'There's the enlargement of the seal – ten by eight, mounted – and three unmounted prints of Dr Jervis's.'

Thorndyke looked at my photographs critically. 'They're excellent, Jervis,' said he. 'The fingerprints are perfectly legible, though faint. I only hope some of them are the right ones. That is my left thumb. I don't see yours. The small one is presumably Miss Blowgrave's. We must take her fingerprints tomorrow, and her father's, too. Then we shall know if we have got any of the robber's.' He ran his eye over my report and nodded approvingly. 'There is plenty there to enable us to identify the typewriter if we can get hold of it, and the paper is very distinctive. What do you think of the seal?' he added, laying the enlarged photograph before me.

'It is magnificent,' I replied, with a grin. 'Perfectly monumental.'

'What are you grinning at?' he demanded.

'I was thinking that you seem to be counting your chickens in pretty good time,' said I. 'You are making elaborate preparations to identify the scarab, but you are rather disregarding the classical advice of the prudent Mrs Glasse.'

'I have a presentiment that we shall get that scarab,' said he. 'At any rate we ought to be in a position to identify it instantly and certainly if we are able to get a sight of it.'

'We are not likely to,' said I. 'Still, there is no harm in providing for the improbable.'

This was evidently Thorndyke's view, and he certainly made ample provision for this most improbable contingency; for, having furnished himself with a drawing-board and a sheet of tracing-paper, he pinned the latter over the photograph on the board and proceeded, with a fine pen and hectograph ink, to make a careful and minute tracing of the intricate and bewildering hieroglyphic inscription on the seal. When he had finished it he transferred it to a clay duplicator and took off half-a-dozen copies, one of which he handed to me. I looked at it dubiously and remarked: 'You have said that the medical jurist must make all knowledge his province. Has he got to be an Egyptologist, too?'

'He will be the better medical jurist if he is,' was the reply, of which I made a mental note for my future guidance. But meanwhile Thorndyke's proceedings were, to me, perfectly incomprehensible. What was his object in making this minute tracing? The seal itself was sufficient for identification. I lingered awhile, hoping that some fresh development might throw a light on the mystery. But his next proceeding was like to have reduced me to stupefaction. I saw him go to the book-shelves and take down a book. As he laid it on the table I glanced at the title, and when I saw that it was *Raper's Navigation Tables* I stole softly out into the lobby, put on my hat and went for a walk.

When I returned the investigation was apparently concluded, for Thorndyke was seated in his easy chair, placidly reading *The Compleat Angler*. On the table lay a large circular protractor, a straight-edge, an architect's scale and a sheet of tracing-paper on which was a tracing in hectograph ink of Shawstead Manor.

'Why did you make this tracing?' I asked. 'Why not take the map itself?'

'We don't want the whole of it,' he replied, 'and I dislike cutting up maps.'

By taking an informal lunch in the train, we arrived at Shawstead Manor by half-past two. Our approach up the drive had evidently been observed, for Blowgrave and his daughter were waiting at the porch to receive us. The former came forward with outstretched hand, but a distinctly woebegone expression, and exclaimed:

'It is most kind of you to come down; but alas! you are too late.'

'Too late for what?' demanded Thorndyke.

'I will show you,' replied Blowgrave, and seizing my colleague by the arm, he strode off excitedly to a little wicket at the side of the house, and, passing through it, hurried along a narrow alley that skirted the garden wall and ended in a large meadow, at one end of which stood a dilapidated windmill. Across this meadow he bustled, dragging my colleague with him, until he reached a heap of freshly turned earth, where he halted and pointed tragically to a spot where the turf had evidently been raised and untidily replaced.

'There!' he exclaimed, stooping to pull up the loose turfs and thereby exposing what was evidently a large hole, recently and hastily filled in. 'That was done last night or early this morning, for I walked over this meadow only yesterday evening and there was no sign of disturbed ground then.'

Thorndyke stood looking down at the hole with a faint smile. 'And what do you infer from that?' he asked.

'Infer!' shrieked Blowgrave. 'Why, I infer that whoever dug this hole was searching for Uncle Reuben and the lost jewels!'

'I am inclined to agree with you,' Thorndyke said calmly. 'He happened to search in the wrong place, but that is his affair.'

'The wrong place!' Blowgrave and his daughter exclaimed in unison. 'How do you know it is the wrong place?'

'Because,' replied Thorndyke, 'I believe I know the right place, and this is not it. But we can put the matter to the test, and we had better do so. Can you get a couple of men with picks and shovels? Or shall we handle the tools ourselves?'

'I think that would be better,' said Blowgrave, who was quivering with excitement. 'We don't want to take anyone into our confidence if we can help it.'

'No,' Thorndyke agreed. 'Then I suggest that you fetch the tools while I locate the spot.'

Blowgrave assented eagerly and went off at a brisk trot, while the young lady remained with us and watched Thorndyke with intense curiosity.

'I mustn't interrupt you with questions,' said she, 'but I can't imagine how you found out where Uncle Reuben was buried.'

'We will go into that later,' he replied; 'but first we have got to find Uncle Reuben.' He laid his research case down on the ground, and opening it, took out three sheets of paper, each bearing a duplicate of his tracing of the map; and on each was marked a spot on this meadow from which a number of lines radiated like the spokes of a wheel.

'You see, Jervis,' he said, exhibiting them to me, 'the advantage of a map. I have been able to rule off these sets of bearings regardless of obstructions, such as those young trees, which have arisen since Silas's day, and mark the spot in its correct place. If the recent obstructions prevent us from taking the bearings, we can still find the spot by measurements with the land-chain or tape.'

'Why have you got three plans?' I asked.

'Because there are three imaginable places. No. 1 is the most likely; No. 2 less likely, but possible; No. 3 is impossible. That is the one that our friend tried last night. No. 1 is among those young trees, and we will now see if we can pick up the bearings in spite of them.'

We moved on to the clump of young trees, where Thorndyke took from the research-case a tall, folding camera-tripod and a large prismatic compass with an aluminium dial. With the latter he made one or two trial bearings and then, setting up the tripod, fixed the compass on it. For some minutes Miss Blowgrave and I watched him as he shifted the tripod from spot to spot, peering through the sight-vane of the compass and glancing occasionally at the map. At length he turned to us and said: 'We are in luck. None of these trees interferes with our bearings.' He took from the research-case a surveyor's arrow, and sticking it in the ground under the tripod, added: 'That is the spot. But we may have to dig a good way round it, for a compass is only a rough instrument.'

At this moment Mr Blowgrave staggered up, breathing hard, and flung down on the ground three picks, two shovels and a spade. 'I won't hinder you, doctor, by asking for explanations,' said he, 'but I am utterly mystified. You must tell us what it all means when we have finished our work.'

This Thorndyke promised to do, but meanwhile he took off his coat, and rolling up his shirt sleeves, seized the spade and began cutting out a large square of turf. As the soil was uncovered, Blowgrave and I attacked it with picks and Miss Blowgrave shovelled away the loose earth.

'Do you know how far down we have to go?' I asked.

'The body lies six feet below the surface,' Thorndyke replied; and as he spoke he laid down his spade, and taking a telescope from the research-case, swept it round the margin of the meadow and finally pointed it at a farmhouse some six hundred yards distant, of which he made a somewhat prolonged inspection, after which he took the remaining pick and fell to work on the opposite corner of the exposed square of earth.

For nearly half-an-hour we worked on steadily, gradually eating our way downwards, plying pick and shovel alternately, while Miss Blowgrave cleared the loose earth away from the edges of the deepening pit. Then a halt was called and we came to the surface, wiping our faces.

'I think, Nellie,' said Blowgrave, divesting himself of his waistcoat, 'a jug of lemonade and four tumblers would be useful, unless our visitors would prefer beer.'

We both gave our votes for lemonade, and Miss Nellie tripped away towards the house, while Thorndyke, taking up his telescope, once more inspected the farmhouse.

'You seem greatly interested in that house,' I remarked.

'I am,' he replied, handing me the telescope. 'Just take a look at the window in the right-hand gable, but keep under the tree.'

I pointed the telescope at the gable and there observed an open window at which a man was seated. He held a binocular glass to his eyes and the instrument appeared to be directed at us.

'We are being spied on, I fancy,' said I, passing the telescope to Blowgrave, 'but I suppose it doesn't matter. This is your land, isn't it?'

'Yes,' replied Blowgrave, 'but still, we didn't want any spectators. That is Harold Bowker,' he added steadying the telescope against a tree, 'my cousin Arthur's nephew, whom I told you about as having inherited the farmhouse. He seems mighty interested in us; but small things interest one in the country.'

Here the appearance of Miss Nellie, advancing across the meadow with an inviting-looking basket, diverted our attention from our inquisitive watcher. Six thirsty eyes were riveted on that basket until it drew near and presently disgorged a great glass jug and four tumblers, when we each took off a long and delicious draught and then jumped down into the pit to resume our labours.

Another half-hour passed. We had excavated in some places to nearly the full depth and were just discussing the advisability of another short rest when Blowgrave, who was working in one corner, uttered a loud cry and stood up suddenly, holding something in his fingers. A glance at the object showed it to be a bone, brown and earth-stained, but evidently a bone. Evidently, too, a human bone, as Thorndyke decided when Blowgrave handed it to him triumphantly.

'We have been very fortunate,' said he, 'to get so near at the first trial. This is from the right great toe, so we may assume that the skeleton lies just outside this pit, but we had better excavate carefully in your corner and see exactly how the bones lie.' This he proceeded to do himself, probing cautiously with the spade and clearing the earth away from the corner. Very soon the remaining bones of the right foot came into view and then the ends of the two leg-bones and a portion of the left foot.

'We can see now,' said he, 'how the skeleton lies, and all we have to do is to extend the excavation in that direction. But there is only room for one to work down here. I think you and Mr Blowgrave had better dig down from the surface.'

On this, I climbed out of the pit, followed reluctantly by Blowgrave, who still held the little brown bone in his hand and was in a state of wild excitement and exultation that somewhat scandalised his daughter.

'It seems rather ghoulish,' she remarked, 'to be gloating over poor Uncle Reuben's body in this way.'

'I know,' said Blowgrave, 'it isn't reverent. But I didn't kill Uncle Reuben, you know, whereas – well it was a long time ago.' With this rather inconsequent conclusion he took a draught of lemonade, seized his pick and fell to work with a will. I, too, indulged in a draught and passed a full tumbler down to Thorndyke. But before resuming my labours I picked up the telescope and once more inspected the farmhouse. The window was still open, but the watcher had apparently become bored with the not very thrilling spectacle. At any rate he had disappeared.

From this time onward every few minutes brought some discovery. First, a pair of deeply rusted steel shoe buckles; then one or two buttons, and presently a fine gold watch with a fob-chain and a bunch of seals, looking uncannily new and fresh and seeming more fraught with tragedy than even the bones themselves. In his cautious digging, Thorndyke was careful not to disturb the skeleton; and looking down into the narrow trench that was growing from the corner of the pit, I could see both legs, with only the right foot missing, projecting from the miniature cliff. Meanwhile our part of the trench was deepening rapidly, so that Thorndyke presently warned us to stop digging and bade us come down and shovel away the earth as he disengaged it.

At length the whole skeleton, excepting the head, was uncovered, though it lay undisturbed as it might have lain in its coffin. And now, as Thorndyke picked away the earth around the head, we could see that the skull was propped forward as if it rested on a high pillow. A little more careful probing with the pick-point served to explain this appearance. For as the earth fell away and disclosed the grinning skull, there came into view the edge and ironbound corners of a small chest.

It was an impressive spectacle; weird, solemn and rather dreadful. There for over a century the ill-fated gambler had lain, his mouldering head pillowed on the booty of unrecorded villainy, booty that had been won by fraud, retrieved by violence, and hidden at last by the final winner with the witness of his crime.

'Here is a fine text for a moralist who would preach on the vanity of riches,' said Thorndyke.

We all stood silent for a while, gazing, not without awe, at the stark figure that lay guarding the ill-gotten treasure. Miss Blowgrave – who had been helped down when we descended – crept closer to her father and murmured that it was 'rather awful'; while Blowgrave himself displayed a queer mixture of exultation and shuddering distaste.

Suddenly the silence was broken by a voice from above, and we all looked up with a start. A youngish man was standing on the brink of the pit, looking down on us with very evident disapproval.

'It seems that I have come just in the nick of time,' observed the newcomer. 'I shall have to take possession of that chest, you know, and of the remains, too, I suppose. That is my ancestor, Reuben Blowgrave.'

'Well, Harold,' said Blowgrave, 'you can have Uncle Reuben if you want him. But the chest belongs to Nellie.'

Here Mr Harold Bowker – I recognised him now as the watcher from the window – dropped down into the pit and advanced with something of a swagger.

'I am Reuben's heir,' said he, 'through my Uncle Arthur, and I take possession of this property and the remains.'

'Pardon me, Harold,' said Blowgrave, 'but Nellie is Arthur's residuary legatee, and this is the residue of the estate.'

'Rubbish!' exclaimed Bowker. 'By the way, how did you find out where he was buried?'

'Oh, that was quite simple,' replied Thorndyke with unexpected geniality. 'I'll show you the plan.' He climbed up to the surface and returned in a few moments with the three tracings and his letter-case. 'This is how we located the spot.' He handed the plan numbered 3 to Bowker, who took it from him and stood looking at it with a puzzled frown.

'But this isn't the place,' he said at length.

'Isn't it?' queried Thorndyke. 'No, of course; I've given you the wrong one. This is the plan.' He handed Bowker the plan marked No. 1, and took the other from him, laying it down on a heap of earth. Then, as Bowker pored gloomily over No. 1, he took a knife and a pencil from his pocket, and with his back to our visitor scraped the lead of the pencil, letting the black powder fall on the plan that he had just laid down. I watched him with some curiosity; and when I observed that the black scrapings fell on two spots near the edges of the paper, a sudden suspicion flashed into my mind, which was confirmed when I saw him tap the paper lightly with his pencil, gently blow away the powder, and quickly producing my photograph of the typewritten letter from his case, hold it for a moment beside the plan.

'This is all very well,' said Bowker, looking up from the plan, 'but how did you find out about these bearings?'

Thorndyke swiftly replaced the letter in his case, and turning round, replied, 'I am afraid I can't give you any further information.'

'Can't you, indeed!' Bowker exclaimed insolently. 'Perhaps I shall compel you to. But, at any rate, I forbid any of you to lay hands on my property.'

Thorndyke looked at him steadily and said in an ominously quiet tone: 'Now, listen to me, Mr Bowker. Let us have an end of this nonsense. You have played a risky game and you have lost. How much you have lost I can't say until I know whether Mr Blowgrave intends to prosecute.'

'To prosecute!' shouted Bowker. 'What the deuce do you mean by prosecute?'

'I mean,' said Thorndyke, 'that on the 7th of June, after nine o'clock at night, you entered the dwelling-house of Mr Blowgrave and stole and carried away certain of his goods and chattels. A part of them you have restored, but you are still in possession of some of the stolen property, to wit, a scarab and a deed-box.'

As Thorndyke made this statement in his calm, level tones, Bowker's face blanched to a tallowy white, and he stood staring at my colleague, the very picture of astonishment and dismay. But he fired a last shot.

'This is sheer midsummer madness,' he exclaimed huskily; 'and you know it.'

Thorndyke turned to our host. 'It is for you to settle, Mr Blowgrave,' said he. 'I hold conclusive evidence that Mr Bowker stole your deed-box. If you decide to prosecute I shall produce that evidence in court and he will certainly be convicted.'

Blowgrave and his daughter looked at the accused man with an embarrassment almost equal to his own.

'I am astounded,' the former said at length; 'but I don't want to be vindictive. Look here, Harold, hand over the scarab and we'll say no more about it.'

'You can't do that,' said Thorndyke. 'The law doesn't allow you to compound a robbery. He can return the property if he pleases and you can do as you think best about prosecuting. But you can't make conditions.'

There was silence for some seconds; then, without another word, the crestfallen adventurer turned, and scrambling up out of the pit, took a hasty departure.

It was nearly a couple of hours later that, after a leisurely wash and a hasty, nondescript meal, we carried the little chest from the dining-room to the study. Here, when he had closed the French window and drawn the curtains, Mr Blowgrave produced a set of tools and we fell to work on the iron fastenings of the chest. It was no light task, though a century's rust had thinned the stout bands, but at length the lid yielded to the thrust of a long case-opener and rose with a protesting creak. The chest was lined with a double thickness of canvas, apparently part of a sail, and contained a number of small leathern bags, which, as we lifted them out, one by one, felt as if they were filled with pebbles. But when we untied the thongs of one and emptied its contents into a wooden bowl, Blowgrave heaved a sigh of ecstasy and Miss Nellie uttered a little scream of delight. They were all cut stones, and most of them of exceptional size; rubies, emeralds, sapphires and a few diamonds. As to their value, we could form but the vaguest guess; but Thorndyke, who was a fair judge of gem-stones, gave it as his opinion that they were fine specimens of their kind, though roughly cut, and that they had probably formed the enrichment of some shrine.

'The question is,' said Blowgrave, gazing gloatingly on the bowl of sparkling gems, 'what are we to do with them?'

'I suggest,' said Thorndyke, 'that Dr Jervis stay here tonight to help you to guard them and that in the morning you take them up to London and deposit them, at your bank.'

Blowgrave fell in eagerly with this suggestion, which I seconded. 'But,' said he, 'that chest is a queer-looking package to be carrying abroad. Now, if we only had that confounded deed-box—'

'There's a deed-box on the cabinet behind you,' said Thorndyke.

Blowgrave turned round sharply. 'God bless us!' he

exclaimed. 'It has come back the way it went. Harold must have slipped in at the window while we were at tea. Well, I'm glad he has made restitution. When I look at that bowl and think what he must have narrowly missed, I don't feel inclined to be hard on him. I suppose the scarab is inside – not that it matters much now.'

The scarab was inside in an envelope; and as Thorndyke turned it over in his hand and examined the hieroglyphics on it through his lens, Miss Blowgrave asked: 'Is it of any value, Dr Thorndyke? It can't have any connection with the secret of the hiding-place, because you found the jewels without it.'

'By the way, doctor, I don't know whether it is permissible for me to ask, but how on earth did you find out where the jewels were hidden? To me it looks like black magic.'

Thorndyke laughed in a quiet, inward fashion. 'There is nothing magical about it,' said he. 'It was a perfectly simple, straightforward problem. But Miss Nellie is wrong. We had the scarab; that is to say we had the wax impression of it, which is the same thing. And the scarab was the key to the riddle. You see,' he continued, 'Silas's letter and the scarab formed together a sort of intelligence test.'

'Did they?' said Blowgrave. 'Then he drew a blank every time.'

Thorndyke chuckled. 'His descendants were certainly a little lacking in enterprise,' he admitted. 'Silas's instructions were perfectly plain and explicit. Whoever would find the treasure must first acquire some knowledge of Egyptian lore and must study the scarab attentively. It was the broadest of hints, but no one – excepting Harold Bowker, who must have heard about the scarab from his Uncle Arthur – seems to have paid any attention to it.

'Now it happens that I have just enough elementary knowledge of the hieroglyphic characters to enable me to spell them out when they are used alphabetically; and as soon as I saw the seal, I could see that these hieroglyphics formed English words. My attention was first attracted by the second group of signs, which spelled the word "Reuben", and then I saw that the first group spelled "Uncle". Of course, the instant I heard Miss Nellie speak of the connection between the scarab and Uncle Reuben, the murder was out. I saw at a glance that the scarab contained all the required information. Last night I made a careful tracing of the hieroglyphics and then rendered them into our own alphabet. This is the result.'

Thorndyke's Tracing of the Impression of the Scarab

The Transliteration of the Hieroglyphics

He took from his letter-case and spread out on the table a duplicate of the tracing which I had seen him make, and of which he had given me a copy. But since I had last seen it, it had received an addition; under each group of signs the equivalents in modern Roman lettering had been written, and these made the following words:

'UNKL RUBN IS IN TH MILL FIELD SKS FT DOWN CHURCH SPIR
NORTH TEN THIRTY EAST DINGL SOUTH GABL NORTH ATY
FORTY FIF WEST GOD SAF KING JORJ.'

Our two friends gazed at Thorndyke's transliteration in blank astonishment. At length Blowgrave remarked: 'But this translation must have demanded a very profound knowledge of the Egyptian writing.'

'Not at all,' replied Thorndyke. 'Any intelligent person could master the Egyptian alphabet in an hour. The language, of course, is quite another matter. The spelling of this is a little crude, but it is quite intelligible and does Silas great credit, considering how little was known in his time.'

'How do you suppose M. Fouquet came to overlook this?' Blowgrave asked.

'Naturally enough,' was the reply. 'He was looking for an Egyptian inscription. But this is not an Egyptian inscription. Does he speak English?'

'Very little. Practically not at all.'

'Then, as the words are English words and imperfectly spelt, the hieroglyphics must have appeared to him mere nonsense. And he was right as to the scarab being an imitation.'

'There is another point,' said Blowgrave. 'How was it that

Harold made that extraordinary mistake about the place? The directions are clear enough. All you had to do was to go out there with a compass and take the bearings just as they were given.'

'But,' said Thorndyke, 'that is exactly what he did, and hence the mistake. He was apparently unaware of the phenomenon known as the Secular Variation of the Compass. As you know, the compass does not – usually – point to true north, but to the Magnetic North; and the Magnetic North is continually changing its position. When Reuben was buried – about 1810—it was twenty-four degrees, twenty-six minutes west of true north; at the present time it is fourteen degrees, forty-eight minutes west of true north. So Harold's bearings would be no less than ten degrees out, which of course, gave him a totally wrong position. But Silas was a ship-master, a navigator, and of course knew all about the vagaries of the compass; and, as his directions were intended for use at some date unknown to him, I assumed that the bearings that he gave were true bearings – that when he said "north" he meant true north, which is always the same; and this turned out to be the case. But I also prepared a plan with magnetic bearings corrected up to date. Here are the three plans: No. 1 – the one we used – showing true bearings; No. 2, showing corrected magnetic bearings which might have given us the correct spot; and No. 3, with uncorrected magnetic bearings, giving us the spot where Harold dug, and which could not possibly have been the right spot.'

On the following morning I escorted the deed-box, filled with the booty and tied up and sealed with the scarab, to Mr Blowgrave's bank. And that ended our connection with the case; excepting that, a month or two later, we attended by request the unveiling in Shawstead churchyard of a fine monument to Reuben Blowgrave. This took the slightly inappropriate form of an obelisk, on which were cut the name and approximate dates, with the added inscription: 'Cast thy bread upon the waters and it shall return after many days'; concerning which Thorndyke remarked dryly that he supposed the exhortation applied equally even if the bread happened to belong to someone else.

The House in Goblin Wood

John Dickson Carr

In Pall Mall, that hot July afternoon three years before the war, an open saloon car was drawn up to the kerb just opposite the Senior Conservatives' Club.

And in the car sat two conspirators.

It was the drowsy post-lunch hour among the clubs, where only the sun remained brilliant. The Rag lay somnolent; the Athenæum slept outright. But these two conspirators, a dark-haired young man in his early thirties and a fair-haired girl perhaps half a dozen years younger, never moved. They stared intently at the Gothic-like front of the Senior Conservatives'.

'Look here, Eve,' muttered the young man, and punched at the steering-wheel, 'do you think this is going to work?'

'I don't know,' the fair-haired girl confessed. 'He absolutely loathes picnics.'

'Anyway, we've probably missed him.'

'Why so?'

'He can't have taken as long over lunch as that!' her companion protested, looking at a wrist-watch. The young man was rather shocked. 'It's a quarter to four! Even if …'

'Bill! There! Look there!'

Their patience was rewarded by an inspiring sight.

Out of the portals of the Senior Conservatives' Club, in awful majesty, marched a large, stout, barrel-shaped gentleman in a white linen suit.

His corporation preceded him like the figurehead of a man-of-war. His shell-rimmed spectacles were pulled down on a broad nose, all being shaded by a Panama hat. At the top of the stone steps he surveyed the street, left and right, with a lordly sneer.

'Sir Henry!' called the girl.

'Hey?' said Sir Henry Merrivale.

'I'm Eve Drayton. Don't you remember me? You knew my father!'

'Oh, ah,' said the great man.

'We've been waiting here a terribly long time,' Eve pleaded. 'Couldn't you see us for just five minutes? – The thing to do,' she whispered to her companion, 'is to keep him in a good humour. Just keep him in a good humour!'

As a matter of fact, H.M. was in a good humour, having just triumphed over the Home Secretary in an argument. But not even his own mother could have guessed it. Majestically, with the same lordly sneer, he began in grandeur to descend the steps of the Senior Conservatives'. He did this, in fact, until his foot encountered an unnoticed object lying some three feet from the bottom.

It was a banana skin.

'Oh, dear!' said the girl.

Now it must be stated with regret that in the old days certain urchins, of what were then called the 'lower orders', had a habit of placing such objects on the steps in the hope that some eminent statesman would take a toss on his way to Whitehall. This was a venial but deplorable practice, probably accounting for what Mr Gladstone said in 1882.

In any case, it accounted for what Sir Henry Merrivale said now.

From the pavement, where H.M. landed in a seated position, arose in H.M.'s bellowing voice such a torrent of profanity, such a flood of invective and vile obscenities, as has seldom before blasted the holy calm of Pall Mall. It brought the hall porter hurrying down the steps, and Eve Drayton flying out of the car.

Heads were now appearing at the windows of the Athenæum across the street.

'Is it all right?' cried the girl, with concern in her blue eyes. 'Are you hurt?'

H.M. merely looked at her. His hat had fallen off, disclosing a large bald head; and he merely sat on the pavement and looked at her.

'Anyway, H.M., get up! Please get up!'

'Yes, sir,' begged the hall porter, 'for heaven's sake get up!'

'Get up?' bellowed H.M., in a voice audible as far as St James's Street. 'Burn it all, how can I get up?'

'But why not?'

'My behind's out of joint,' said H.M. simply. 'I'm hurt

awful bad. I'm probably goin' to have spinal dislocation for the rest of my life.'

'But, sir, people are looking!'

H.M. explained what these people could do. He eyed Eve Drayton with a glare of indescribable malignancy over his spectacles.

'I suppose, my wench, *you're* responsible for this?'

Eve regarded him in consternation.

'You don't mean the banana skin?' she cried.

'Oh, yes, I do,' said H.M., folding his arms like a prosecuting counsel.

'But we – we only wanted to invite you to a picnic!'

H.M. closed his eyes. 'That's fine,' he said in a hollow voice. 'All the same, don't you think it'd have been a subtler kind of hint just to pour mayonnaise over my head or shove ants down the back of my neck? Oh, lord love a duck!'

'I didn't mean that! I meant ...'

'Let me help you up, sir,' interposed the calm, reassuring voice of the dark-haired and blue-chinned young man who had been with Eve in the car.

'So you want to help too, hey? And who are *you*?'

'I'm awfully sorry!' said Eve. 'I should have introduced you! This is my fiancé, Dr William Sage.'

H.M.'s face turned purple.

'I'm glad to see,' he observed, 'you had the uncommon decency to bring along a doctor. I appreciate that, I do. And the car's there, I suppose, to assist with the examination when I take off my pants?'

The hall porter uttered a cry of horror.

Bill Sage, either from jumpiness and nerves or from sheer inability to keep a straight face, laughed loudly.

'I keep telling Eve a dozen times a day,' he said, 'that I'm not to be called "doctor". I happen to be a surgeon—'

(Here H.M. really did look alarmed.)

'—but I don't think we need operate. Nor, in my opinion,' Bill gravely addressed the hall porter, 'will it be necessary to remove Sir Henry's trousers in front of the Senior Conservatives' Club.'

'Thank you very much, sir.'

'We had an infernal nerve to come here,' the young man confessed to H.M. 'But I honestly think, Sir Henry, you'd be more comfortable in the car. What about it? Let me give you a hand up?'

Yet even ten minutes later, when H.M. sat glowering in the back of the car and two heads were craned round towards him, peace was not restored.

'All right!' said Eve. Her pretty, rather stolid face was flushed; her mouth looked miserable. 'If you won't come to the picnic, you won't. But I did believe you might do it to oblige me.'

'Well … now!' muttered the great man uncomfortably.

'And I did think, too, you'd be interested in the other person who was coming with us. But Vicky's – difficult. She won't come either, if you don't.'

'Oh? And who's this other guest?'

'Vicky Adams.'

H.M.'s hand, which had been lifted for an oratorical gesture, dropped to his side.

'Vicky Adams? That's not the gal who …?'

'Yes!' Eve nodded. 'They say it was one of the great mysteries, twenty years ago, that the police failed to solve.'

'It was, my wench,' H.M. agreed sombrely. 'It was.'

'And now Vicky's grown up. And we thought if you of all people went along, and spoke to her nicely, she'd tell us what really happened on that night.'

H.M.'s small, sharp eyes fixed disconcertingly on Eve. 'I say, my wench. What's your interest in all this?'

'Oh, reasons.' Eve glanced quickly at Bill Sage, who was again punching moodily at the steering-wheel, and checked herself. 'Anyway, what difference does it make now? If you won't go with us …'

H.M. assumed a martyred air.

'I never said I wasn't goin' with you, did I?' he demanded. (This was inaccurate, but no matter.) 'Even after you practically made a cripple of me, I never said I *wasn't* goin'.' His manner grew flurried and hasty. 'But I got to leave now,' he added apologetically. 'I got to get back to my office.'

'We'll drive you there, H.M.'

'No, no, no,' said the practical cripple, getting out of the car with surprising celerity. 'Walkin' is good for my stomach if it's not so good for my behind. I'm a forgivin' man. You pick me up at my house tomorrow morning. G'bye.'

And he lumbered off in the direction of the Haymarket.

It needed no close observer to see that H.M. was deeply abstracted. He remained so abstracted, indeed, as to be nearly murdered by a taxi at the Admiralty Arch; and he was halfway down Whitehall before a familiar voice stopped him.

'Afternoon, Sir Henry!'

Burly, urbane, buttoned up in blue serge, with his bowler hat and his boiled blue eye, stood Chief Inspector Masters.

'Bit odd,' the Chief Inspector remarked affably, 'to see you taking a constitutional on a day like this. And how are you, sir?'

'Awful,' said H.M. instantly. 'But that's not the point. Masters, you crawlin' snake! You're the very man I wanted to see.'

Few things startled the Chief Inspector. This one did.

'You', he repeated, 'wanted to see *me*?'

'Uh-huh.'

'And what about?'

'Masters, do you remember the Victoria Adams case about twenty years ago?'

The Chief Inspector's manner suddenly changed and grew wary.

'Victoria Adams case?' he ruminated. 'No, sir, I can't say I do.'

'Son, you're lyin'! You were sergeant to old Chief Inspector Rutherford in those days, and well I remember it!'

Masters stood on his dignity. 'That's as may be, sir. But twenty years ago …'

'A little girl of twelve or thirteen, the child of very wealthy parents, disappeared one night out of a country cottage with all the doors and windows locked on the inside. A week later, while everybody was havin' screaming hysterics, the child reappeared again: through the locks and bolts, tucked up in her bed as usual. And to this day nobody's ever known what really happened.'

There was a silence, while Masters shut his jaws hard.

'This family, the Adamses,' persisted H.M., 'owned the

cottage, down Aylesbury way, on the edge of Goblin Wood, opposite the lake. Or was it?'

'Oh, ah,' growled Masters. 'It was.'

H.M. looked at him curiously.

'They used the cottage as a base for bathin' in summer, and ice-skatin' in winter. It was black winter when the child vanished, and the place was all locked up inside against drafts. They say her old man nearly went loopy when he found her there a week later, lying asleep under the lamp. But all she'd say, when they asked her where she'd been, was, "*I don't know*."'

Again there was a silence, while red buses thundered through the traffic press of Whitehall.

'You've got to admit, Masters, there was a flaming public rumpus. I say: did you ever read Barrie's *Mary Rose*?'

'No.'

'Well, it was a situation straight out of Barrie. Some people, y'see, said that Vicky Adams was a child of faerie who'd been spirited away by the pixies …'

Whereupon Masters exploded.

He removed his bowler hat and wiped his forehead. He made remarks about pixies; in detail, which could not have been bettered by H.M. himself.

'I know, son, I know.' H.M. was soothing. Then his big voice sharpened. 'Now tell me. Was all this talk strictly true?'

'What talk?'

'Locked windows? Bolted doors? No attic-trap? No cellar? Solid walls and floor?'

'Yes, sir,' answered Masters, regaining his dignity with a powerful effort, 'I'm bound to admit it *was* true.'

'Then there wasn't any jiggery-pokery about the cottage?'

'In your eye there wasn't,' said Masters.

'How d'ye mean?'

'Listen, sir.' Masters lowered his voice. 'Before the Adamses took over that place, it was a hideout for Chuck Randall. At that time he was the swellest of the swell mob; we lagged him a couple of years later. Do you think Chuck wouldn't have rigged up some gadget for a getaway? Just so! Only …'

'Well? Hey?'

'We couldn't find it,' grunted Masters.

'And I'll bet that pleased old Chief Inspector Rutherford?'

'I tell you straight: he was fair up the pole. Especially as the kid herself was a pretty kid, all big eyes and dark hair. You couldn't help trusting her.'

'Yes,' said H.M. 'That's what worries me.'

'Worries you?'

'Oh, my son!' said H.M. dismally. 'Here's Vicky Adams, the spoiled daughter of dotin' parents. She's supposed to be "odd" and "fey". She's even encouraged to be. During her adolescence, the most impressionable time of her life, she gets wrapped round with the gauze of a mystery that people talk about even yet. What's that woman like now, Masters? What's that woman like now?'

'Dear Sir Henry!' murmured Miss Vicky Adams in her softest voice.

She said this just as William Sage's car, with Bill and Eve Drayton in the front seat, and Vicky and H.M. in the back seat, turned off the main road. Behind them lay the smoky-red roofs of Aylesbury, against a brightness of late afternoon. The car turned down a side road, a damp tunnel of greenery, and into another road which was little more than a lane between hedgerows.

H.M. – though cheered by three good-sized picnic hampers from Fortnum & Mason, their wickerwork lids bulging with a feast – did not seem happy. Nobody in that car was happy, with the possible exception of Miss Adams herself.

Vicky, unlike Eve, was small and dark and vivacious. Her large light-brown eyes, with very black lashes, could be arch and coy; or they could be dreamily intense. The late Sir James Barrie might have called her a sprite. Those of more sober views would have recognised a different quality: she had an inordinate sex appeal, which was as palpable as a physical touch to any male within yards. And despite her smallness, Vicky had a full voice like Eve's. All these qualities she used even in so simple a matter as giving traffic directions.

'First right,' she would say, leaning forward to put her hands on Bill Sage's shoulders. 'Then straight on until the next traffic light. Ah, clever boy!'

'Not at all, not at all!' Bill would disclaim, with red ears and rather an erratic style of driving.

'Oh, yes, you are!' And Vicky would twist the lobe of his ear, playfully, before sitting back again.

(Eve Drayton did not say anything. She did not even turn round. Yet the atmosphere, even of that quiet English picnic party, had already become a trifle hysterical.)

'Dear Sir Henry!' murmured Vicky, as they turned down into the deep lane between the hedgerows. 'I do wish you wouldn't be so materialistic! I do, really. Haven't you the tiniest bit of spirituality in your nature?'

'Me?' said H.M. in astonishment. 'I got a very lofty spiritual nature. But what I want just now, my wench, is grub. – Oi!'

Bill Sage glanced round.

'By that speedometer,' H.M. pointed, 'we've now come forty-six miles and a bit. We didn't even leave town until people of decency and sanity were having their tea. Where are we *goin'*?'

'But didn't you know?' asked Vicky, with wide-open eyes. 'We're going to the cottage where I had such a dreadful experience when I was a child.'

'Was it such a dreadful experience, Vicky dear?' inquired Eve.

Vicky's eyes seemed far away.

'I don't remember, really. I was only a child, you see. I didn't understand. I hadn't developed the power for myself then.'

'What power?' H.M. asked sharply.

'To dematerialise,' said Vicky. 'Of course.'

In that warm, sun-dusted lane, between the hawthorn hedges, the car jolted over a rut. Crockery rattled.

'Uh-huh. I see,' observed H.M. without inflection. 'And where do you go, my wench, when you dematerialise?'

'Into a strange country. Through a little door. You wouldn't understand. Oh, you *are* such Philistines!' moaned Vicky. Then, with a sudden change of mood, she leaned forward and her whole physical allurement flowed again towards Bill Sage. '*You* wouldn't like me to disappear, would you, Bill?'

(Easy! Easy!)

'Only', said Bill, with a sort of wild gallantry, 'if you promised to reappear again straightaway.'

'Oh, I should have to do that.' Vicky sat back. She was trembling. 'The power wouldn't be strong enough. But even a poor little thing like me might be able to teach you a lesson. Look there!'

And she pointed ahead.

On their left, as the lane widened, stretched the ten-acre gloom of what is fancifully known as Goblin Wood. On their right lay a small lake, on private property and therefore deserted.

The cottage – set well back into a clearing of the wood so as to face the road, screened from it by a line of beeches – was in fact a bungalow of rough-hewn stone, with a slate roof. Across the front of it ran a wooden porch. It had a seedy air, like the long, yellow-green grass of its front lawn. Bill parked the car at the side of the road, since there was no driveway.

'It's a bit lonely, ain't it?' demanded H.M. His voice boomed out against that utter stillness, under the hot sun.

'Oh, yes!' breathed Vicky. She jumped out of the car in a whirl of skirts. 'That's why *they* were able to come and take me. When I was a child.'

'They?'

'Dear Sir Henry! Do I need to explain?'

Then Vicky looked at Bill.

'I must apologise,' she said, 'for the state the house is in. I haven't been out here for months and months. There's a modern bathroom, I'm glad to say. Only paraffin lamps, of course. But then,' a dreamy smile flashed across her face, 'you won't need lamps, will you? Unless ...'

'You mean,' said Bill, who was taking a black case out of the car, 'unless you disappear again?'

'Yes, Bill. And promise me you won't be frightened when I do.'

The young man uttered a ringing oath which was shushed by Sir Henry Merrivale, who austerely said he disapproved of profanity. Eve Drayton was *very* quiet.

'But in the meantime,' Vicky said wistfully, 'let's forget it all, shall we? Let's laugh and dance and sing and pretend we're children! And surely our guest must be even more hungry by this time?'

It was in this emotional state that they sat down to their picnic.

H.M., if the truth must be told, did not fare too badly. Instead of sitting on some hummock of ground, they dragged a table and chairs to the shaded porch. All spoke in strained voices. But no word of controversy was said. It was only afterwards, when the cloth was cleared, the furniture and hampers pushed indoors, the empty bottles flung away, that danger tapped a warning.

From under the porch Vicky fished out two half-rotted deckchairs, which she set up in the long grass of the lawn. These were to be occupied by Eve and H.M., while Vicky took Bill Sage to inspect a plum tree of some remarkable quality she did not specify.

Eve sat down without comment. H.M., who was smoking a black cigar opposite her, waited some time before he spoke.

'Y'know,' he said, taking the cigar out of his mouth, 'you're behaving remarkably well.'

'Yes,' Eve laughed. 'Aren't I?'

'Are you pretty well acquainted with this Adams gal?'

'I'm her first cousin,' Eve answered simply. 'Now that her parents are dead, I'm the only relative she's got. I know *all* about her.'

From far across the lawn floated two voices saying something about wild strawberries. Eve, her fair hair and fair complexion vivid against the dark line of Goblin Wood, clenched her hands on her knees.

'You see, H.M.,' she hesitated, 'there was another reason why I invited you here. I – I don't quite know how to approach it.'

'I'm the old man,' said H.M., tapping himself impressively on the chest. 'You tell me.'

'Eve, darling!' interposed Vicky's voice, crying across the ragged lawn. 'Coo-ee! Eve!'

'Yes, dear?'

'I've just remembered,' cried Vicky, 'that I haven't shown Bill over the cottage! You don't mind if I steal him away from you for a little while?'

'No, dear! Of course not!'

It was H.M., sitting so as to face the bungalow, who saw Vicky and Bill go in. He saw Vicky's wistful smile as she closed the door after them. Eve did not even look round. The sun was declining, making fiery chinks through the thickness of Goblin Wood behind the cottage.

'I won't let her have him,' Eve suddenly cried. 'I won't! I won't! I won't!'

'Does she want him, my wench? Or, which is more to the point, does he want her?'

'He never has,' Eve said with emphasis. 'Not really. And he never will.'

H.M., motionless, puffed out cigar smoke.

'Vicky's a faker,' said Eve. 'Does that sound catty?'

'Not necessarily. I was just thinkin' the same thing myself.'

'I'm patient,' said Eve. Her blue eyes were fixed. 'I'm terribly, terribly patient. I can wait years for what I want. Bill's not making much money now, and I haven't got a bean. But Bill's got great talent under that easy-going manner of his. He *must* have the right girl to help him. If only …'

'If only the elfin sprite would let him alone. Hey?'

'Vicky acts like that,' said Eve, 'towards practically every man she ever meets. That's why she never married. She says it leaves her soul free to commune with other souls. This occultism—'

Then it all poured out, the family story of the Adamses. This repressed girl spoke at length, spoke as perhaps she had never spoken before. Vicky Adams, the child who wanted to attract attention, her father, Uncle Fred, and her mother, Aunt Margaret, seemed to walk in vividness as the shadows gathered.

'I was too young to know her at the time of the "disappearance", of course. But, oh, I knew her afterwards! And I thought …'

'Well?'

'If I could get *you* here,' said Eve, 'I thought she'd try to show off with some game. And then you'd expose her. And Bill would see what an awful faker she is. But it's hopeless! It's hopeless!'

'Looky here,' observed H.M., who was smoking his third cigar. He sat up. 'Doesn't it strike you those two are being a rummy-awful long time just in lookin' through a little bungalow?'

Eve, roused out of a dream, stared back at him. She sprang to her feet. She was not now, you could guess, thinking of any disappearance.

'Excuse me a moment,' she said curtly.

Eve hurried across to the cottage, went up on the porch, and opened the front door. H.M. heard her heels rap down the length of the small passage inside. She marched straight back again, closed the front door, and rejoined H.M.

'All the doors of the rooms are shut,' she announced in a high voice. 'I really don't think I ought to disturb them.'

'Easy, my wench!'

'I have absolutely no interest,' declared Eve, with the tears coming into her eyes, 'in what happens to either of them now. Shall we take the car and go back to town without them?'

H.M. threw away his cigar, got up, and seized her by the shoulders.

'I'm the old man,' he said, with a leer like an ogre. 'Will you listen to me?'

'No!'

'If I'm any reader of the human dial,' persisted H.M., 'that young feller's no more gone on Vicky Adams than I am. He was scared, my wench. Scared.' Doubt, indecision crossed H.M.'s face. 'I dunno what he's scared of. Burn me, I don't! But …'

'Hoy!' called the voice of Bill Sage. It did not come from the direction of the cottage.

They were surrounded on three sides by Goblin Wood, now blurred with twilight. From the north side the voice bawled at them, followed by crackling in dry undergrowth. Bill, his hair and sports coat and flannels more than a little dirty, regarded them with a face of bitterness.

'Here are her blasted wild strawberries,' he announced, extending his hand. 'Three of 'em. The fruitful (excuse me) result of three-quarters of an hour's hard labour. I absolutely refuse to chase 'em in the dark.'

For a moment Eve Drayton's mouth moved without speech. 'Then you weren't … in the cottage all this time?'

'In the cottage?' Bill glanced at it. 'I was in that cottage,' he said, 'about five minutes. Vicky had a woman's whim. She wanted some wild strawberries out of what she called the "forest".'

'Wait a minute, son!' said H.M. very sharply. 'You didn't come out that front door. Nobody did.'

'No! I went out the back door! It opens straight on the wood.'

'Yes. And what happened then?'

'Well, I went to look for these damned …'

'No, no! What did *she* do?'

'Vicky? She locked and bolted the back door on the inside. I remember her grinning at me through the glass panel. She—'

Bill stopped short. His eyes widened, and then narrowed, as though at the impact of an idea. All three of them turned to look at the rough-stone cottage.

'By the way,' said Bill. He cleared his throat vigorously. 'By the way, have you seen Vicky since then?'

'No.'

'This couldn't be ...?'

'It could be, son,' said H.M. 'We'd all better go in there and have a look.'

They hesitated for a moment on the porch. A warm, moist fragrance breathed up from the ground after sunset. In half an hour it would be completely dark.

Bill Sage threw open the front door and shouted Vicky's name. That sound seemed to penetrate, reverberating, through every room. The intense heat and stuffiness of the cottage, where no window had been raised in months, blew out at them. But nobody answered.

'Get inside,' snapped H.M. 'And stop yowlin'.' The Old Maestro was nervous. 'I'm dead sure she didn't get out by the front door; but we'll just make certain there's no slippin' out now.'

Stumbling over the table and chairs they had used on the porch, he fastened the front door. They were in a narrow passage, once handsome with parquet floor and pine-panelled walls, leading to a door with a glass panel at the rear. H.M. lumbered forward to inspect this door, and found it locked and bolted, as Bill had said.

Goblin Wood grew darker.

Keeping well together, they searched the cottage. It was not large, having two good-sized rooms on one side of the passage, and two small rooms on the other side, so as to make space for bathroom and kitchenette. H.M., raising fogs of dust, ransacked every inch where a person could possibly hide.

And all the windows were locked on the inside. And the chimney flues were too narrow to admit anybody.

And Vicky Adams wasn't there.

'Oh, my eye!' breathed Sir Henry Merrivale.

They had gathered, by what idiotic impulse not even H.M. could have said, just outside the open door of the bathroom. A bath-tap dripped monotonously. The last light through a frosted-glass window showed three faces hung there as though disembodied.

'Bill,' said Eve in an unsteady voice, 'this is a trick. Oh, I've longed for her to be exposed! This is a trick!'

'Then where is she?'

'H.M. can tell us! Can't you, H.M.?'

'Well … now,' muttered the great man.

Across H.M.'s Panama hat was a large black handprint, made there when he had pressed down the hat after investigating the chimney. He glowered under it.

'Son,' he said to Bill, 'there's just one question I want you to answer in all this hokey-pokey. When you went out pickin' wild strawberries, will you swear Vicky Adams didn't go with you?'

'As God is my Judge, she didn't,' returned Bill, with fervency and obvious truth. 'Besides, how the devil could she? Look at the lock and bolt on the back door!'

H.M. made two more violent black handprints on his hat.

He lumbered forward, his head down, two or three paces in the narrow passage. His foot half-skidded on something that had been lying there unnoticed, and he picked it up. It was a large, square section of thin, waterproof oilskin, jagged at one corner.

'Have you found anything?' demanded Bill in a strained voice. 'No. Not to make any sense, that is. But just a minute!'

At the rear of the passage, on the left-hand side, was the bedroom from which Vicky Adams had vanished as a child. Though H.M. had searched this room once before, he opened the door again.

It was now almost dark in Goblin Wood.

He saw dimly a room twenty years before: a room of flounces, of lace curtains, of once-polished mahogany, its mirrors glimmering against white-papered walls. H.M. seemed especially interested in the windows.

He ran his hands carefully round the frame of each, even climbing laboriously up on a chair to examine the tops. He borrowed a box of matches from Bill; and the little spurts of light, following the rasp of the match, rasped against nerves as well. The hope died out of his face, and his companions saw it.

'H.M.,' Bill said for the dozenth time, 'where is she?'

'Son,' replied H.M. despondently, 'I don't know.'

'Let's get out of here,' Eve said abruptly. Her voice was a small scream. 'I kn-know it's all a trick! I know Vicky's a faker! But let's get out of here. For God's sake let's get out of here!'

'As a matter of fact,' Bill cleared his throat, 'I agree. Anyway, we won't hear from Vicky until tomorrow morning.'

'*Oh, yes, you will,*' whispered Vicky's voice out of the darkness. Eve screamed.

They lighted a lamp.

But there was nobody there.

Their retreat from the cottage, it must be admitted, was not very dignified.

How they stumbled down that ragged lawn in the dark, how they piled rugs and picnic hampers into the car, how they eventually found the main road again, is best left undescribed.

Sir Henry Merrivale has since sneered at this – 'a bit of a goosy feeling; nothin' much' – and it is true that he has no nerves to speak of. But he can be worried, badly worried, and that he was worried on this occasion may be deduced from what happened later.

H.M., after dropping in at Claridge's for a modest late supper of lobster and *Pêche Melba*, returned to his house in Brook Street and slept a hideous sleep. It was three o'clock in the morning, even before the summer dawn, when the ringing of the bedside telephone roused him.

What he heard sent his blood pressure soaring. 'Dear Sir Henry!' crooned a familiar and sprite-like voice.

H.M. was himself again, full of gall and bile. He switched on the bedside lamp and put on his spectacles with care, so as adequately to address the phone.

'Have I got the honour,' he said with dangerous politeness, 'of addressin' Miss Vicky Adams?'

'Oh, yes!'

'I sincerely trust,' said H.M., 'you've been havin' a good time? Are you materialised yet?'

'Oh, yes!'

'Where are you now?'

'I'm afraid' – there was coy laughter in the voice – 'that must be a little secret for a day or two. I want to teach you a really *good* lesson. Blessings, dear.'

And she hung up the receiver.

H.M. did not say anything. He climbed out of bed. He stalked up and down the room, his corporation majestic under an old-fashioned nightshirt stretching to his heels. Then, since he himself had been waked up at three o'clock in the morning, the obvious course was to wake up somebody else; so he dialled the home number of Chief Inspector Masters.

'No, sir,' retorted Masters grimly, after coughing the frog out of his throat, 'I do *not* mind you ringing up. Not a bit of it!' He spoke with a certain pleasure. 'Because I've got a bit of news for you.'

H.M. eyed the phone suspiciously.

'Masters, are you trying to do me in the eye again?'

'It's what you always try to do to me, isn't it?'

'All right, all right!' growled H.M. 'What's the news?'

'Do you remember mentioning the Vicky Adams case to me yesterday?'

'Sort of. Yes.'

'Oh, ah! Well, I had a word or two round among our people. I was tipped the wink to go and see a certain solicitor. He was old Mr Fred Adams's solicitor before Mr Adams died about six or seven years ago.'

Here Masters's voice grew suave with triumph.

'I always said, Sir Henry, that Chuck Randall had planted some gadget in that cottage for a quick getaway. And I was right. The gadget was …'

'You were quite right, Masters. The gadget was a trick window.'

The telephone so to speak, gave a start.

'What's that?'

'A trick window.' H.M. spoke patiently. 'You press a spring. And the whole frame of the window, two leaves locked together, slides down between the walls far enough so you can climb over. Then you push it back up again.'

'*How in lum's name do you know that?*'

'Oh, my son! They used to build windows like it in country houses during the persecution of Catholic priests. It was a good enough second guess. Only ... it won't work.'

Masters seemed annoyed. 'It won't work now,' he agreed. 'And do you know why?'

'I can guess. Tell me.'

'Because, just before Mr Adams died, he discovered how his darling daughter had flummoxed him. He never told anybody except his lawyer. He took a handful of four-inch nails, and sealed up the top of that frame so tight an orang-outang couldn't move it, and painted 'em over so they wouldn't be noticed.'

'Uh-huh. You can notice 'em now.'

'I doubt if the young lady herself ever knew. But, by George!' Masters said savagely, 'I'd like to see anybody try the same game now!'

'You would, hey? Then will it interest you to know that the same gal has just disappeared out of the same house AGAIN?'

H.M. began a long narrative of the facts, but he had to break off because the telephone was raving.

'Honest, Masters,' H.M. said seriously, 'I'm not joking. She didn't get out through the window. But she did get out. You'd better meet me' – he gave directions – 'tomorrow morning. In the meantime, son, sleep well.'

It was, therefore, a worn-faced Masters who went into the Visitors' Room at the Senior Conservatives' Club just before lunch on the following day.

The Visitors' Room is a dark, sepulchral place, opening on an air-well, where the visitor is surrounded by pictures of dyspeptic-looking gentlemen with beards. It has a pervading mustiness of wood and leather. Though whisky and soda stood on the table, H.M. sat in a leather chair far away from it, ruffling his hands across his bald head.

'Now, Masters, keep your shirt on!' he warned. 'This business may be rummy. But it's not a police matter – yet.'

'I know it's not a police matter,' Masters said grimly. 'All the same, I've had a word with the Superintendent at Aylesbury.'

'Fowler?'

'You know him?'

'Sure. I know everybody. Is he goin' to keep an eye out?'

'He's going to have a look at that ruddy cottage. I've asked for any telephone calls to be put through here. In the meantime, sir—'

It was at this point, as though diabolically inspired, that the telephone rang. H.M. reached it before Masters.

'It's the old man,' he said, unconsciously assuming a stance of grandeur. 'Yes, yes! Masters is here, but he's drunk. You tell me first. What's that?'

The telephone talked thinly.

'Sure I looked in the kitchen cupboard,' bellowed H.M. 'Though I didn't honestly expect to find Vicky Adams hidin' there. What's that? Say it again! Plates? Cups that had been ...'

An almost frightening change had come over H.M.'s

expression. He stood motionless. All the posturing went out of him. He was not even listening to the voice that still talked thinly, while his eyes and his brain moved to put together facts. At length (though the voice still talked) he hung up the receiver.

H.M. blundered back to the centre table, where he drew out a chair and sat down.

'Masters,' he said very quietly, 'I've come close to makin' the silliest mistake of my life.'

Here he cleared his throat.

'I shouldn't have made it, son, I really shouldn't. But don't yell at me for cuttin' off Fowler. I can tell you now how Vicky Adams disappeared. And she said one true thing when she said she was going into a strange country.'

'How do you mean?'

'She's dead,' answered H.M.

The word fell with heavy weight into that dingy room, where the bearded faces look down.

'Y'see,' H.M. went on blankly, 'a lot of us were right when we thought Vicky Adams was a faker. She was. To attract attention to herself, she played that trick on her family with the hocused window. She's lived and traded on it ever since. That's what sent me straight in the wrong direction. I was on the alert for some trick Vicky Adams might play. So it never occurred to me that this elegant pair of beauties, Miss Eve Drayton and Mr William Sage, were deliberately conspirin' to murder *her*.'

Masters got slowly to his feet.

'Did you say … murder?'

'Oh, yes.'

Again H.M. cleared his throat.

'It was all arranged beforehand for me to be a witness. They knew Vicky Adams couldn't resist a challenge to disappear, especially as Vicky always believed she could get out by the trick window. They wanted Vicky to *say* she was goin' to disappear. They never knew anything about the trick window, Masters. But they knew their own plan very well.

'Eve Drayton even told me the motive. She hated Vicky, of course. But that wasn't the main point. She was Vicky Adams's only relative; she'd inherit an awful big scoopful of money. Eve said she could be patient. (And, burn me, how her eyes meant it when she said that!) Rather than risk any slightest suspicion of murder, she was willing to wait seven years until a disappeared person can be presumed dead.

'Our Eve, I think, was the fiery drivin' force of that conspiracy. She was only scared part of the time. Sage was scared all of the time. But it was Sage who did the real dirty work. He lured Vicky Adams into that cottage, while Eve kept me in close conversation on the lawn ...'

H.M. paused.

Intolerably vivid in the mind of Chief Inspector Masters, who had seen it years before, rose the picture of the rough-stone bungalow against the darkening wood.

'Masters,' said H.M., 'why should a bath-tap be dripping in a house that hadn't been occupied for months?'

'Well?'

'Sage, y'see, is a surgeon. I saw him take his black case of instruments out of the car. He took Vicky Adams into that house. In the bathroom he stabbed her, he stripped her, and *he dismembered her body in the bath-tub. – Easy, son!*'

'Go on,' said Masters, without moving.

'The head, the torso, the folded arms and legs, were wrapped up in three large square pieces of thin, transparent oilskin. Each was sewed up with coarse thread so the blood wouldn't drip. Last night I found one of the oilskin pieces he'd ruined when his needle slipped at the corner. Then he walked out of the house, with the back door still standin' unlocked, to get his wild-strawberry alibi.'

'Sage went out of there,' shouted Masters, 'leaving the body in the house?'

'Oh, yes,' agreed H.M.

'But where did he leave it?'

H.M. ignored this.

'In the meantime, son, what about Eve Drayton? At the end of the arranged three-quarters of an hour, she indicated there was hanky-panky between her fiancé and Vicky Adams. She flew into the house. But what did she do?

'She walked to the back of the passage. I heard her. *There she simply locked and bolted the back door.* And then she marched out to join me with tears in her eyes. And these two beauties were ready for investigation.'

'Investigation?' said Masters. 'With that body still in the house?'

'Oh, yes.'

Masters lifted both fists.

'It must have given young Sage a shock,' said H.M., 'when I found that piece of waterproof oilskin he'd washed but dropped. Anyway, these two had only two more bits of hokey-pokey. The "vanished" gal had to speak – to show she was still alive. If you'd been there, son, you'd have noticed that Eve Drayton's got a voice just like Vicky Adams's. If somebody speaks in a dark room, carefully imitatin' a coy tone she never uses herself, the illusion's goin' to be pretty good. The same goes for a telephone.

'It was finished, Masters. All that had to be done was remove the body from the house, and get it far away from there ...'

'But that's just what I'm asking you, sir! Where was the body all this time? And who in blazes did remove the body from the house?'

'All of us did,' answered H.M.

'What's that?'

'Masters,' said H.M., 'aren't you forgettin' the picnic hampers?'

And now, the Chief Inspector saw, H.M. was as white as a ghost. His next words took Masters like a blow between the eyes.

'Three good-sized wickerwork hampers, with lids. After our big meal on the porch, those hampers were shoved inside the house, where Sage could get at 'em. He had to leave most of the used crockery behind, in the kitchen cupboard. But three wickerwork hampers from a picnic, and three butcher's parcels to go inside 'em. I carried one down to the car myself. It felt a bit funny ...'

H.M. stretched out his hand, not steadily, towards the whisky.

'Y'know,' he said, 'I'll always wonder whether I was carrying the – head.'

The Oracle of the Dog

G. K. Chesterton

'Yes,' said Father Brown, 'I always like a dog, so long as he isn't spelt backwards.'

Those who are quick in talking are not always quick in listening. Sometimes even their brilliancy produces a sort of stupidity. Father Brown's friend and companion was a young man with a stream of ideas and stories, an enthusiastic young man named Fiennes, with eager blue eyes and blond hair that seemed to be brushed back, not merely with a hair-brush but with the wind of the world as he rushed through it. But he stopped in the torrent of his talk in a momentary bewilderment before he saw the priest's very simple meaning.

'You mean that people make too much of them?' he said. 'Well, I don't know. They're marvellous creatures. Sometimes I think they know a lot more than we do.'

Father Brown said nothing; but continued to stroke the

head of the big retriever in a half-abstracted but apparently soothing fashion.

'Why,' said Fiennes, warming again to his monologue, 'there was a dog in the case I've come to see you about; what they call the "Invisible Murder Case", you know. It's a strange story, but from my point of view the dog is about the strangest thing in it. Of course, there's the mystery of the crime itself, and how old Druce can have been killed by somebody else when he was all alone in the summer-house—'

The hand stroking the dog stopped for a moment in its rhythmic movement; and Father Brown said calmly, 'Oh, it was a summer-house, was it?'

'I thought you'd read all about it in the papers,' answered Fiennes. 'Stop a minute; I believe I've got a cutting that will give you all the particulars.' He produced a strip of newspaper from his pocket and handed it to the priest, who began to read it, holding it close to his blinking eyes with one hand while the other continued its half-conscious caresses of the dog. It looked like the parable of a man not letting his right hand know what his left hand did.

> 'Many mystery stories, about men murdered behind locked doors and windows, and murderers escaping without means of entrance and exit, have come true in the course of the extraordinary events at Cranston on the coast of Yorkshire, where Colonel Druce was found stabbed from behind by a dagger that has entirely disappeared from the scene, and apparently even from the neighbourhood.
>
> 'The summer-house in which he died was indeed accessible at one entrance, the ordinary doorway which looked down the central walk of the garden towards the house. But

by a combination of events almost to be called a coincidence, it appears that both the path and the entrance were watched during the crucial time, and there is a chain of witnesses who confirm each other. The summer-house stands at the extreme end of the garden, where there is no exit or entrance of any kind. The central garden path is a lane between two ranks of tall delphiniums, planted so close that any stray step off the path would leave its traces; and both path and plants run right up to the very mouth of the summer-house, so that no straying from that straight path could fail to be observed, and no other mode of entrance can be imagined.

'Patrick Floyd, secretary of the murdered man, testified that he had been in a position to overlook the whole garden from the time when Colonel Druce last appeared alive in the doorway to the time when he was found dead; as he, Floyd, had been on the top of a step-ladder clipping the garden hedge. Janet Druce, the dead man's daughter, confirmed this, saying that she had sat on the terrace of the house throughout that time and had seen Floyd at his work. Touching some part of the time, this is again supported by Donald Druce, her brother, who overlooked the garden standing at his bedroom window in his dressing-gown, for he had risen late. Lastly the account is consistent with that given by Dr Valentine, a neighbour, who called for a time to talk with Miss Druce on the terrace, and by the Colonel's solicitor, Mr Aubrey Traill, who was apparently the last to see the murdered man alive – presumably with the exception of the murderer.

'All are agreed that the course of events was as follows: about half-past three in the afternoon, Miss Druce went down the path to ask her father when he would like tea; but he said he did not want any and was waiting to see Traill, his lawyer, who was to be sent to him in the summer-house. The girl then came away and met Traill coming down the path; she directed him to her father and he went in as directed. About half an hour afterwards he came out again, the Colonel coming with him to the door and showing himself to all appearance in health and even high spirits. He had been somewhat annoyed earlier in the day by his son's irregular hours, but seemed to recover his temper in a perfectly normal fashion, and had been rather markedly genial in receiving other visitors, including two of his nephews who came over for the day. But as these were out walking during the whole period of the tragedy, they had no evidence to give. It is said, indeed, that the Colonel was not on very good terms with Dr Valentine, but that gentleman only had a brief interview with the daughter of the house, to whom he's supposed to be paying serious attentions.

'Traill, the solicitor, says he left the Colonel entirely alone in the summer-house, and this is confirmed by Floyd's bird's-eye view of the garden, which showed nobody else passing the only entrance. Ten minutes later Miss Druce again went down the garden and had not reached the end of the path, when she saw her father, who was conspicuous by his white linen coat, lying in a heap on the floor. She uttered a scream which brought others to the spot, and on entering the place they found the Colonel lying dead beside his basket-chair, which was also upset. Dr Valentine, who was still in the immediate neighbourhood, testified that the wound was made by some sort of stiletto, entering under the shoulder-blade and piercing the heart. The police have searched the neighbourhood for such a weapon, but no trace of it can be found.'

'So Colonel Druce wore a white coat, did he?' said Father Brown as he put down the paper.

'Trick he learnt in the tropics,' replied Fiennes with some wonder. 'He'd had some queer adventures there, by his own account; and I fancy his dislike of Valentine was connected with the doctor coming from the tropics, too. But it's all an infernal puzzle. The account there is pretty accurate; I didn't see the tragedy, in the sense of the discovery; I was out walking with the young nephews and the dog – the dog I wanted to tell you about. But I saw the stage set for it as described: the straight lane between the blue flowers right up to the dark entrance, and the lawyer going down it in his blacks and his silk hat, and the red head of the secretary showing high above the green hedge as he worked on it with his shears. Nobody could have mistaken that red head at any distance; and if people say they saw it there all the time, you may be sure they did. This red-haired secretary Floyd is quite a character; a breathless, bounding sort of fellow, always doing everybody's work as he was doing the gardener's. I think he is an American; he's certainly got the American view of life; what they call the viewpoint, bless 'em.'

'What about the lawyer?' asked Father Brown.

There was a silence and then Fiennes spoke quite slowly for him. 'Traill struck me as a singular man. In his fine black clothes he was almost foppish, yet you can hardly call him fashionable. For he wore a pair of long, luxuriant black whiskers such as haven't been seen since Victorian times. He had rather a fine grave face and a fine grave manner, but every now and then he seemed to remember to smile. And when he showed his white teeth he seemed to lose a little of his dignity and there was something faintly fawning about him. It may have been only embarrassment, for he would also fidget with his cravat and his tie-pin, which were at once handsome and unusual, like himself. If I could think of anybody – but what's the good, when the whole thing's impossible? Nobody knows who did it. Nobody knows how it could be done. At least there's only one exception I'd make, and that's why I really mentioned the whole thing. The dog knows.'

Father Brown sighed and then said absently: 'You were there as a friend of young Donald, weren't you? He didn't go on your walk with you?'

'No,' replied Fiennes smiling. 'The young scoundrel had gone to bed that morning and got up that afternoon. I went with his cousins, two young officers from India, and our conversation was trivial enough. I remember the elder, whose name I think is Herbert Druce and who is an authority on horse-breeding, talked about nothing but a mare he had bought and the moral character of the man who sold her – while his brother Harry seemed to be brooding on his bad luck at Monte Carlo. I only mention it to show you, in the light of what happened on our walk, that there was nothing psychic about us. The dog was the only mystic in our company.'

'What sort of a dog was he?' asked the priest.

'Same breed as that one,' answered Fiennes. 'That's what started me off on the story, your saying you didn't believe in believing in a dog. He's a big black retriever named Nox, and a suggestive name too; for I think what he did a darker mystery than the murder. You know Druce's house and garden are by the sea; we walked about a mile from it along the sands and then turned back, going the other way. We passed a rather curious rock called the Rock of Fortune, famous in the neighbourhood because it's one of those examples of one stone barely balanced on another, so that a touch would knock it over. It is not really very high, but the hanging outline of it makes it look a little wild and sinister; at least it made it look so to me, for I don't imagine my jolly young companions were afflicted with the picturesque. But it may be that I was beginning to feel an atmosphere; for just then the question arose of whether it was time to go back to tea, and even then I think I had a premonition that time counted for a good deal in the business. Neither Herbert Druce nor I had a watch, so we called out to his brother, who was some paces behind, having stopped to light his pipe under the hedge. Hence it happened that he shouted out the hour, which was twenty past four, in his big voice through the growing twilight; and somehow the loudness of it made it sound like the proclamation of something tremendous. His unconsciousness seemed to make it all the more so; but that was always the way with omens; and particular ticks of the clock were really very ominous things that afternoon. According to Dr Valentine's testimony, poor Druce had actually died just about half-past four.

'Well, they said we needn't go home for ten minutes, and we walked a little farther along the sands, doing nothing in particular – throwing stones for the dog and throwing sticks into the sea for him to swim after. But to me the twilight seemed to grow oddly oppressive and the very shadow of the top-heavy Rock of Fortune lay on me like a load. And then the curious thing happened. Nox had just brought back Herbert's walking-stick out of the sea and his brother had thrown his in also. The dog swam out again, but just about what must have been the stroke of the half-hour, he stopped swimming. He came back again on to the shore and stood in front of us. Then he suddenly threw up his head and sent up a howl or wail of woe, if ever I heard one in the world.

'"What the devil's the matter with the dog?" asked Herbert; but none of us could answer. There was a long silence after the brute's wailing and whining died away on the desolate shore; and then the silence was broken. As I live, it was broken by a faint and far-off shriek, like the shriek of a woman from beyond the hedges inland. We didn't know what it was then; but we knew afterwards. It was the cry the girl gave when she first saw the body of her father.'

'You went back, I suppose,' said Father Brown patiently. 'What happened then?'

'I'll tell you what happened then,' said Fiennes with a grim emphasis. 'When we got back into that garden the first thing we saw was Traill the lawyer; I can see him now with his black hat and black whiskers relieved against the perspective of the blue flowers stretching down to the summer-house, with the sunset and the strange outline of the Rock of Fortune in the distance. His face and figure were in shadow against the sunset; but I swear the white teeth were showing in his head and he was smiling.

'The moment Nox saw that man, the dog dashed forward and stood in the middle of the path barking at him madly, murderously, volleying out curses that were almost verbal in their dreadful distinctness of hatred. And the man doubled up and fled along the path between the flowers.'

Father Brown sprang to his feet with a startling impatience.

'So the dog denounced him, did he?' he cried. 'The oracle of the dog condemned him. Did you see what birds were flying, and are you sure whether they were on the right hand or the left? Did you consult the augurs about the sacrifices? Surely you didn't omit to cut open the dog and examine his entrails. That is the sort of scientific test you heathen humanitarians seem to trust when you are thinking of taking away the life and honour of a man.'

Fiennes sat gaping for an instant before he found breath to say, 'Why, what's the matter with you? What have I done now?'

A sort of anxiety came back into the priest's eyes – the anxiety of a man who has run against a post in the dark and wonders for a moment whether he has hurt it.

'I'm most awfully sorry,' he said with sincere distress. 'I beg your pardon for being so rude; pray forgive me.'

Fiennes looked at him curiously. 'I sometimes think you are more of a mystery than any of the mysteries,' he said. 'But anyhow, if you don't believe in the mystery of the dog, at least you can't get over the mystery of the man. You can't deny that at the very moment when the beast came back from the sea and bellowed, his master's soul was driven out of his body by the blow of some unseen power that no mortal man can trace or even imagine. And as for the lawyer, I don't go only by the dog; there are other curious details too. He struck me as a smooth, smiling, equivocal sort of person; and one of his tricks seemed like a sort of hint. You know the doctor and the police were on the spot very quickly; Valentine was brought back when walking away from the house, and he telephoned instantly. That, with the secluded house, small numbers, and enclosed space, made it pretty possible to search everybody who could have been near; and everybody was thoroughly searched – for a weapon. The whole house, garden, and shore were combed for a weapon. The disappearance of the dagger is almost as crazy as the disappearance of the man.'

'The disappearance of the dagger,' said Father Brown, nodding. He seemed to have become suddenly attentive.

'Well,' continued Fiennes, 'I told you that man Traill had a trick of fidgeting with his tie and tie-pin – especially his tie-pin. His pin, like himself, was at once showy and old-fashioned. It had one of those stones with concentric coloured rings that look like an eye; and his own concentration on it got on my nerves, as if he had been a Cyclops with one eye in the middle of his body. But the pin was not only large but long; and it occurred to me that his anxiety about its adjustment was because it was even longer than it looked; as long as a stiletto in fact.'

Father Brown nodded thoughtfully. 'Was any other instrument ever suggested?' he asked.

'There was another suggestion,' answered Fiennes, 'from one of the young Druces – the cousins, I mean. Neither Herbert nor Harry Druce would have struck one at first as likely to be of assistance in scientific detection; but while Herbert was really the traditional type of heavy Dragoon, caring for nothing but horses and being an ornament to the

Horse Guards, his younger brother Harry had been in the Indian Police and knew something about such things. Indeed in his own way he was quite clever; and I rather fancy he had been too clever; I mean he had left the police through breaking some red-tape regulations and taking some sort of risk and responsibility of his own. Anyhow, he was in some sense a detective out of work, and threw himself into this business with more than the ardour of an amateur. And it was with him that I had an argument about the weapon – an argument that led to something new. It began by his countering my description of the dog barking at Traill; and he said that a dog at his worst didn't bark, but growled.'

'He was quite right there,' observed the priest.

'This young fellow went on to say that, if it came to that, he'd heard Nox growling at other people before then; and among others at Floyd the secretary. I retorted that his own argument answered itself; for the crime couldn't be brought home to two or three people, and least of all to Floyd, who was as innocent as a harum-scarum schoolboy, and had been seen by everybody all the time perched above the garden hedge with his fan of red hair as conspicuous as a scarlet cockatoo. "I know there's difficulties anyhow," said my colleague, "but I wish you'd come with me down the garden a minute. I want to show you something I don't think anyone else has seen." This was on the very day of the discovery, and the garden was just as it had been: the step-ladder was still standing by the hedge, and just under the hedge my guide stooped and disentangled something from the deep grass. It was the shears used for clipping the hedge, and on the point of one of them was a smear of blood.'

There was a short silence, and then Father Brown said suddenly, 'What was the lawyer there for?'

'He told us the Colonel sent for him to alter his will,' answered Fiennes. 'And, by the way, there was another thing about the business of the will that I ought to mention. You see, the will wasn't actually signed in the summer-house that afternoon.'

'I suppose not,' said Father Brown; 'there would have to be two witnesses.'

'The lawyer actually came down the day before and it was signed then; but he was sent for again next day because the old man had a doubt about one of the witnesses and had to be reassured.'

'Who were the witnesses?' asked Father Brown.

'That's just the point,' replied his informant eagerly, 'the witnesses were Floyd the secretary and this Dr Valentine, the foreign sort of surgeon or whatever he is; and the two have a quarrel. Now I'm bound to say that the secretary is something of a busybody. He's one of those hot and headlong people whose warmth of temperament has unfortunately turned mostly to pugnacity and bristling suspicion; to distrusting people instead of to trusting them. That sort of red-haired red-hot fellow is always either universally credulous or universally incredulous; and sometimes both. He was not only a Jack of all trades, but he knew better than all tradesmen. He not only knew everything, but he warned everybody against everybody. All that must be taken into account in his suspicions about Valentine; but in that particular case there seems to have been something behind it. He said the name of Valentine was not really Valentine. He said he had seen him elsewhere known by the name of De Villon. He said it would invalidate the will; of course he was kind enough to explain to the lawyer what the law was on that point. They were both in a frightful wax.'

Father Brown laughed. 'People often are when they are to witness a will,' he said, 'for one thing, it means that they can't have any legacy under it. But what did Dr Valentine say? No doubt the universal secretary knew more about the doctor's name than the doctor did. But even the doctor might have some information about his own name.'

Fiennes paused a moment before he replied.

'Dr Valentine took it in a curious way. Dr Valentine is a curious man. His appearance is rather striking but very foreign. He is young but wears a beard cut square; and his face is very pale, dreadfully pale and dreadfully serious. His eyes have a sort of ache in them, as if he ought to wear glasses or had given himself a headache with thinking; but he is quite handsome and always very formally dressed, with a top hat and a dark coat and a little red rosette. His manner is rather cold and haughty, and he has a way of staring at you which is very disconcerting. When thus charged with having changed his name, he merely stared like a sphinx and then said with a little laugh that he supposed Americans had no names to change. At that I think the Colonel also got into a fuss and said all sorts of angry things to the doctor; all the more angry because of the doctor's pretensions to a future place in his family. But I shouldn't have thought much of that but for a few words that I happened to hear later, early in the afternoon of the tragedy. I don't want to make a lot of them, for they weren't the sort of words on which one would like, in the ordinary way, to play the eavesdropper. As I was passing out towards the front gate with my two companions and the dog, I heard voices which told me that Dr Valentine and Miss Druce had withdrawn for a moment into the shadow of the house, in an angle behind a row of flowering plants, and were talking to each other in passionate whisperings – sometimes almost like hissings; for it was something of a lovers' quarrel as well as a lovers' tryst. Nobody repeats the sort of things they said for the most part; but in an unfortunate business like this I'm bound to say that there was repeated more than once a phrase about killing somebody. In fact, the girl seemed to be begging him not to kill somebody, or saying that no provocation could justify killing anybody; which seems an unusual sort of talk to address to a gentleman who has dropped in to tea.'

'Do you know,' asked the priest, 'whether Dr Valentine seemed to be very angry after the scene with the secretary and the Colonel – I mean about witnessing the will?'

'By all accounts,' replied the other, 'he wasn't half so angry as the secretary was. It was the secretary who went away raging after witnessing the will.'

'And now,' said Father Brown, 'what about the will itself?'

'The Colonel was a very wealthy man, and his will was important. Traill wouldn't tell us the alteration at that stage, but I have since heard, only this morning in fact, that most of the money was transferred from the son to the daughter. I told you that Druce was wild with my friend Donald over his dissipated hours.'

'The question of motive has been rather overshadowed by the question of method,' observed Father Brown thoughtfully. 'At that moment, apparently, Miss Druce was the immediate gainer by the death.'

'Good God! What a cold-blooded way of talking,' cried Fiennes, staring at him. 'You don't really mean to hint that she ...'

'Is she going to marry that Dr Valentine?' asked the other.

'Some people are against it,' answered his friend. 'But he is liked and respected in the place and is a skilled and devoted surgeon.'

'So devoted a surgeon,' said Father Brown, 'that he had surgical instruments with him when he went to call on the young lady at tea-time. For he must have used a lancet or something, and he never seems to have gone home.'

Fiennes sprang to his feet and looked at him in a heat of inquiry. 'You suggest he might have used the very same lancet—'

Father Brown shook his head. 'All these suggestions are fancies just now,' he said. 'The problem is not who did it or what did it, but how it was done. We might find many men and even many tools – pins and shears and lancets. But how did a man get into the room? How did even a pin get into it?'

He was staring reflectively at the ceiling as he spoke, but as he said the last words his eye cocked in an alert fashion as if he had suddenly seen a curious fly on the ceiling.

'Well, what would you do about it?' asked the young man. 'You have a lot of experience, what would you advise now?'

'I'm afraid I'm not much use,' said Father Brown with a sigh. 'I can't suggest very much without having ever been near the place or the people. For the moment you can only go on with local inquiries. I gather that your friend from the

Indian Police is more or less in charge of your inquiry down there. I should run down and see how he is getting on. See what he's been doing in the way of amateur detection. There may be news already.'

As his guests, the biped and the quadruped, disappeared, Father Brown took up his pen and went back to his interrupted occupation of planning a course of lectures on the Encyclical Rerum Novarum. The subject was a large one and he had to recast it more than once, so that he was somewhat similarly employed some two days later when the big black dog again came bounding into the room and sprawled all over him with enthusiasm and excitement. The master who followed the dog shared the excitement if not the enthusiasm. He had been excited in a less pleasant fashion, for his blue eyes seemed to start from his head and his eager face was even a little pale.

'You told me,' he said abruptly and without preface, 'to find out what Harry Druce was doing. Do you know what he's done?'

The priest did not reply, and the young man went on in jerky tones:

'I'll tell you what he's done. He's killed himself.'

Father Brown's lips moved only faintly, and there was nothing practical about what he was saying – nothing that had anything to do with this story or this world.

'You give me the creeps sometimes,' said Fiennes. 'Did you – did you expect this?'

'I thought it possible,' said Father Brown; 'that was why I asked you to go and see what he was doing. I hoped you might not be too late.'

'It was I who found him,' said Fiennes rather huskily. 'It was the ugliest and most uncanny thing I ever knew. I went down that old garden again and I knew there was something new and unnatural about it besides the murder. The flowers still tossed about in blue masses on each side of the black entrance into the old grey summer-house; but to me the blue flowers looked like blue devils dancing before some dark cavern of the underworld. I looked all around; everything seemed to be in its ordinary place. But the queer notion grew on me that there was something wrong with the very shape of the sky. And then I saw what it was. The Rock of Fortune always rose in the background beyond the garden hedge and against the sea. And the Rock of Fortune was gone.'

Father Brown had lifted his head and was listening intently.

'It was as if a mountain had walked away out of a landscape or a moon fallen from the sky; though I knew, of course, that a touch at any time would have tipped the thing over. Something possessed me and I rushed down that garden path like the wind and went crashing through that hedge as if it were a spider's web. It was a thin hedge really, though its undisturbed trimness had made it serve all the purposes of a wall. On the shore I found the loose rock fallen from its pedestal; and poor Harry Druce lay like a wreck underneath it. One arm was thrown round it in a sort of embrace as if he had pulled it down on himself; and on the broad brown sands beside it, in large crazy lettering, he had scrawled the words, "The Rock of Fortune falls on the Fool."'

'It was the Colonel's will that did that,' observed Father Brown. 'The young man had staked everything on profiting himself by Donald's disgrace, especially when his uncle sent for him on the same day as the lawyer, and welcomed him with so much warmth. Otherwise he was done; he'd lost his police job; he was beggared at Monte Carlo. And he killed himself when he found he'd killed his kinsman for nothing.'

'Here, stop a minute!' cried the staring Fiennes. 'You're going too fast for me.'

'Talking about the will, by the way,' continued Father Brown calmly, 'before I forget it, or we go on to bigger things, there was a simple explanation, I think, of all that business about the doctor's name. I rather fancy I have heard both names before somewhere. The doctor is really a French nobleman with the title of the Marquis de Villon. But he is also an ardent Republican and has abandoned his title and fallen back on the forgotten family surname. "With your Citizen Riquetti you have puzzled Europe for ten days."'

'What is that?' asked the young man blankly.

'Never mind,' said the priest. 'Nine times out of ten it is a rascally thing to change one's name; but this was a piece of fine fanaticism. That's the point of his sarcasm about Americans having no names – that is, no titles. Now in England the Marquis of Hartington is never called Mr Hartington; but in France the Marquis de Villon is called M. de Villon. So it might well look like a change of name. As for the talk about killing, I fancy that also was a point of French etiquette. The doctor was talking about challenging Floyd to a duel, and the girl was trying to dissuade him.'

'Oh, I see,' cried Fiennes slowly. 'Now I understand what she meant.'

'And what is that about?' asked his companion, smiling.

'Well,' said the young man, 'it was something that

happened to me just before I found that poor fellow's body; only the catastrophe drove it out of my head. I suppose it's hard to remember a little romantic idyll when you've just come on top of a tragedy. But as I went down the lanes leading to the Colonel's old place, I met his daughter walking with Dr Valentine. She was in mourning of course, and he always wore black as if he were going to a funeral; but I can't say that their faces were very funereal. Never have I seen two people looking in their own way more respectably radiant and cheerful. They stopped and saluted me and then she told me they were married and living in a little house on the outskirts of the town, where the doctor was continuing his practice. This rather surprised me, because I knew that her old father's will had left her his property; and I hinted at it delicately by saying I was going along to her father's old place and had half expected to meet her there. But she only laughed and said, "Oh, we've given up all that. My husband doesn't like heiresses." And I discovered with some astonishment they really had insisted on restoring the property to poor Donald; so I hope he's had a healthy shock and will treat it sensibly. There was never much really the matter with him; he was very young and his father was not very wise. But it was in connection with that that she said something I didn't understand at the time; but now I'm sure it must be as you say. She said with a sort of sudden and splendid arrogance that was entirely altruistic: "I hope it'll stop that red-haired fool from fussing any more about the will. Does he think my husband, who has given up a crest and a coronet as old as the Crusades for his principles, would kill an old man in a summer-house for a legacy like that?"

Then she laughed again and said, "My husband isn't killing anybody except in the way of business. Why, he didn't even ask his friends to call on the secretary." Now, of course, I see what she meant.'

'I see part of what she meant, of course,' said Father Brown. 'What did she mean exactly by the secretary fussing about the will?'

Fiennes smiled as he answered. 'I wish you knew the secretary, Father Brown. It would be a joy to you to watch him make things hum, as he calls it. He made the house of mourning hum. He filled the funeral with all the snap and zip of the brightest sporting event. There was no holding him, after something had really happened. I've told you how he used to oversee the gardener as he did the garden, and how he instructed the lawyer in the law. Needless to say, he also instructed the surgeon in the practice of surgery; and as the surgeon was Dr Valentine, you may be sure it ended in accusing him of something worse than bad surgery. The secretary got it fixed in his red head that the doctor had committed the crime; and when the police arrived he was perfectly sublime. Need I say that he became on the spot the greatest of all amateur detectives? Sherlock Holmes never towered over Scotland Yard with more Titanic intellectual pride and scorn than Colonel Druce's private secretary over the police investigating Colonel Druce's death. I tell you it was a joy to see him. He strode about with an abstracted air, tossing his scarlet crest of hair and giving curt impatient replies. Of course it was his demeanour during these days that made Druce's daughter so wild with him. Of course he had a theory. It's just the sort of theory a man would have in a book; and Floyd is the sort of man who ought to be in a book. He'd be better fun and less bother in a book.'

'What was his theory?' asked the other.

'Oh, it was full of pep,' replied Fiennes gloomily. 'It would have been glorious copy if it could have held together for ten minutes longer. He said the Colonel was still alive when they found him in the summer-house and the doctor killed him with the surgical instrument on pretence of cutting the clothes.'

'I see,' said the priest. 'I suppose he was lying flat on his face on the mud floor as a form of siesta.'

'It's wonderful what hustle will do,' continued his informant. 'I believe Floyd would have got his great theory into the papers at any rate, and perhaps had the doctor arrested, when all these things were blown sky high as if by dynamite by the discovery of that dead body lying under the Rock of Fortune. And that's what we come back to after all. I suppose the suicide is almost a confession. But nobody will ever know the whole story.'

There was a silence, and then the priest said modestly, 'I rather think I know the whole story.'

Fiennes stared. 'But look here,' he cried, 'how do you come to know the whole story, or to be sure it's the true story? You've been sitting here a hundred miles away writing a sermon; do you mean to tell me you really know what happened already? If you've really come to the end, where in the world do you begin? What started you off with your own story?'

Father Brown jumped up with a very unusual excitement and his first exclamation was like an explosion.

'The dog!' he cried. 'The dog, of course! You had the whole story in your hands in the business of the dog on the beach, if you'd only noticed the dog properly.'

Fiennes stared still more. 'But you told me before that my feelings about the dog were all nonsense, and the dog had nothing to do with it.'

'The dog had everything to do with it,' said Father Brown, 'as you'd have found out if you'd only treated the dog as a dog and not as God Almighty judging the souls of men.'

He paused in an embarrassed way for a moment, and then said, with a rather pathetic air of apology:

'The truth is, I happen to be awfully fond of dogs. And it seemed to me that in all this lurid halo of dog superstitions nobody was really thinking about the poor dog at all. To begin with a small point, about his barking at the lawyer or growling at the secretary. You asked how I could guess things a hundred miles away; but honestly it's mostly to your credit, for you described people so well that I know the types. A man like Traill who frowns usually and smiles suddenly, a man who fiddles with things, especially at his throat, is a nervous, easily embarrassed man. I shouldn't wonder if Floyd, the efficient secretary, is nervy and jumpy too; those Yankee hustlers often are. Otherwise he wouldn't have cut his fingers on the shears and dropped them when he heard Janet Druce scream.

'Now dogs hate nervous people. I don't know whether they make the dog nervous too; or whether, being after all a brute, he is a bit of a bully; or whether his canine vanity (which is colossal) is simply offended at not being liked. But anyhow there was nothing in poor Nox protesting against those people, except that he disliked them for being afraid of him. Now I know you're awfully clever, and nobody of sense sneers at cleverness. But I sometimes fancy, for instance, that you are too clever to understand animals. Sometimes you are too clever to understand men, especially when they act almost as simply as animals. Animals are very literal; they live in a world of truisms. Take this case; a dog barks at a man and a man runs away from a dog. Now you do not seem to be quite simple enough to see the fact; that the dog barked because he disliked the man and the man fled because he was frightened of the dog. They had no other motives and they needed none. But you must read psychological mysteries into it and suppose the dog had super-normal vision, and was a mysterious mouthpiece of doom. You must suppose the man was running away, not from the dog but from the hangman. And yet, if you come to think of it, all this deeper psychology is exceedingly improbable. If the dog really could completely and consciously realise the murderer of his master, he wouldn't stand yapping as he might at a curate at a tea-party; he's much more likely to fly at his throat. And on the other hand, do you really think a man who had hardened his heart to murder an old friend and then walk about smiling at the old friend's family, under the eyes of his old friend's daughter and post-mortem doctor – do you think a man like that would be doubled up by mere remorse because a dog barked? He might feel the tragic irony of it; it might shake his soul, like any other tragic trifle. But he wouldn't rush madly the length of a garden to escape from the only witness whom he knew to be unable to talk. People have a panic like that when they are frightened, not of tragic ironies, but of teeth. The whole thing is simpler than you can understand.

'But when we come to that business by the seashore, things are much more interesting. As you stated then, they were much more puzzling. I didn't understand that tale of the dog going in and out of the water; it didn't seem to me a doggy thing to do. If Nox had been very much upset about something else, he might possibly have refused to go after the stick at all. He'd probably go off nosing in whatever direction he suspected the mischief. But when once a dog is actually chasing a thing, a stone or a stick or a rabbit, my experience is that he won't stop for anything but the most peremptory command, and not always for that. That he should turn around because his mood changed seems to me unthinkable.'

'But he did turn around,' insisted Fiennes, 'and came back without the stick.'

'He came back without the stick for the best reason in the world,' replied the priest. 'He came back because he couldn't find it. He whined because he couldn't find it. That's the sort of thing a dog really does whine about. A dog is a devil of a ritualist. He is as particular about the precise routine of a game as a child about the precise repetition of a fairy-tale. In this case something had gone wrong with the game. He came back to complain seriously of the conduct of the stick. Never had such a thing happened before. Never had an eminent and distinguished dog been so treated by a rotten old walking-stick.'

'Why, what had the walking-stick done?' inquired the young man.

'It had sunk,' said Father Brown.

Fiennes said nothing, but continued to stare, and it was the priest who continued:

'It had sunk because it was not really a stick, but a rod of steel with a very thin shell of cane and a sharp point. In other words, it was a sword-stick. I suppose a murderer never got rid of a bloody weapon so oddly and yet so naturally as by throwing it into the sea for a retriever.'

'I begin to see what you mean,' admitted Fiennes; 'but even if a sword-stick was used, I have no guess of how it was used.'

'I had a sort of guess,' said Father Brown, 'right at the beginning when you said the word summer-house. And another when you said that Druce wore a white coat. As long as everybody was looking for a short dagger, nobody thought of it; but if we admit a rather long blade like a rapier, it's not so impossible.'

He was leaning back, looking at the ceiling, and began like one going back to his own first thoughts and fundamentals.

'All that discussion about detective stories like the Yellow Room, about a man found dead in sealed chambers which no one could enter, does not apply to the present case, because it is a summer-house. When we talk of a Yellow Room, or any room, we imply walls that are really homogeneous and impenetrable. But a summer-house is not made like that; it is often made, as it was in this case, of closely interlaced but still separate boughs and strips of wood, in which there are chinks here and there. There was one of them just behind Druce's back as he sat in his chair up against the wall. But just as the room was a summer-house, so the chair was a basket-chair. That also was a lattice of loopholes. Lastly, the summer-house was close up under the hedge; and you have just told me that it was really a thin hedge. A man standing outside it could easily see, amid a network of twigs and branches and canes, one white spot of the Colonel's coat as plain as the white of a target.

'Now, you left the geography a little vague; but it was possible to put two and two together. You said the Rock of Fortune was not really high; but you also said it could be seen dominating the garden like a mountain-peak. In other words, it was very near the end of the garden, though your walk had taken you a long way round to it. Also, it isn't likely the young lady really howled so as to be heard half a mile. She gave an ordinary involuntary cry, and yet you heard it on the shore. And among other interesting things that you told me, may I remind you that you said Harry Druce had fallen behind to light his pipe under a hedge.'

Fiennes shuddered slightly. 'You mean he drew his blade there and sent it through the hedge at the white spot. But surely it was a very odd chance and a very sudden choice. Besides, he couldn't be certain the old man's money had passed to him, and as a fact it hadn't.'

Father Brown's face became animated.

'You misunderstand the man's character,' he said, as if he himself had known the man all his life. 'A curious but not unknown type of character. If he had really known the money would come to him, I seriously believe he wouldn't have done it. He would have seen it as the dirty thing it was.'

'Isn't that rather paradoxical?' asked the other.

'This man was a gambler,' said the priest, 'and a man in disgrace for having taken risks and anticipated orders. It was probably for something pretty unscrupulous, for every imperial police is more like a Russian secret police than we like to think. But he had gone beyond the line and failed. Now, the temptation of that type of man is to do a mad thing precisely because the risk will be wonderful in retrospect. He wants to say, "Nobody but I could have seized that chance or seen that it was then or never. What a wild and wonderful guess it was, when I put all those things together; Donald in disgrace; and the lawyer being sent for; and Herbert and I sent for at the same time – and then nothing more but the way the old man grinned at me and shook hands. Anybody would say I was mad to risk it; but that is how fortunes are made, by the man mad enough to have a little foresight." In short, it is the vanity of guessing. It is the megalomania of the gambler. The more incongruous the coincidence, the more instantaneous the decision, the more likely he is to snatch the chance. The accident, the very triviality, of the white speck and the hole in the hedge intoxicated him like a vision of the world's desire. Nobody clever enough to see such a combination of accidents could be cowardly enough not to use them! That is how the devil talks to the gambler. But the devil himself would hardly have induced that unhappy man to go down in a dull, deliberate way and kill an old uncle from whom he'd always had expectations. It would be too respectable.'

He paused a moment; and then went on with a certain quiet emphasis.

'And now try to call up the scene, even as you saw it yourself. As he stood there, dizzy with his diabolical opportunity, he looked up and saw that strange outline that might have been the image of his own tottering soul; the one great crag poised perilously on the other like a pyramid on its point, and remembered that it was called the Rock of Fortune. Can you guess how such a man at such a moment would read such a signal? I think it strung him up to action and even to vigilance. He who would be a tower must not fear to be a toppling tower. Anyhow, he acted; his next difficulty was to cover his tracks. To be found with a sword-stick, let alone a blood-stained sword-stick, would be fatal in the search that was certain to follow. If he left it anywhere, it would be found and probably traced. Even if he threw it into the sea the action might be noticed, and thought noticeable – unless indeed he could think of some more natural way of covering the action. As you know, he did think of one, and a very good one. Being the only one of you with a watch, he told you it was not yet time to return, strolled a little farther and started the game of throwing in sticks for the retriever. But how his eyes must have rolled darkly over all that desolate seashore before they alighted on the dog!'

Fiennes nodded, gazing thoughtfully into space. His mind seemed to have drifted back to a less practical part of the narrative.

'It's queer,' he said, 'that the dog really was in the story after all.'

'The dog could almost have told you the story, if he could talk,' said the priest. 'All I complain of is that because he couldn't talk, you made up his story for him, and made him talk with the tongues of men and angels. It's part of something I've noticed more and more in the modern world, appearing in all sorts of newspaper rumours and conversational catch-words; something that's arbitrary without being authoritative. People readily swallow the untested claims of this, that, or the other. It's drowning all your old rationalism and scepticism, it's coming in like a sea; and the name of it is superstition.' He stood up abruptly, his face heavy with a sort of frown, and went on talking almost as if he were alone. 'It's the first effect of not believing in God that you lose your common sense, and can't see things as they are. Anything that anybody talks about, and says there's a good deal in it, extends itself indefinitely like a vista in a nightmare. And a dog is an omen and a cat is a mystery and a pig is a mascot and a beetle is a scarab, calling up all the menagerie of polytheism from Egypt and old India; Dog Anubis and great green-eyed Pasht and all the holy howling Bulls of Bashan; reeling back to the bestial gods of the beginning, escaping into elephants and snakes and crocodiles; and all because you are frightened of four words: "He was made Man."'

The young man got up with a little embarrassment, almost as if he had overheard a soliloquy. He called to the dog and left the room with vague but breezy farewells. But he had to call the dog twice, for the dog had remained behind quite motionless for a moment, looking up steadily at Father Brown as the wolf looked at St Francis.

The Exploding Battleship

Michael Innes

Sitting in front of Florian's café in Venice, Lady Appleby counted her resources. She began with her remaining traveller's cheques, went on to Italian banknotes, and ended up with small change. Her husband divided his attention between watching this operation tolerantly – Judith was always extremely businesslike on holidays – and surveying the tourists who thronged the Piazza San Marco.

It was the height of the season. There were Germans fathoms deep in guidebooks, Americans obsessively intent on peering into cameras, and English with their brows furrowed in various degrees of that financial anxiety which Judith herself was evincing. There were also some Italians. These, Appleby thought, appeared agreeably carefree.

'And six days to go,' Judith said. She had arrived at her grand total. 'Of course, we have to remember the children's presents. I've got a list.' She produced a notebook. 'A mechanical mouse that squeaks and runs; a hunting-crop that turns into a stiletto; an exploding battleship; an atomic submarine; a bone or some other bit of an old saint or martyr; and three caskets in gold, silver, and lead.'

'I'm surprised,' Appleby said, 'that Bobby didn't add an heiress: Portia as well as her caskets. "In Belmont is a lady richly left." It sounds most attractive. But don't you think they all sound rather unlikely objects to pick up in Venice? Even the lethal hunting-crop.'

'Pardon me.' A polite American voice sounded in the Applebys' ears. 'But I guess I'd like to know what is meant by an exploding battleship.'

The American was at the next table. He was elderly and had the air of feeling lonesome. He was also – Appleby decided with his policeman's habit of rapid appraisal – wealthy, unsophisticated, and highly intelligent.

'An exploding battleship?' Appleby turned his chair round and addressed the stranger companionably. 'It's built up, I think, in a number of interlocking sections, and there's some sort of simple spring-mechanism inside. You shoot at it with a little gun. And when you hit the vital spot, the spring is released, and the whole thing flies into bits.'

'Sure.' The American produced this monosyllable thoughtfully and with much deliberation. Then he turned to Judith. 'Marm,' he said courteously, 'I can direct you to that mechanical mouse. The small toy-store at this end of the Merceria dell' Orologio.' He paused, and then addressed Appleby. 'Would you be in the way, sir, of buying objects of antique art in this remarkable town?'

'Well, no.' Appleby was amused by this question. 'I used

to pick up very modest things here once upon a time. But I don't nowadays.'

The stranger nodded wisely.

'In that case,' he said, 'I needn't communicate to you a certain darned nasty suspicion building up in my mind right now!'

And with this cryptic remark the elderly American stood up, made Judith Appleby a careful bow, and walked away.

Four days later Appleby received an unexpected request to call on the Chief of Police. He made his way in some perplexity to the Fondamenta San Lorenzo, and was received with great politeness.

'My dear Sir John,' the functionary said, 'it was decided by one of my officers that you must be questioned. But when I discovered in you a distinguished colleague, I ventured to give myself the pleasure of inviting you to call. You were well acquainted with Mr Conklin?'

'Conklin?' Appleby was perplexed.

'An American visitor with whom one of our *vigili* happened to observe you in conversation in the Piazza on Monday.' The Chief of Police spread out his hands expressively. 'A most elusive and unobtrusive man. He proved to be unaccompanied by a wife or other companion. We can discover almost nothing about him, so far. Except, indeed, that the gentleman was a millionaire.'

'*Was?*' Appleby said.

'Alas, yes. His body has been recovered from the lagoon. And almost certainly there has been foul play. A perplexing affair. We do not like unresolved mysteries in Venice.'

'Nor do we care for them in London, my dear sir. But what you tell me is most surprising. Mr Conklin seemed a most inoffensive man, quite unlikely to get into trouble.' Appleby reflected for a moment. 'You know nothing about him?'

'It appears that he was something of an art-collector. Not, perhaps, among the more highly informed in the field. But – as I have said – a millionaire.'

'In other words, a ready-made dupe?'

'It is sad, Sir John.' The Chief of Police again made his expressive gesture. 'But they have much wealth, these people. And they come among us, who have little wealth, but much colourable junk lying ready to our hand. I command very poor English, I fear. But at least I make myself comprehensible?'

'Certainly you do. And you feel, I think, that drowning the dupes is going rather too far?'

'It is my sentiment in the matter. Decidedly.'

Again Appleby reflected.

'My encounter with this unfortunate man,' he said, 'was of the slightest, as I shall explain. But I believe I can possibly help you, all the same.'

'My dear Sir John, I am enchanted.'

'Only I am afraid it may cost money. Or at least *look* as if it were costing money.'

'*Non importa*,' the Chief of Police said.

Appleby began by buying – or appearing to buy – a genuine Tintoretto. He followed this up with a clamantly spurious Carpaccio, and then with a Guardi so authentically lovely that he could hardly bear to reflect on how fictitious his purchase really was. Judith sometimes watched him covertly from over the way. It intrigued her to think that she might really have married an American precisely like this.

It was on the third day that Appleby made the acquaintance of the Conte Alfonso Forobosco. This gentleman's conversation, casually offered over a *cappuccino*, showed him to be familiarly acquainted not only with his fellow members of the Italian aristocracy but also with the President of the Republic, the exiled Royal Family, and most of the more important dignitaries in the Vatican. All of which didn't prevent Conte Alfonso from being hard up. This fact, emerging in due season and with delightful candour, precluded the further revelation that he was even constrained, from time to time, to part with a few of the innumerable artistic treasures which had descended to him from his ancestors.

All this was extremely impressive. And so was the speed with which the Conte worked. Half an hour later, Appleby found himself in a gaunt and semi-derelict *palazzo* on the Grand Canal.

'The goblets,' Conte Alfonso said, 'belonged to Machiavelli. The pistols were Mazzini's. The writing-table was used by Manzoni.'

Appleby made the sort of responses he judged appropriate in a wealthy American. The *palazzo* – or its *piano nobile* at least – had been well stocked with a variety of imposing objects. And presently the Conte came to the most imposing of the lot: a species of elaborately convoluted urn in Venetian glass. Appleby doubted whether anything more completely hideous had ever issued from the glass-factories on Murano.

'The poison-vase of Lucrezia Borgia,' the Conte said, pointing to it on a table. 'Take it – but carefully – and hold it up to the light.'

Appleby did as he was told. But even as he raised the precious object in his two hands there was an ominous crack. And then he was looking at its shattered fragments lying at his feet.

Conte Alfonso gave an agonised cry. Then, with a gesture magnificently magnanimous, he stopped, picked up the pieces, strode to a window, and pitched them into the Grand Canal of Venice.

'*Non fa niente*,' he said. 'No matter. An accident. And you are my guest.'

Appleby went through a pantomime of extreme contrition and dismay. The least he could do, he intimated, was to pay up. The Conte protested. Appleby insisted. Reluctantly the Conte named a sum – a nominal sum, a bare million lire. And then Appleby led him to the window.

'At least,' he said, 'I may get back the bits.'

And this seemed true. Several police launches were diverting the *vaporetti* and other traffic on the canal. Just beneath the window a frogman was already at work. It would have been possible to reflect that there was an authentic Carpaccio depicting a very similar scene.

'And now I think you have visitors,' Appleby said, turning round. 'Including your Chief of Police himself.'

'It was this so-called Conte Alfonso's regular racket?' Judith asked afterwards.

'Certainly it was.' Appleby paused in the task of packing

his suitcase. 'The fellow had a steady supply of Lucrezia Borgia's teapots, or whatever. Two seconds after you picked them up, the spring went off and shattered them. And then, of course, the problem was to get rid of the evidence. But there lay the advantage of having the scene of the operation on the Grand Canal. The Conte made detection impossible simply by putting on that aristocratic turn of gathering up the bits and chucking them into the water. Our friend Conklin, however, was a shrewd chap in his way, and he suspected he'd been had. When I explained about the exploding battleship, the full truth flashed on him.'

'So he went back and taxed the Conte with the fraud?'

'Just that. And the scoundrel – rather an engaging scoundrel if he hadn't gone so decidedly too far – liquidated him at once. Quite in the antique Venetian manner, I suppose one may say. But, apart from that, there was certainly nothing genuinely antique about him.'

A knock came at the bedroom door, and a hotel servant handed in a parcel. Appleby received it, regarded it doubtfully, and then opened it up. What lay inside was the little Guardi.

'John!' – Judith was very startled – 'you haven't really gone and bought the thing?'

'Of course not.' Appleby had opened a letter. 'It's a present – call it from the Doge and the Serenissimi.'

'Meaning from the mayor and city council?'

'That does make it sound a good deal more prosaic. But remember for how long Venice held the gorgeous East in fee. She seems capable of decidedly regal behaviour still.'

The Flowers that Bloom in the Spring

Julian Symons

The outsider, Bertie Mays was fond of saying, sees most of the game. In the affair of the Purchases and the visiting cousin from South Africa he saw quite literally all of it. But the end was enigmatic and a little frightening, at least as seen through Bertie's eyes. It left with him the question whether there had been a game at all.

Bertie had retired early from his unimportant and uninteresting job in the Ministry of Welfare. He had a private income, he was unmarried, and his only extravagance was a passion for travel, so why go on working? Bertie gave up his London flat and settled down in the cottage in the Sussex countryside which he had bought years earlier as a weekend place. It was quite big enough for a bachelor, and Mrs Last from the village came in two days a week to clean the place. Bertie himself was an excellent cook.

It was a fine day in June when he called next door to offer Sylvia Purchase a lift to the tea party at the Hall. She was certain to have been asked, and he knew that she would need a lift because he had seen her husband Jimmy putting a case into the boot of their ancient Morris. Jimmy was some sort of freelance journalist, and often went on trips, leaving Sylvia on her own. Bertie, who was flirtatious by nature, had asked if she would like him to keep her company, but she did not seem responsive to the suggestion. Linton House, which the Purchases had rented furnished a few months earlier, was a rambling old place with oak beams and low ceilings. There was an attractive garden, some of which lay between the house and Bertie's cottage, and by jumping over the fence between them Bertie could walk across this garden. He did so that afternoon, taking a quick peek into the sitting room as he went by. He could never resist such peeks, because he always longed to know what people might be doing when they thought that nobody was watching. On this occasion the sitting room was empty. He found Sylvia in the kitchen, washing dishes in a half-hearted way.

'Sylvia, you're not ready.' She had on a dirty old cardigan with the buttons done up wrongly. Bertie himself was, as always, dressed very suitably for the occasion in a double-breasted blue blazer with brass buttons, fawn trousers and a neat bow tie. He always wore bow ties, which he felt gave a touch of distinction and individuality.

'Ready for what?'

'Has the Lady of the Manor not bidden you to tea?' That was his name for Lady Hussey up at the Hall.

She clapped hand to forehead, leaving a slight smudge.

'I'd forgotten all about it. Don't think I'll go, can't stand those bun fights.'

'But I have called specially to collect you. Let me be your chauffeur. Your carriage awaits.' Bertie made a sketch of a bow, and Sylvia laughed. She was a blonde in her early thirties, attractive in a slapdash sort of way.

'Bertie, you are a fool. All right, give me five minutes.'

The women may call Bertie Mays a fool, Bertie thought, but how they adore him.

'Oh,' Sylvia said. She was looking behind Bertie, and when he turned he saw a man standing in the shadow of the door. At first glance he thought it was Jimmy, for the man was large and square like Jimmy, and had the same gingery fair colouring. But the resemblance went no further, for as the man stepped forward he saw that their features were not similar.

'This is my cousin Alfred Wallington. He's paying us a visit from South Africa. Our next-door neighbour, Bertie Mays.'

'Pleased to meet you.' Bertie's hand was firmly gripped. The two men went into the sitting room, and Bertie asked whether this was Mr Wallington's first visit.

'By no means. I know England pretty well. The south, anyway.'

'Ah, business doesn't take you up north?' Bertie thought of himself as a tactful but expert interrogator, and the question should have brought a response telling him Mr Wallington's occupation. In fact, however, the other man merely said that was so.

'In the course of my work I used to correspond with

several firms in Cape Town,' Bertie said untruthfully. Wallington did not comment. 'Is your home near there?'

'No.'

The negative was so firm that it gave no room for further conversational manoeuvre. Bertie felt slightly cheated. If the man did not want to say where he lived in South Africa of course he was free to say nothing, but there was a certain finesse to be observed in such matters, and a crude 'no' was not at all the thing. He was able to establish at least that this was the first time Wallington had visited Linton House.

On the way up to the Hall he said to Sylvia that her cousin seemed a dour fellow.

'Alf?' Bertie winced at the abbreviation. 'He's all right when you get to know him.'

'He said he was often in the south. What's his particular sphere of interest?'

'I don't know, I believe he's got some sort of export business around Durban. By the way, Bertie, how did you know Jimmy was away?'

'I saw him waving goodbye to you.' It would hardly do to say that he had been peeping through the curtains.

'Did you now? I was in bed when he went. You're a bit of a fibber I'm afraid, Bertie.'

'Oh, I can't remember *how* I knew.' Really, it was too much to be taken up on every little point.

When they drove into the great courtyard and Sylvia got out of the car, however, he reflected that she looked very slenderly elegant, and that he was pleased to be with her. Bertie liked pretty women and they were safe with him, although he would not have thought of it that way. He might have said, rather, that he would never have compromised a lady, with the implication that all sorts of things might be said and done providing that they stayed within the limits of discretion. It occurred to him that Sylvia was hardly staying within those limits when she allowed herself to be alone at Linton House with her South African cousin. Call me old-fashioned, Bertie said to himself, but I don't like it.

The Hall was a nineteenth-century manor house and by no means, as Bertie had often said, an architectural gem, but the lawns at the back where tea was served were undoubtedly fine. Sir Reginald Hussey was a building contractor who had been knighted for some dubious service to the export drive. He was in demand for opening fêtes and fund-raising enterprises, and the Husseys entertained a selection of local people to parties of one kind or another half a dozen times a year. The parties were always done in style, and this afternoon there were maids in white caps and aprons, and a kind of major domo who wore a frock coat and white gloves. Sir Reginald was not in evidence, but Lady Hussey presided in a regal manner.

Of course Bertie knew that it was all ridiculously vulgar and ostentatious, but still he enjoyed himself. He kissed Lady Hussey's hand and said that the scene was quite entrancing, like a Victorian period picture, and he had an interesting chat with Lucy Broadhinton, who was the widow of an Admiral. Lucy was the president and Bertie the secretary of the local historical society, and they were great friends. She told him now in the strictest secrecy about the outrageous affair Mrs Monro was having with somebody who must be nameless, although from the details given Bertie was quite able to guess his identity. There were other titbits too, like the story of the scandalous misuse of the Church Restoration Fund money. It was an enjoyable afternoon, and he fairly chortled about it on the way home.

'They're such snobby affairs,' Sylvia said. 'I don't know why I went.'

'You seemed to be having a good time. I was quite jealous.'

Sylvia had been at the centre of a very animated circle of three or four young men. Her laughter at their jokes had positively rung out across the lawns, and Bertie had seen Lady Hussey give more than one disapproving glance in the direction of the little group. There was something undeniably attractive about Sylvia's gaiety and about the way in which she threw back her head when laughing, but her activities had a recklessness about them which was not proper for a lady. He tried to convey something of this as he drove back, but was not sure that she understood what he meant. He also broached delicately the impropriety of her being alone in the house with her cousin by asking when Jimmy would be coming back. In a day or two, she said casually. He refused her invitation to come in for a drink. He had no particular wish to see Alf Wallington again.

On the following night at about midnight, when Bertie was in bed reading, he heard a car draw up next door. Doors were closed, there was the sound of voices. Just to confirm that Jimmy was back, Bertie got out of bed and lifted an edge of the curtain. A man and a woman were coming out of the garage. The woman was Sylvia. The man had his arm round her, and as Bertie watched bent down and kissed her neck. Then they moved towards the front door, and the man laughed and said something. From his general build he might, seen in the dim light, have been Jimmy, but the voice had the distinctive South African accent of Wallington.

Bertie drew away from the window as though he had been scalded.

It was a feeling of moral responsibility that took him round to Linton House on the following day. To his surprise Jimmy Purchase opened the door.

'I – ah – thought you were away.'

'Got back last night. What can I do for you?'

Bertie said that he would like to borrow the electric hedge clippers, which he knew were in the garden shed. Jimmy led the way there and handed them over. Bertie said that he had heard the car coming back at about midnight.

'Yeah.' Jimmy had a deplorably Cockney voice, not at all out of the top drawer. 'That was Sylvia and Alf. He took her to a dance over at Ladersham. I was too fagged out, just wanted to get my head down.'

'Her cousin from South Africa?'

'Yeah, right, from the Cape. He's staying here for a bit. Plenty of room.'

Was he from the Cape or from Durban? Bertie did not fail to notice the discrepancy.

Bertie's bump of curiosity was even stronger than his sense of propriety. It became important, even vital, that he should know just what was going on next door. When he returned the hedge cutters he asked them all to dinner, together with Lucy Broadhinton to make up the number. He took pains in preparing a delicious cold meal. The salmon was cooked to perfection, and the hollandaise sauce had just the right hint of something tart beneath its blandness.

The evening was not a success. Lucy had on a long dress and Bertie wore a very smart velvet jacket, but Sylvia was dressed in sky-blue trousers and a vivid shirt, and the two men wore open-necked shirts and had distinctly unkempt appearances. They had obviously been drinking before they arrived. Wallington tossed down Bertie's expensive hock as though it were water, and then said that South African wine had more flavour than that German stuff.

'You're from Durban, I believe, Mr Wallington.' Lucy fixed him with her Admiral's lady glance. 'My husband and I were there in the sixties, and thought it delightful. Do you happen to know the Morrows or the Page-Manleys? Mary Page-Manley gave such delightful parties.'

Wallington looked at her from under heavy brows. 'Don't know them.'

'You have an export business in Durban?'

'That's right.'

There was an awkward pause. Then Sylvia said, 'Alf's trying to persuade us to pay him a visit out there.'

'I'd like you to come out. Don't mind about him.' Wallington jerked a thumb at Jimmy. 'Believe me, we'd have a good time.'

'I do believe you, Alf.' She gave her head-back laugh, showing the fine column of her neck. 'It's something we've forgotten here, how to have a good time.'

Jimmy Purchase had been silent during dinner. Now he said, 'People here just don't have the money. Like the song says, it's money makes the world go round.'

'The trouble in Britain is that too much money has got into the wrong hands.' Lucy looked round the table. Nobody seemed inclined to argue the point. 'There are too many grubby little people with sticky fingers.'

'I wish some of the green stuff would stick to my fingers,' Jimmy said, and hiccuped. Bertie realised with horror that he was drunk. 'We're broke, Sylvie, old girl.'

'Oh, shut up.'

'You don't believe me?' And he actually began to empty out his pockets. What appalling creatures the two men were, each as bad as the other. Bertie longed for the evening to end, and was delighted when Lucy rose to make a stately departure. He whispered an apology in the hall, but she told him not to be foolish, it had been fascinating.

When he returned Wallington said, 'What an old battle axe. *Did you happen to know the Page-Manleys.* Didn't know they were still around, people like that.'

Sylvia was looking at Bertie. 'Alf, you're shocking our host.'

'Sorry, man, but honest, I thought they kept her sort in museums. Stuffed.'

'You mustn't say stuffed. That'll shock Bertie too.'

Bertie said stiffly, 'I am not in the least shocked, but I certainly regard it as the height of bad manners to criticise a guest in such a manner. Lucy is a very dear friend of mine.'

Sylvia at least had some understanding of his feelings. She said sorry and smiled, so that he was at once inclined to forgive her. Then she said it was time she took her rough diamonds home.

'Thanks for the grub,' Wallington said. Then he leaned

across the dining table and shouted, 'Wake up, man, it's tomorrow morning already.' Jimmy had fallen asleep in his chair. He was hauled to his feet and supported across the garden.

Bertie called up Lucy the next morning and apologised again. She said that he should think no more about it. 'I didn't take to that South African feller, though. Shouldn't be surprised if he turns out to be a bad hat. And I didn't care too much for your neighbours, if you don't mind my being frank.'

Bertie said of course not, although he reflected that there seemed to be a sudden spasm of frankness among his acquaintances. Mrs Purchase, Lucy said, had a roving eye. She left it at that, and they went on to discuss the agenda for the next meeting of the historical society.

Later in the morning there was a knock on the door. Jimmy was there, hollow-eyed and slightly green. ''Fraid we rather blotted our copybook last night. Truth is, Alf and I were fairly well loaded before we came round. Can't remember too much about it, but Syl said apologies were in order.'

Bertie asked when Sylvia's cousin was leaving. Jimmy Purchase shrugged and said he didn't know. Bertie nearly said that the man should not be left alone with Sylvia, but refrained. He might be inquisitive, but he was also discreet.

A couple of nights later he was doing some weeding in the garden when he heard voices raised in Linton House. One was Jimmy's, the other belonged to Sylvia. They were in the sitting room shouting at each other, not quite loudly enough for the words to be distinguishable. It was maddening not to know what was being said. Bertie moved along the fence separating the gardens, until he was as near as he could get without being seen. He was now able to hear a few phrases.

'Absolutely sick of it … drink because it takes my mind off … told you we have to wait …' That was Jimmy. Then Sylvia's voice, shrill as he had never heard it, shrill and sneering.

'Tell me the old old story … how long do we bloody well wait then … you said it would be finished by now.' An indistinguishable murmur from Jimmy. 'None of your business,' she said. More murmuring. 'None of your business what I do.' Murmur murmur. 'You said yourself we're broke.' To this there was some reply. Then she said clearly, 'I shall do what I like.'

'*All right*,' Jimmy said, so loudly that Bertie fairly jumped. There followed a sharp crack, which sounded like hand on flesh.

Sylvia said, 'You bastard, that's it, then.'

Nothing more. No sound, no speech. Bertie waited five minutes and then tiptoed away, fearful of being seen. Once indoors again he felt quite shaky, and had to restore himself by a nip of brandy. What had the conversation meant? Much of it was plain enough. Sylvia was saying that it was none of her husband's business if she carried on an affair. But what was it they had to wait for, what was it that should have been finished? A deal connected with the odious Alf? And where was Alf, who as Bertie had noticed went out into the village very little?

He slept badly, and was wakened in the middle of the night by a piercing, awful scream. He sat up in bed quivering, but the sound was not repeated. He decided that he must have been dreaming.

On the following day the car was not in the garage. Had Jimmy gone off again? He met Sylvia out shopping in the village, and she said that he had been called to an assignment at short notice.

'What sort of assignment?' He had asked before for the name of the paper Jimmy worked on, to be told that he was a freelance.

'A Canadian magazine. He's up in the Midlands, may be away a few days.'

Should he say something about the row? But that would have been indiscreet, and in any case Sylvia had such a wild look in her eye that he did not care to ask further questions. It was on this morning that he read about the Small Bank Robbers.

The Small Bank Robbers had been news for some months. They specialised in fast, well organised raids on banks, and had carried out nearly twenty of these in the past year. Several men were involved in each raid. They were armed, and did not hesitate to use coshes or revolvers when necessary. In one bank a screaming woman customer had suffered a fractured skull when hit over the head, and in another a guard who resisted the robbers had been shot and killed. The diminutive applied to them referred to the banks they robbed, not to their own physical dimensions. A bank clerk who admitted giving information to the gang had asked why they were interested in his small branch bank, and had been told that they always raided small banks because they were much more vulnerable than large ones.

After the arrest of this clerk the robbers seemed to have gone to ground. There had been no news of them for the last three or four weeks.

Bertie had heard about the Small Bank Robbers, but took no particular interest in them. He was a nervous man, and did not care for reading about crime. On this morning, however, his eye was caught by the heading: *Small Bank Robbers. The South African Connection*. The story was a feature by the paper's crime reporter, Derek Holmes. He said that Scotland Yard knew the identities of some of the robbers, and described his own investigations, which led to the conclusion that three or four of them were in Spain. The article continued:

> But there is another connection, and a sinister one. The men in Spain are small fry. My researches suggest that the heavy men who organised the robberies, and were very ready to use violence, came from South Africa. They provided the funds and the muscle. Several witnesses who heard the men talking to each other or giving orders during the raids have said that they used odd accents. This has been attributed to the sound distortion caused by the stocking masks they wore, but two men I spoke to, both of whom have spent time in South Africa, said that they had no doubt the accent was South African.

The writer suggested that these men were now probably back in South Africa. But supposing that one of them was still in England, that he knew Jimmy and Sylvia and had a hold over them? Supposing, even, that they were minor members of the gang themselves? The thought made Bertie shiver with fright and excitement. What should or could he do about it? And where had Jimmy Purchase gone?

Again he slept badly, and when he did fall into a doze it was a short one. He woke to find Wallington knocking on the door. Once inside the house he drew out a huge wad of notes, said that there was enough for everybody, and counted out bundles which he put on the table between them with a small decisive thwack. A second bundle, thwack, and a third, thwack. How many more? He tried to cry out, to protest, but the bundles went on, thwack, thwack, thwack …

He sat up in bed, crying out something inaudible. The thin grey light of early morning came through the curtains. There was a sound in the garden outside, a sound regularly repeated, the *thwack* of his dream. It took him in his slightly dazed state a little while to realise that if he went to the window he might see what was causing the sound. He tiptoed across the room and raised the curtain. He was trembling.

It was still almost dark, and whatever was happening was taking place at the back of Linton House, so that he could not see it. But as he listened to the regularly repeated sound, he had no doubt of its nature. Somebody was digging out there. The sound of the spade digging earth had entered his dream, and there was an occasional clink when it struck a stone. Why would somebody be digging at this time in the morning? He remembered that terrible cry on the previous night, the cry he had thought to be a dream. Supposing it had been real, who had cried out?

The digging stopped and two people spoke, although he could not hear the words or even the tones. One, light and high in pitch, was no doubt Sylvia, but was the other voice Wallington's? And if it was, had Jimmy Purchase gone away at all? In the half-light a man and woman were briefly visible before they passed into the house. The man carried a spade, but his head was down and Bertie could not see his face, only his square bulky figure. He had little doubt that the man was Wallington.

That morning he went up to London. He had visited the city rarely since his retirement, finding that on each visit he was more worried and confused. The place seemed continually to change, so that what had been a landmark of some interest was a kebab or hamburger restaurant. The article had appeared in the *Banner*, and their offices had moved from Fleet Street to somewhere off the Gray's Inn Road. He asked for Arnold Grayson, a deputy editor he had known slightly, to be told that Grayson had moved to another paper. He had to wait almost an hour before he was able to talk to Derek Holmes. The crime reporter remained staring at his desk while he listened to Bertie's story. During the telling of it he chewed gum and said 'Yup' occasionally.

'Yup,' he said again at the end. 'Okay, Mr Mays. Thanks.'

'What are you going to do about it?'

Holmes removed his gum and considered the question. 'Know how many people been in touch about that piece, saying they've seen the robbers, their landlord's one of them, they heard two South Africans talking in a bus about how the loot should be split, etcetera? One hundred and eleven. Half of 'em are sensationalists, the other half plain crazy.'

'But this is different.'

'They're all different. I shouldn'ta seen you only you mentioned Arnie, and he was a good friend. But what's it amount to? Husband and wife have a shindig, husband goes off, South African cousin's digging a flowerbed—'

'At that time in the morning?'

The reporter shrugged. 'People are funny.'

'Have you got pictures of the South Africans you say are involved in the robberies? If I could recognise Wallington—'

Holmes put another piece of gum in his mouth, chewed on it meditatively, and then produced half a dozen photographs. None of them resembled Wallington. Holmes shuffled the pictures together, put them away. 'That's it then.'

'But aren't you going to come down and look into it? I tell you I believe murder has been done. Wallington is her lover. Together they have killed Purchase.'

'If Wallington's lying low with his share of the loot, the last thing he'd do is get involved in this sort of caper. You know your trouble, Mr Mays? You've got an overheated imagination.'

If only he knew somebody at Scotland Yard! But there was no reason to think that they would take him any more seriously than the newspaper man had done. He returned feeling both chastened and frustrated. To his surprise Sylvia got out of another carriage on the train. She greeted him cheerfully.

'Hallo Bertie. I've just been seeing Alf off.'

'Seeing Alf off?' he echoed stupidly.

'Back to South Africa. He had a letter saying they needed him back there.'

'Back in Durban?'

'That's right.'

'Jimmy said he was from the Cape.'

'Did he? Jimmy often gets things wrong.'

It was not in Bertie's nature to be anything but gallant to a lady, even one he suspected of being a partner in murder. 'Now that you are a grass widow again, you must come in and have a dish of tea.'

'That would be lovely.'

'Tomorrow?'

'It's a date.'

They had reached his cottage. She pressed two fingers to her lips, touched his cheek with them. Inside the cottage the telephone was ringing. It was Holmes.

'Mr Mays? Thought you'd like to know. Your chum Purchase is just what he said, a freelance journalist. One or two of the boys knew him. Not too successful from what I hear.'

'So you did pay some attention to what I told you,' Bertie said triumphantly.

'Always try and check a story out. Nothing to this one, far as I can see.'

'Wallington has gone back to South Africa. Suddenly, just like that.'

'Has he now? Good luck to him.'

Triumph was succeeded by indignation. He put down the telephone without saying goodbye.

Was it all the product of an overheated imagination? He made scones for Sylvia's visit next day, and served them with his homemade blackcurrant conserve. Then he put the question that still worried him. He would have liked to introduce it delicately, but somehow didn't manage that.

'What was all that digging in the garden early the other morning?'

Sylvia looked startled, and then exclaimed as a fragment of the scone she was eating dropped on to her dress. When it had been removed she said, 'Sorry you were disturbed. It was Timmy.'

'Timmy?'

'Our tabby. He must have eaten something poisoned and he died. Poor Timmy. Alf dug a grave and we gave him Christian burial.' With hardly a pause she went on, 'We're clearing out at the end of the week.'

'Leaving?' For a moment he could hardly believe it.

'Right. I'm a London girl at heart you know, always was. The idea of coming here was that Jimmy would be able to do some writing of his own, but that never seemed to work out, he was always being called away. If I'm in London I can get a job, earn some money. Very necessary at the moment. If Alf hadn't helped out, I don't know what we'd have done. It was a crazy idea coming down here, but then we're crazy people.'

And at the end of the week Sylvia went. Since the house had been rented furnished, she had only suitcases to take away. She came to say goodbye. There was no sign of Jimmy, and Bertie asked about him.

'Still up on that job. But anyway he wouldn't have wanted to come down and help, he hates things like that. Goodbye, Bertie, we'll meet again I expect.' A quick kiss on the cheek and she was driving off in her hired car.

She departed leaving all sorts of questions unanswered when Bertie came to think about it, mundane ones like an address if anybody should want to get in touch with her or with Jimmy, and things he would have liked to know, such as the reason for digging the cat's grave at such an extraordinary hour. He found himself more and more suspicious of the tale she had told. The row he had overheard could perhaps be explained by lack of money, but it seemed remarkable that Jimmy Purchase had not come back. Linton House was locked up and empty, but it was easy enough to get into the garden. The area dug up was just inside the boundary fence. It was difficult to see how much had been dug because there were patches of earth at either side, but it looked a large area to bury a cat.

On impulse one day, a week after Sylvia had gone, Bertie took a spade into the garden and began to dig. It proved to be quite hard work, and he went down two feet before reaching the body. It was that of a cat, one he vaguely remembered seeing in the house, but Sylvia's story of its death had been untrue. Its head was mangled, shattered by one or two heavy blows.

Bertie looked at the cat with distaste – he did not care for seeing dead things – returned it, and had just finished shovelling back the earth when he was hailed from the road. He turned, and with a sinking heart saw the local constable, P.C. Harris, standing beside his bicycle.

'Ah, it's you, Mr Mays. I was thinking it might be somebody with burglarious intent. Somebody maybe was going to dig a tunnel to get entrance into the house. But perhaps it was your *own* house you was locked out of.' P.C. Harris was well known as a local wag, and nobody laughed more loudly at his own jokes. He laughed heartily now. Bertie joined in feebly.

'But what *was* you doing digging in the next-door garden, may I ask?'

What could he say? I was digging for a man, but only found a cat? Desperately Bertie said, 'I'd – ah – lost something and thought it might have got in here. I was just turning the earth.'

The constable shook his head. 'You was trespassing, Mr Mays. This is not your property.'

'No, of course not. It won't happen again. I'd be glad if you could forget it.' He approached the constable, a pound note in his hand.

'No need for that, sir, which might be construed as a bribe and hence an offence in itself. I shall not be reporting the matter on this occasion, nor enquiring further into the whys and wherefores, but would strongly advise you in future to keep within the bounds of your own property.'

Pompous old fool, Bertie thought, but said that of course he would do just that. He scrambled back into his own garden, aware that he made a slightly ludicrous figure. P.C. Harris mounted his bicycle in a stately manner and rode away.

That was almost, but not quite, the end of the story. Linton House was empty for a few weeks and then let again, to a family called Hobson who had two noisy children. Bertie had as little to do with them as possible. He was very conscious of having been made to look a fool, and there was nothing he disliked more than that. He was also aware of a disinclination in himself to enter Linton House again.

In the late spring of the following year he went to Sardinia for a holiday, driving around on his own, looking at the curious nuraghi and the burial places made from gigantic blocks of stone which are called the tombs of the giants. He drove up the western coast in a leisurely way, spending long mornings and afternoons over lunches and dinners in the small towns, and then moving inland to bandit country. He was sitting nursing a drink in a square at Nuoro, which is the capital of the central province, when he heard his name called.

It was Sylvia, so brown that he hardly recognised her. 'Bertie, what are you doing here?'

He said that he was on holiday, and returned the question.

'Just come down to shop. We have a house up in the hills, you must come and see it. Darling, look who's here.'

A bronzed Jimmy Purchase approached across the square. Like Sylvia he seemed in fine spirits, and endorsed enthusiastically the suggestion that Bertie should come out to their house. It was a few miles from the city on the slopes of Mount Ortobene, a long low white modern house at the end of a rough track. They sat in a courtyard and ate grilled fish, with which they drank a hard dry local white wine. Bertie felt his natural curiosity rising. How could he ask questions without appearing to be – well – nosy? Over coffee he said that he supposed Jimmy was out here on an assignment.

It was Sylvia who answered. 'Oh no, he's given all that up since the book was published.'

'The book?'

'Show him, Jimmy.'

Jimmy went into the house. He returned with a book

which said on the cover *My Tempestuous Life. As told by Anita Sorana to Jimmy Purchase.*

'You've heard of her?'

It would have been difficult not to have heard of Anita Sorana. She was a screen actress famous equally for her temperament, her five well publicised marriages, and the variety of her love affairs.

'It was fantastic luck when she agreed that Jimmy should write her autobiography. It was all very hush hush and we had to pretend that he was off on assignments when he was really with Anita.'

Jimmy took it up. 'Then she'd break appointments, say she wasn't in the mood to talk. A few days afterwards she'd ask to see me at a minute's notice. Then Sylvia started to play up—'

'I thought he was having an affair with her. She certainly fancied him. He swears he wasn't, but I don't know. Anyway, it was worth it.' She yawned.

'The book was a success?'

Jimmy grinned, teeth very white in his brown face. 'I'll say. Enough for me to shake off the dust of Fleet Street.'

So the quarrel was explained, and Jimmy's sudden absences, and his failure to return. After a glass of some fiery local liqueur Bertie felt soporific, conscious that he had drunk a little more than usual. There was some other question he wanted to ask, but he did not remember it until they were driving him down the mountain, back to his hotel in Nuoro.

'How is your cousin?'

Jimmy was driving. 'Cousin?'

'Mr Wallington, Sylvia's cousin from South Africa.'

Sylvia, from the back of the car, said 'Alf 's dead.'

'Dead!'

'In a car accident. Soon after he got back to South Africa. Wasn't it sad?'

Very few more words were spoken before they reached the hotel and said goodbye. The heat of the hotel room and the wine he had drunk made him fall asleep at once. After a couple of hours he woke, sweating, and wondered if he believed what he had been told. Was it possible to make enough money from 'ghosting' (he had heard that was the word) a life story to retire to Sardinia? It seemed unlikely. He lay on his back in the dark room, and it seemed to him that he saw with terrible clarity what had happened.

Wallington was one of the Small Bank Robbers, and he had come to the Purchases looking for a safe place to stay. He had his money, what Holmes had called the loot, with him, and they had decided to kill him for it. The quarrel had been about when Wallington would be killed, the sound that wakened him in the night had been Wallington's death cry. Jimmy had merely pretended to go away that night, and had returned to help Sylvia dispose of the body. Jimmy dug the grave and they put Wallington in it. Then the cat had been killed and put into a shallow grave on top of the body. It was the killing of the cat, those savage blows on its head, that somehow horrified Bertie most.

He cut short his holiday, took the next plane back. At home he walked round to the place where he had dug up the cat. The Hobsons had put in bedding plants, and the wallflowers were flourishing. He had read somewhere that flowers always flourished over a grave.

'Not thinking of trespassing again, I hope, Mr Mays?'

It was P.C. Harris, red-faced and jovial.

Bertie shook his head. What he had imagined in the hotel room might be true, but then again it might not. Supposing that he went to the police, supposing he was able to convince them that there was something in his story, supposing they dug up the flower bed and found nothing but the cat? He would be the laughing stock of the neighbourhood.

Bertie Mays knew that he would say nothing.

'I reckon you was feeling a little bit eccentric that night you was doing the digging,' P.C. Harris said sagely.

'Yes, I think I must have been.'

'They make a fine show, them wallflowers. Makes you more cheerful, seeing spring flowers.'

'Yes,' said Bertie Mays meekly. 'They make a fine show.'

Dead Mountain Lion

Ellis Peters

Toiling up the ash-white traverses of the Langkofeljoch, with his eyes bent steadily on the zigzags of the path ahead, Edward Stanier came over the brow of the pass and looked up from the sudden grey heaving of rock round his elbows, into a boiling cauldron of cloud. The cliffs of the Langkofel soared clean out of sight, foaming with leaden coils of cloud, and screaming with ravens.

Edward stopped and, turning his back on the forbidding cavern of the Langkofelkar, looked back down the dizzy chute of scree, into the rock town behind the Rifugio Passo Sella.

Down there was the warmth of July, and the drowsy sunset of Italy. Up here he stood on the edge of a slanting snowfield, with the vaporous hands of an imminent storm brushing damply at his shoulders. Against his will he felt a small contraction of discomfort inside him. It was all downhill now to the Rifugio Vicenza, low down there in the invisible bowl of the group. Surely there wasn't a shadow of risk attached to the mere slither down the scree and snow to find it, and with it his bed for the night.

Still, he had to admit that he disliked the look of it almost as much as he disliked the idea of turning back. He could tackle anything, provided he could see it; but here the limit of vision went backward before him grudgingly, a step at a time. Between the twin copper cliffs the palpable presence of storm coiled and writhed, and the ravens screamed and wheeled in it invisibly.

He had come all the way up from Bolzano in the orderly manner he preferred, sticking to his timetable as tenaciously as he stuck to his syllabus all through a three-year tutorial; and if he did not reach Vicenza tonight his whole programme would be thrown out of gear. The very thought made him give a determined hitch to his rucksack and plunge on.

Within the darkening shelter of the Five Fingers a tall snowfield slanted upward and instantly he stopped in his tracks, for somehow at this hour he had not expected the Langkofelkar to be inhabited.

There was a girl on the snowfield. She was not paying any attention to him; she had not yet seen him, nor heard his approach. She was wholly absorbed in what she was doing, and to Edward's staid mind her occupation was so astonishing that he became wholly absorbed in it, too, and stood staring like a halfwit.

She was dressed in slacks and a thick orange-coloured sweater, with her trouser-ends tucked into multicoloured socks above ski boots, and she was engaged in running full tilt up the steep snowfield as high as she could before losing impetus, and then sliding down again, eccentrically poised with spread arms on the dimpled and soiled surface.

She was playing devotedly, in the middle of a terrifying solitude of rock and stormcloud, as unimpressed by the vastness and violence of the Dolomites and the crying flight of the ravens as a child, or a cat. And, indeed, there was something of both child and cat in her perfect concentration and absolute unselfconsciousness. Edward held his breath, and did not realise that he was holding it for fear she should become aware of him, and be disconcerted. Children and cats do not like being watched.

She was young, and beautifully built, strong and slender. She had hair of the light, honeyed gold which is not uncommon in North Italy, and her face was oval and smooth, and tanned to a deep bronze-gold, noticeably darker than the hair. This gold and bronze colouring was all he could see of her, until she took a wilder plunging fall, rolled down the snowfield, and sat up in a flurry of white, beating snow from her sleeves. She was facing the rocks where he stood, and she saw him.

He need not have been afraid; she was not startled. She got up unconcernedly, and came towards him at a light run and said in a clear, rather high voice: '*Buona sera!*' as if they were meeting and passing on some frequented road; and then as blithely, in case he had not understood: '*Bon soir, monsieur!* Good evening!'

Edward, who had never been more taken aback in his life, nevertheless managed to reply with correct gravity: 'Good evening!'

He shifted his rucksack uneasily, and looked down the wavering track which was trodden downhill through the snow.

'Where are you bound for?' she asked.

'The Rifugio Vicenza. And you?'

'Oh, back to Sella,' she said, shaking back the heavy, soft mass of her swinging hair. 'I came up here only for an hour, to get an appetite for dinner. From where have you come today?'

'From Pordoi.' It did not sound a very impressive day's work; he wondered how he had managed to take so long over it.

'To Vicenza is too far,' she said, shaking her head gravely. 'The weather is not good, and it will be dark before you can reach the *rifugio*. You should turn back to Sella.'

'How long does it take from here to Vicenza?'

'Even in good conditions, more than one hour. Down to Sella it is only half an hour, and very easy. I think you should not go on tonight, it will not be safe. At the Rifugio Sella they will find you a bed. I am staying there myself. It is full, but they will not send you away.'

He knew that she was giving him sensible advice, but his mind could find only dismay in such an adjustment of his holiday.

'I'm going back now,' she said. 'If you are wise, you will come, too.' But she did not wait to see if he would follow her.

Edward turned resolutely, and walked across the almost level basin towards the next broken barrier of rocks. He began the descent gingerly, but maintained it for no more than five minutes. Darkness was closing too quickly upon the Langkofelkar. The girl was right, he ought to go back. It was the only sane thing to do.

He went down the slope more soberly than she had done. The first drops of a heavy shower spattered round him as he drew near to the large white bulk of the *rifugio*.

He clumped into the wide wooden hall. People and dogs were seething in and out of the doors as furiously as the cloud boiled in and out of the darkening blowhole of the mountain above. Most of the people, Edward judged, were Italians, and of a certain quite clearly indicated kind. Not the rich and fashionable, but the comfortably off and self-confident. The few who were just coming in, in climbing kit of the cheap, unaesthetic but efficient ex-army type, struck him as being the few foreigners, Austrian, German or English. The rest were better-dressed, but for admiration rather than action. As for the dogs, they were mostly a litter of half-grown boxers which seemed to belong to the house. Children shrilly pursued and tormented them. The din was almost confusing, after the immense quietness on the mountain.

He used his best German on a girl behind the counter in the little shop, where all the musical boxes and wooden toys from the Val Gardena waited for purchasers. She told him that the rooms were all taken, but hesitated and glanced at the darkening windows, and he knew she would not turn him away. There was a bed in one of the top landings.

It proved to be a large corner in a wilderness of dark recesses like open rooms, warm still from the hot sunshine which had poured upon the roof most of the day. A bathroom was not far distant, and the place had more privacy by far than he would have found in the chalet used by the climbers. He accepted it gladly, and shut himself into the bathroom to wash and shave, in some haste, for the gong had already sounded for dinner, and he was hungry.

The dining-room at the Rifugio Passo Sella was large, bright and noisy. As soon as Edward entered, he was met by a very diminutive waitress, with a flashing smile, who waved him after her to a table in a corner.

It was laid for six people, but only one person was yet seated, an elderly, lean-faced man, with cheeks the colour of teak, and far-sighted blue eyes. He was dressed in an ancient and disreputable tweed jacket, knickerbockers, and a khaki shirt without a tie, and his large hands, knotted before him on the plastic tablecloth, were like the roots of trees.

'Good evening!' said the elderly man. '*Thought* you were English! Sit down – where you like!' He pushed the carafe of red wine across the table. 'Staying long?'

'Only overnight. I was a bit too late to get over to Vicenza, or I shouldn't be here now. The weather was against me.'

'Oh! Just walking!' A little of the bright, speculative interest faded out of the blue eyes. 'You don't climb?'

'I'm afraid not.'

'Pity! But you couldn't have better country for learning,' he said, brightening. 'I've got a couple of keen beginners up on the Grohmann today. I'd have been with 'em now if I hadn't pulled a muscle on the Sella yesterday. Why not stay a few days, and join up with us?'

Edward devoted himself to his soup, and muttered apologetically that he had to get over to Siusi as soon as possible.

'All your party are English?' he inquired.

'Yes. Palgrave and his wife have been coming out here with me – various places, you know – for several years. This year we brought out two of my undergraduates. Promising lads, too! Climbed with 'em in England often, but they're new to the Dolomites.'

Edward warmed to find himself in the company of a fellow don. They exchanged names, and plunged into involved comparisons of provincial universities.

Professor Lacey's light blue eyes roved round the room speculatively. 'I see our star turn's missing!'

Edward suppressed a guilty start, convinced for a moment that this sharp old gossip had probed the recesses of his mind, and surprised the image of the golden girl inconveniently insistent there. But when he followed the shrewd gaze he saw that his companion's thoughts were elsewhere. He was watching the antics of a large party of obvious Italians, round a table in the middle of the room. They were all of them notably overdressed, and were making a considerable amount of noise. There was only one vacant place, a pretty, distrait little dark woman sitting anxiously beside it, her eyes forever on her watch.

'Her husband,' explained the Professor simply. 'It seems very quiet without him,' he added.

'Why, who is he?' asked Edward.

'Oh, just one of those people with over-active glands. We always call him the Lion. The rest run after him making adoring noises. They're all from the same place – somewhere in the Veneto; I think it's Padua.'

He sniffed; his opinion of the Paduan party was plainly not a very high one. Probably none of them climbed.

'Pretty wife he's got, at any rate,' said Edward, watching her look sadly from her watch to the empty chair beside her. 'Fond of him, too!'

'Best-looking of the whole bunch, and the only one he never takes any notice of. There isn't a woman in the place he hasn't made a pass at – most of them successful! Until Olimpia arrived, he didn't mind handling three or four at a time. But, of course, with Olimpia in sight, the rest more or less vanish.' He lifted his long nose, sniffing appreciatively in the direction of the door. 'Speak of the angel! Now *there's* a woman!'

The golden girl from the Langkofelkar came in slowly, and moved to her place on the other side of the room. She had changed into a black silk skirt, and sandals, and a matt white blouse cut very low on the shoulders, and out of its thick opaque whiteness her golden shoulders sailed with the aplomb of a lily growing. Her arms were long, rounded and beautiful. Her skin was as sleekly smooth as polished bronze.

The only disquieting thing about her was the presence at her shoulder of a large man in an expensive summer suiting, a bulky blond of impressive physique and indeterminate age. Somewhere between thirty and forty, clean-shaven, heavy-featured, one of those inert faces behind which a formidable temper can sometimes conceal itself. Worst of all, his hand at the girl's elbow was casual and possessive.

Edward's eyes followed her steadily until she was seated. He swallowed hard, and asked as casually as he could:

'Who is she?'

'That's Olimpia! Signora Montesanto – I'm afraid!' Edward caught Professor Lacey's too penetrating eye, and quickly averted his own.

'Yes,' said the Professor with candid sympathy, 'he's her husband. Sometimes I'm not sure that she's any better pleased about it than the rest of us. A lovely creature, isn't she? There isn't a man in the place who hasn't made a play for her.'

'Including your Lion,' said Edward, struggling manfully to look no more concerned about Signor Montesanto's unwelcome existence than the next man.

'Oh, he can't understand that any woman could resist him.'

'She'd have made a magnificent lioness,' said Edward, on an irresponsible impulse.

'So the Lion seems to think. I must say, she hasn't shown any sign of thinking so herself, for all the success he's had elsewhere. No doubt she's found out that it's the only way to keep the peace, with a possessive person like her husband around.'

Some of the tables were already emptying. Giulia Leoni was twisting a handkerchief between her anxious fingers, and looking over her shoulder towards the door at every sound of a step entering the wooden hall. She was certainly no lioness. A charming little black kitten, perhaps, nothing more deadly than that.

They were halfway through coffee when a red head was thrust in at the door, and dark young eyes in a dirty face signalled across to them imperatively.

'Young Crowther,' said Professor Lacey, stubbing out his cigarette without hesitation. 'Something wrong!' he added in the same quiet tone, and got up and made for the door. Edward went after him, because the boy's eyes had seemed to include him in the summons. He began to talk, in a soft, laborious voice of shock, the moment they were within range.

'Prof, something ghastly's happened! He would climb alone! My God, of all the idiots! And who's going to tell his wife?'

The big, brown, quiet woman who was kneeling in the middle of the floor said kindly, but firmly: 'Shut up, Bill! Go and get a drink, and bring one for Tony, too.'

There were four of them grouped round something on the floor; the woman, who must be Mrs Palgrave, and a shaggy middle-aged man in a dark green sweater, who was most probably her husband; the other undergraduate, a thickset boy in an ex-army windproof jacket; and the guide Johann, who was slight and wiry, and looked the part rather less perfectly than Lacey did.

They were bending over a long bundle, the unmistakable shape of a man, from which Johann was just carefully unwinding the nylon rope which had afforded a means of carrying the burden.

'Took us all this time to get him down the scree,' said Palgrave, looking up sombrely into Lacey's face. 'We marked out the position we found him in, in case they can make anything of it, but Bill's right, it looks as if he was fooling about on the Grohmann by himself. Betty tried some photographs, too, in what was left of the light.'

'We'd better get the doctor, at any rate. He's in the dining-room now.'

'I'll go,' said Tony promptly, and made for the door.

'And the manager! Ask Sabina to find him.' Lacey watched the layers of padding fall away with the rope, and asked: 'Dead?'

'Stone dead! Dead when we found him.'

The figure took shape, seemed to grow larger. Edward saw the body of a big and shapely man, a young, lusty, arrogant body, in well-made mountain clothes of a rough light cloth, good boots, a white silk shirt open about a brown, brawny throat. A sweater was peeled away gently from the face. One of those bold, over-pronounced faces, full of bone, with large, deep eyelids, half-open upon dark eyes, a strong jaw, and a mouth whose forward thrust suggested large and immaculate teeth. He had a short russet beard, nicely trimmed about the full and passionate mouth.

They stood looking down at him for an instant in awed silence. 'Better a live dog!' said Professor Lacey, and added upon a sharper tone: 'He doesn't seem to have had much of a fall!'

He fell on his knees beside Johann, who was already unbuttoning the tweed jacket. 'Not a mark on him! No obvious fractures! What the devil *did* happen to him?'

They had all drawn closer, Edward fascinated but silent on the fringe of the circle.

'The snow under him,' said Mrs Palgrave suddenly, 'it was hardly dented! Close to the rocks, too – if he'd fallen far he'd have been embedded in it feet deep. There must be nearly two metres of snow there—'

Johann turned back the jacket. There was a thick pullover under it; he felt at it above the dead man's heart, and drew back his fingers faintly stained. He turned up the pullover to disclose the soft white shirt. Close above the heart was a small, neat, unmistakable hole, so small that in the dark wool they had failed to see it at all. There was hardly any blood, only a few stained inches of silk. The wool had absorbed the rest as it oozed out from the wound.

'No,' said Professor Lacey, softly out of the stunned silence. 'He didn't fall far – just off his own two feet. Somebody put a bullet in him at pretty short range. I think,' he said, 'I'd better go and break it to the manager that we're going to need the police.'

Edward never knew how far the police had to come but by nine o'clock they were there and in possession. The small points of light moving about high in the air to westward were the torches of the policemen plying up the traverses to the col. Within the house the little office was given over to the use of two more officers, the only refuge anywhere within doors from Giulia's tears and despair.

The English party told their story first, and it was brief enough. They had been all day up on the Langkofelkar. They had been entirely absorbed in the pitches of their climb and the coaching of the novices, and had seen no human beings below them, nor heard anything which could make them think of a revolver shot. Descending, in light considerably worse than they had expected, they had found the body. They had thought it best to bring it down with them, but had marked out its position with stones, and left a coloured handkerchief wedged flaglike into a cleft of the rock above to make discovery easy.

The deceptive light had prevented them from seeing too clearly, and the very meagre flow of blood had all been absorbed within his clothes. Moreover, as they realised now, his jacket had been buttoned after he was shot, for the cloth was not marked by any hole over the spot where his pullover and shirt were perforated. Not until they had eased him laboriously all the way down the scree, and brought him into the light of the hotel, did they discover how he had died.

Edward, for his part, had come from Pordoi the long but easy way. At the top, about a quarter to seven, he had encountered Signora Montesanto, who had advised him to turn back to Sella because of the bad weather and the fading light, and after a very brief pause for consideration he had done so. That was all he knew.

When they had made their statements, which Professor Lacey translated into Italian, they were dismissed from the office. The dining-room was a chaos, the boxer pups unchecked under everybody's feet, the doctor, an inoffensive little man on holiday from a practice in Cremona, in weary attendance on Giulia. As soon as she was fit to answer questions the police would see her, so that she could be put to bed, and escape something, at least, of the horror of the evening. Meantime, she sat clutching at the nearest friendly arm, her handkerchief at her lips, the tears raining effortlessly from her large, purple-black eyes.

Several of the other Paduan women were also in tears, but voluble between their bouts of weeping, and the noise they produced sounded to Edward as bitter and angry as it was shrill. The men of the party were nervous and sullen, padding backwards and forwards between the bar and their table, and accosting one another in sudden explosive outbursts as they drank.

'They sound as if they're quarrelling,' said Edward, in Professor Lacey's pricked and capacious ear.

'They are. Not much comradeship left in that little fraternity now. All the women were jealous of the least attention the Lion paid to any other woman, and the husbands divided their time between envying him, being scared of him, and hating his guts. He was an eminently murderable person,' sighed Professor Lacey, almost with respect, almost with regret, 'in spite of being irrepressibly likeable.'

'How did a man like that manage to get into the Langkofelkar entirely alone? I suppose he did! I should have thought there'd always be a few of the faithful under his feet.'

'Oh, he could kick when he liked. People didn't hang around the Lion when he told them to go to hell! Everybody claims to have been miles away all afternoon, and they're all busy casting doubts on the claims of all the others. Nobody seems to have seen the Lion turn back from Rodella and go up into the Langkofelkar.'

'That could be true enough,' said Palgrave, looking up from his belated dinner. 'In country on this fantastic scale it's amazing how you can lose a hundred people – all still within sight.'

'Oh, it could be true! So he came back alone and unnoticed – or maybe he didn't come back, but worked up along the contour from Rodella, and on to the scree from there.'

'Did he leave his wife with as little ceremony as the rest of the party?' asked Edward.

'With a damned sight less. Why should he waste finesse on her? He already had her. Besides, Giulia doesn't walk. Everybody knows it. No, he brought her here, and after that she had to fend for herself. It would have been rather a sensation if he *had* been seen out with her, as a matter of fact.'

'Then where did she spend her afternoon? I suppose they'll have to ask her, too.' She was gone from the dining-room, as he saw when he looked round again; she must be in the office with the police at this moment.

'She took one of the cars, and went off down the valley by herself after breakfast. It seems she's been down in Santa Cristina, shopping. I saw her bringing the parcels in when she got back, about twenty past seven or somewhere around that time.'

The red-headed Bill said, somewhat uncomfortably: 'There's a path up from Santa Cristina – it works up round the back of the Langkofel.'

'It's two good hours' walking, and the scramble at the end,' said Tony. 'And Giulia doesn't walk. And even if she really could tackle ground like that, she couldn't have got back to pick up her car in the time.'

'How do you know she couldn't? We don't know what time he was shot.'

Edward looked at the Professor, who certainly would not have forgotten to sound the doctor upon the subject. 'What time *was* he shot?'

'He's too cautious to commit himself too deeply. Probably between half-past four and half-past six, he says.'

'So, on the earlier limit, it *would* be a possibility for her to walk back to Santa Cristina, pick up the car, and still be back here by twenty-past seven.'

'It would for anyone but Giulia. Maybe she's not so helpless on her feet as she claims, but no one's ever seen her take more than a peaceful little promenade on the grass verge along the road.'

'You didn't notice her shoes?' asked Mrs Palgrave.

'No, I can't say I did. She wears good stout walking shoes. They're the thing here, and you can trust all that party to do whatever is the thing.'

'She wouldn't have hurt him!' said Tony, suddenly laying down his fork as if his appetite had suffered a serious check. 'She's crazy about him. And look what she's put up with already, without a murmur of complaint!'

Giulia came out of the office, her handkerchief to her eyes, the sympathetic arm of one of her friends supporting her tenderly towards the stairs. It was curious that they all looked at her shoes now. They saw foolish little sandals, with three-inch heels. Exactly the shoes one would bring to Sella to support a reputation for never walking anywhere.

The manager, hovering anxiously upon the threshold of the office, lifted an imploring finger, and whispered: 'Signora Montesanto!'

Olimpia rose, smiled at him reassuringly across the room, and crushed out her cigarette in the ashtray. She walked towards the open door and the waiting policemen with the beautiful, alert vehemence with which she had launched herself down the snowfield.

Edward said: 'I suppose there wouldn't be any objection

to our getting a breath of air, would there, provided we stay within call?'

He went towards the door, and since no one attempted to stop him, opened it and went out into the night. He took the path which lay between the hotel and the little chapel, and walked into the cold, pale, stony borders of the rock town. Far above him the vague shape of the Langkofel, fantastically high and close, blotted out whole galaxies of stars.

He lit a cigarette, and found himself a sheltered corner among the rocks. The air had almost the snap of frost, and he was shivering by the time he turned back slowly towards the *rifugio*.

Out of the dimness something white moved vaguely towards him upon the path. His senses leaped to recognition as if he had willed her rather than merely encountered her. After the whiteness of her blouse he was aware of the light, amber gleam of her eyes. They had not kept her long; but then, she had nothing to tell them. He heard her sudden, indrawn breath, the long, soft sigh.

'Oh, it's you!'

The high, clear voice could be almost as still as silence itself.

'You'll be very cold!' said Edward, disturbingly aware of her naked golden shoulders so close to him. 'I'll go and get you a coat – or, if you'll have mine—'

The short hair tossed violently as she shook her head. 'No, not cold! May I have a cigarette, please?' As he sheltered the little flame of the lighter assiduously between their bodies, his heart thumping at her nearness, she shut her hand suddenly over his, and clung to it with cool, tremulous fingers.

In the pure oval of her face her eyes clung to his as fiercely. 'Not cold – just afraid!'

'You're very kind,' she added softly, 'and I am glad you are here. But there is nothing you can do for me except be here, and be kind.'

He did not know how it had happened, but his arm was about her shoulders, and he was trembling as violently as she, and stammering incoherent reassurances into her ear. They clung together in the hushed and magical night.

'You can tell me,' he said vaingloriously. 'You can trust me! If there's something frightening you—'

He held her to his swelling heart, and waited.

'If I'd known – if we *could* know what people will do – I wouldn't have let him out of my sight today! Ever since I married him it has been like this! He looks for wrongs, wrongs, wrongs, everywhere, always. But I have grown used to that,' she said in a shuddering whisper, 'and I thought it would just go on like that always. I never thought that something bad would happen – like this!'

'You think your husband may have – may know something about Leoni's death?' Edward baulked at the word 'murder'. She lifted her beautiful face, so softly and deeply moulded in the darkness, and he saw the fixed golden shining of her eyes.

'We were out together all morning on the Cir. We went at dawn. When we came back to lunch I was tired, and so was he, and I went to my room and slept. When I dressed and came down to look for him I could not find him. I thought I would just go up to the col before dinner. It was after five o'clock, I know, when I went out, but I am not sure how much after – perhaps Sabina will know, she saw me go out. When I came back – you know when that was – Tonino still had not come in. He did not come until almost eight o'clock.'

'But he must be able to prove where he was all the afternoon,' said Edward reasonably.

'He *says* that he took the meadow path over the pass, by Valentini's Inn, and went down towards Ganazei. You know that path? For a long way it is so open you could see and recognise a man on it as much as half a mile away from you. There are huts, too, and part of the meadow is only just being mown. Do you think a man could go that way, and meet nobody? Oh, it is possible, it could happen to one man in a thousand men, but—'

'But you're afraid he was up there in the Langkofelkar with Leoni! Is that it? You think he was there when you climbed up the same path, and that he waited until we'd both gone before he ventured down?'

'It could have been like that,' she said, almost inaudibly.

His eyes dwelt upon hers in consternation and dismay. '*Has* he a gun?'

'Yes. I have seen it – but I do not know about guns. It is only small, but I don't know the … calibre? Is that right? It may be the wrong kind of gun. Only, I am afraid—'

Edward was shaken with a tremor of alarm which seemed to originate within his own heart rather than in any look or word of hers. He took her suddenly by the shoulders, aware of the silken unexpectedness of her cool skin under his palms, but past anything so trivial as embarrassment. 'He won't hurt *you*? If there's any fear of that – if there's any possibility—'

Olimpia smiled, slowly and wryly, with the smoke of the cigarette curling from her lips. She looked at him steadily, and he thought he saw amusement in her eyes, but was sure he saw tenderness. 'You are very sweet,' she said, so softly that he hardly heard the words.

'But if he's crazy with jealousy like that – if he thinks that – that you—'

'He thinks I have betrayed him with Paolo Leoni,' she said, in a voice which had strongly recovered its calm, 'and with at least a dozen men before him. I think he has dealt with Paolo for it. But that is not the kind of thing one tells the police unless one is sure.'

She dropped the butt of her cigarette, and put her foot upon it. Her hand closed tightly over his for a moment, and she was turning abruptly away when he caught her back suddenly into his arms.

'Olimpia—'

He didn't know what he had wanted to say, he was groping without any words, her startled face upturned to him, glimmering in the dark, the rich, soft lips parted, the shining eyes wide. He felt for her mouth partly out of sheer desperation, because he was at a loss for anything to say which would not be utterly fatuous. Her mouth quivered, made to maintain its startled quiescence, and then could not. She fastened upon him insatiably, clinging and trembling.

Somewhere not very far distant, upon the path, a stone rolled and a foot stumbled. A voice, heavy and still like valley air, said loudly: 'Olimpia!'

She pulled herself out of Edward's arms. Her face was quite calm. She shook her head, forbidding him to accompany her, but she made no secret of his presence, for as she walked firmly towards her husband she called back: 'Good night!' over her shoulder in deliberate English.

Edward stood where she had left him. He strained his ears to catch the tone of the encounter, ready to spring to her rescue at the first hint of a threat.

The deep voice, inexpressibly weary and bitter, said with the faintest note of surprise: 'An Englishman this time?' copying her firm pronunciation. 'Well, why not? I have been cuckolded in every other major language.' It was, in its way, a blow, but it was not the voice of a man immediately dangerous.

They were gone. For an instant, when they reached the light from the windows of the dining-room, he saw them as two black shapes silhouetted on the yellow, walking apart, scrupulously drawn back from touching each other. Their careful movements infected him with a totally unexpected frenzy of pain.

Then they vanished, and he was alone. Far up the scree the torches of the police were threading a zigzag way downward, like arrested lightning flowing painfully towards the earth.

Edward watched the police thread their way through the rocks towards the *rifugio*, which was still blazing with lights. They had not the knowledge he had just acquired, nor his urgent reasons for wanting the case cleared up at all costs. For the only possible way to extricate Olimpia Montesanto from her unbearable situation was to prove her husband a murderer, and wrest her away from him once and for all, or prove him innocent, and set her mind at rest.

He stood looking back towards the lighted windows for a few minutes after the policemen had passed by, and then he swung round suddenly, and began to stride rapidly up through the rocks towards the base of the zigzag path which climbed the scree.

The sky had cleared, and stars, very small and pinched, pricked the dark blue expanse of sky with pinpoints of light. The *rifugio* was only a tiny lamp below him now, shining upon a short, lambent, pallid coil of road. Suddenly he saw himself for the incredible fool he was, charging romantically up a mountain at eleven o'clock at night to find some evidence which would put a man, hitherto unknown to him even by name, in goal, and set his wife free – free for what? Free to accept Edward Stanier's protection and admiration? He was appalled by the unexpectedness of the vision.

The rocks soared about him quite suddenly, a sort of closing in of the arms of the mountain round his strenuously bent shoulders. The cliffs were awesome in the night, and the silence was withering.

The first glimmering snowfield fell away on his left, within the arena of rocks. He was glad that his climbing boots were Italian, and almost certainly of the same pattern as many which had passed this way already, probably including some of those worn by the policemen. He must not cut up the marked area of snow too crudely, but if he took care his tracks would pass among the rest.

It had not occurred to him until then that someone might

have been left on guard there, and he halted for a moment in his reckless slide down the snow, in consternation at the possibility. But no, on second thoughts it was unlikely enough. The night was already very cold; before morning there would be several degrees of frost up here; and who was likely to invade the mountain at night, in any case?

The place was not so hard to find. There it was, the shape of a man roughly marked out on the dimpled surface and a flutter of coloured cloth above.

Stepping lightly and steadily, to leave no deeper indentations than he need, he went inch by inch over the ground where the body had lain.

One of the stones placed by Johann's party heeled away silently. He righted it, playing his torch closely into the hollow; and in the thin beam of light he saw something black in the crumbling whiteness within.

He pulled out a soft, narrow leather strap, a bit of black kid about eight inches long, with two small steel half-hoops sewn into a loop in one end of it. He did not know what he had expected; it meant nothing to him now that he had it. Just a strip of kid, with a few frayed threads of cotton where it had been sewn to something else. And yet there was something about it that made his fingertips tingle as he held it.

The leather was fresh, supple and brightly black, and his cold hands could detect in it none of the internal stiffness of damp. It could not have kept this condition for so much as a single day in the hollow of snow. Either one of Johann's party had shed the thing when they lifted the body or else it had been dropped by someone shortly before Leoni was shot. So shortly, thought Edward, shivering in the thin, frosty wind, that he could hardly be anyone else but the murderer.

The place was neither on nor near any path; he had had to swing inward a long way from the track to reach it. He could hardly believe that some other, some innocent person had chosen exactly the same spot to linger in, on the same day. No, what he had in his hand belonged to one of the climbing party who had moved the body, or to the murderer.

He found nothing else, though he hunted doggedly for ten minutes more about the disturbed area of snow. He was shivering violently with the cold, and it was growing very late. He pushed the strap into his pocket, for more exact examination later, and began the laborious climb back to the col.

It was past midnight when he crept quietly through the town, but the lights were still on in the hall and the office, and the doors still unfastened.

He got himself to bed and lay for a long time sleepless, trembling and trying to get warm.

Tomorrow he must somehow contrive to get a word with Olimpia alone, and show her the strap. If she could connect it with her husband, there would be something, at least, on which the police could take action.

When Edward came downstairs next morning, the dining-room curtains were still closely drawn, so he went out and strolled back and forth on the green verge of the road, where he could keep an eye upon the stairs every time he passed the door. The first sunlight, salmon pink, flushed the upper cliffs of the Langkofel. It was going to be a beautiful day.

Professor Lacey came out with the rest, hitched his shapeless hat, decorated with a frayed end of nylon rope, forward over his mahogany brow, and sniffed appreciatively at the glittering air. Then he went back to muster his party, and presently they emerged in a tight little organised knot of British efficiency, and made purposefully for the dining-room, which was now open.

They called a greeting to Edward as they approached the doorway, and lingered as though they expected him to join them at once; but he did not go in until he had seen Olimpia come down the stairs and enter the dining-room, her husband close at her elbow, his hand touching her arm. No luck there! She passed in through the little anteroom as though she had not seen Edward standing in the sunlight beside the road; but he felt in his heart that she had, that she was deeply aware of him, and would have come to him if she could have shaken off that forbidding hand.

At least from his place at the corner table he could watch her across the room. While he fended off the Professor's efforts to inveigle him into their plans for the day's climb, he was covertly studying the slender, erect figure, the long brown hands and the swinging honey-coloured hair. She was in knickerbockers and a white shirt this morning, her hooded windjacket hanging on the arm of her chair. So they were going out, and on an active expedition, too.

The thought terrified him. How could he let her go off into the desolate lunar craters of disintegrating rock about these mountains, alone, with a wretched unbalanced creature who had probably killed once out of his insane jealousy, and might do so again? He could not bear to think of the miles and miles of faint, bewildering greys and greens and pinks of stone and scree, unpopulated, deceptive, silent, where a body could lie for weeks and weeks undiscovered since only colour and movement together ever served to call attention even to the living.

The Professor was nudging him, urging something, he didn't know what, he hadn't been listening. Distrait, he parried at a venture:

'Perhaps we shan't be allowed to go off the premises. I mean – the police—'

'My dear fellow! Approximately one hundred and eighty people, most of them with only the flimsiest acquaintance with the Lion! How can they all be kept here? No, we can all go where we like, as long as they're reasonably sure we're coming back again. You'd much better come with us.'

Edward fought them off with much more decision than he could ever have shown for his own sake. His eyes were on the silent couple across the room, the girl with her warm bronze skin exquisite against the white silk of her shirt, and her eyes cast down desultorily upon the plate she had hardly touched.

He wondered that the tension between himself and her was not as perceptible to everyone in the room as it was to him. She kept her eyes resolutely lowered because if she raised them it would be to fix their wide, golden, fearful appeal upon him, and that look would be one Tonino would read instantly, and translate into something shameful.

Edward had to let them pass through the doorway before he dared excuse himself hurriedly and follow. They were going towards the stairs again. He saw Olimpia check suddenly, heard her say something about stamps, drawing her arm from Tonino's grasp with an easy and natural recoil towards the little shop; but instead of going up the staircase without her, he came back at her heels, stood by her at the counter, still touching her remindingly with the ends of long, inexorable fingers. He was not going to let her out of his sight, that was plain. 'Neither will I!' said Edward grimly to himself. 'Not until I can get her safely away from you!'

He met her eyes full for an instant, light yellow flames of fear in the mask-like calm of her lovely face, and flashed back at her, as convincingly as he could when the greater part of himself was a molten panic of infatuation and bewilderment, his service and reassurance.

He watched them move off across the road, and take a thinly trodden path diagonally over the open meadow, heading straight for the cliffs of the Sella, which loomed immense against the washed blue sky, palest pink above, shadowy russet and bluish grey below. As soon as he was sure of their direction he went back into the equipment room, where the English party were just girding themselves with the most casual set of ropes and *kletterschuhe* he had ever seen.

'Is there a quick way up into the Sella plateau this side? There's a path that makes off directly into the cliffs just opposite here. I wondered about taking that. It must take hours off the Val Lasties route if it's practicable.'

'Oh yes, much the most direct way up.' Professor Lacey knotted a pair of dingy tennis shoes at his belt, and looked round with mildly quickening interest. 'Just across the meadows here – the path's liable to vanish, but keep more or less on the contour, and scout along the cliff there, and you can't miss it. Takes you up to Piz Selva in a few hours. Interesting route, too!'

'Is it very difficult?'

'Hardly a scramble. Where it gets rather steep and exposed there are wire ropes fixed and some hand-holds.'

'Only you have to watch out for the ropes in places,' supplemented Mrs Palgrave cheerfully. 'Some of them aren't too safe. There's a lot of weathering on those faces.'

Edward withdrew with somewhat nervous thanks, and went out to the vast green undulation of meadow again. The two dwindling figures were walking steadily along the invisible track, some distance away now, their faces towards the mountain, but the space between was so open that he could not follow them without becoming as conspicuous as a sore finger against the empty sweep of grass.

After a few irresolute moments he set off uphill by the road, cutting the corners of the boggy grass, towards the crest of the pass. He had not thought what he could do. The first thing was to be close to her, and feel the desperate valour her eyes had given him filling his mild heart with fury and resolution.

He lost sight of them from time to time from the undulations of the cliff-face, which leaped out of the meadow almost as cleanly as a wall, with only here and there a few fallen boulders to soften its fabulous outlines. He dared not go many yards from the shelter of the rock, for fear of becoming visible to the two who were gradually converging with him across the meadow.

He slowed down, edging yard by yard along, and waiting for the first sounds of their nearness. They were not speaking at all. Presently he could hear their steps in the grass; and for a moment, before they vanished into the rock, he saw Olimpia's face clearly, intent, aware, and very still, the eyes flaring unfocused, as though all her powers were concentrated on listening. Listening, he thought, for him.

When their leisurely, deliberate movements no longer sent him any echoes, he ventured along the cliff perhaps twenty yards more, and came upon the gully, doubling steeply backward into the rock mass. It was narrow enough to be easily missed unless one looked back at the right angle, complicated with masses of fallen stones for a while, but clear of scree, and he could move silently and fairly quickly up it, for there was plenty of cover.

From rock to rock and corner to corner he pulled strenuously upwards until he could hear them moving ahead of him and catch an occasional glimpse of them as they bent their backs in the long, easy, untiring stride of practised mountaineers.

Once they halted, and sat down where there was an open window on the pass, to smoke their first cigarette; but as soon as the ends were trodden out against the stones they were off again. He stayed in close attendance on them, dangerously close, wherever there was cover, but sometimes he had to fall back as much as a hundred yards to remain hidden, and then his fear began to beat upward in his throat urgently, tugging him onward towards her for dear life, her life, which had become so crazily dear to him.

They were well up now, and coming to some of the more

exposed places, where the path, if it could be called a path, crawled outward to the exterior faces of the group.

At any other time he would have been gravely discomfited by the plucking of the air, and the almost sheer drop of several hundred feet on his right hand; now he was too furiously intent to notice his own uneasy situation. Compared with the two people he was shadowing, he was an abject amateur. To them this was indeed an easy scramble, and nothing more. Edward watched Olimpia's movements whenever the chance offered, envious of her ease and precision. He knew how her mind leaned back to him in its anxiety, and yet her body seemed as relaxed and competent as a cat's.

Her husband went before her, leaning back to give her a hand occasionally where the reach was long and difficult. Now the route had tacked, and they were crossing Edward's position on a higher level. He clung flattened against the rock, listening intently as the methodical, measured movements of their feet were stepped out above his head.

For the first time within Edward's hearing, Tonino had spoken to her. Her high, clear voice, curiously flattened and wary, said something mildly in return; it sounded like an obedient agreement to whatever he had said. Then a foot slid suddenly along the rock, a protesting sound; there were two cries so simultaneous that they might have been only the two dominant tones of a dreadful natural disharmony. Then a shadow flung outward on the air above Edward's head like a swooping bird, and something went by his cringing shoulders with a rushing sigh, turning, plying its arms vainly against the unsustaining wind, down, down, over the sheer edge of the cliff-face, plunging towards the meadows far below.

Crouched hard against his rock, frozen with horror, he saw something else fall with it, something tiny and thin and between black and bright, that rang on the edge of the fall with a metallic note, and bounced outward from his sight to vanish after Tonino Montesanto's body.

His senses, recoiling in self-defence, slammed a door upon reality and left him hanging there blind and deaf for a moment, and then he tore himself out of his paralysis to hear the thin, terrifying sound of Olimpia screaming. He forgot the nine hundred feet of vertigo below him, and the thirty-seven years of physical mediocrity behind him, and clawed his way up to her with heroic haste. She was spread out against the rock, her face pressed into her shoulder, wailing like a crazy child. Not far above her right hand he could see the place where the iron staple was newly broken out of the rock.

He came to her side very gently and warily, anchored her to the rock with a firm arm, and began to talk to her softly, choosing words so calm and tender that she had to hear their authoritative sound, if not their sense.

'It's all over now, you're quite safe with me. I'll take you down again safely. I'll take you home. Don't worry any more. I'm with you.'

She braced herself a little, and drew closer to him, huddling against his breast.

'It wasn't your fault. Don't think of it, it's all over now. Just hold on to me.'

'He tried to kill me,' she said indistinctly into his coat, her voice a child's whimper of protest against injustice. 'He leaned down to give me his hand and he took hold of the iron hold instead, and broke it out, and it fell – I don't know what happened – he must have lost his balance—'

She detached one hand from its frantic clutch on the rock, and took hold of his coat instead, clinging convulsively. 'He wanted to kill me!' she sobbed, relaxing from her quivering rigidity into the sustaining circle of his arm. 'He was smiling, and then he pulled the staple out and let it fall – and all at once he slipped, and the smile went away from his face – and then he fell, too—'

He held and soothed her until she ceased to tremble, and visibly drew herself together again, raising her face dazedly to his.

'He was mad, wasn't he?' she said suddenly, when they were nearing the last stony cleft which brought them into the meadow. 'It wasn't his fault – he didn't know what he was doing.'

'No,' said Edward tenderly, 'he didn't know what he was doing. He wasn't normal.'

He knew he had to find the body. When they reached the grass he wanted to leave her sitting against the safe, solid rocks while he prospected to the left, where he was pretty sure it would have fallen; but though her knees were shaking under her, she would not be left alone. She followed at his elbow, her hand reaching out to him, so that he turned back impulsively and gathered her to him again. Her face was too still, her eyes too hectically bright in it. He was afraid she might collapse in the reaction from terror and shock.

What was left of Tonino was lying in a small, hard field of stones below the sheer face, about thirty yards to the left of the mouth of the cleft. He looked remarkably intact still, only without bones, as limp and abandoned as a rag doll, and insubstantial inside the deflated bulk of his windjacket. Not ten yards from him the iron staple was lying in the thin grass between the stones.

'He's dead?' asked Olimpia, through stiff lips.

'Instantly. Maybe before he even hit the ground. He wouldn't know, Olimpia, he wouldn't have time to feel anything but one great blow. You mustn't think of it. You have to think of yourself now.'

'I'm all right,' she said, and swayed on her feet.

He got her to a comfortable spot with her back against a smooth stone, and wrapped her in her own jacket and his, and told her to shut her eyes and wait there while he ran to the *rifugio*, and not to try to move until he came back with help.

He thought for fully five minutes, as he ran across the meadow, that she was going to obey him. But at the end of that time, looking back again, he saw her stumbling after him at a reckless run, and calling after him with a sad little cry.

He turned back, sick with devotion, and took her into his arms. She was crying, the tears pouring from her eyes; and her face had recovered something of its live warmth with the relief of it. She was ashamed and apologetic, flushing under her tan as she entreated: 'Don't leave me behind! I'm sorry – I'm so sorry! But don't make me stay there—'

He kissed her wet cheeks, not like a lover at all, more like a father picking up a hurt child; and slowly, gently, he helped and coaxed her all across the interminable waste of meadow towards the *rifugio*.

The porter, Edward, and four policemen, went out to bring back the remains of Tonino Montesanto. It was not quite noon when they picked him out of the blood-stained stones, and went carefully over his disarticulated body, picked up the fallen iron staple he had wrenched from its place the better to tip his wife to her death, and put together the whole story of the morning from Edward's account.

The police officer in charge – Edward never knew what his title might be – felt at the deep inside pockets of the gaberdine windjacket before he unzipped it. His hand halted upon the left breast, felt along the outline of something hard there. He was interested.

What came out of the pocket was a small, snub-nosed revolver, which he lifted forth in the folds of a handkerchief, and regarded with alert satisfaction. The make and calibre, to judge by his face, was right. There was a silencer grooved into the barrel. The individual markings and the fingerprints, if any, should settle the matter.

Edward wondered where the gun would have been by now, if it had been Olimpia, and not Tonino, who had fallen. With all the terrace of the Sella for its grave, it would have taken some resurrecting.

Had Olimpia known more than she had confided to him last night? Had she discovered more since then, enough to make her death desirable for other reasons besides Othello's demented vengeance? He was never going to ask her. She was alive, and out of her nightmare. That was all that mattered.

They carried the stretcher back to the *rifugio*, decently covered from sight, and it was taken into the little office and the policemen went in after it, and shut the door on all the rest of the world. And yet within an hour or two the news had gone round.

The gun which had shot Paolo Leoni was the one which had been found, wiped clean of all prints, in Tonino Montesanto's pocket. There was no mystery now, it was all over. The murderer was dead, as dead as his victim. A wretched husband unbalanced by groundless jealousy – they knew well how to understand a tragedy like that.

Giulia Leoni came down in the afternoon, when it was quiet in the sun by the little chapel. She was drawn with weeping, but quiet and calm, her pretty dark curls conscientiously arranged about her little erect head. She went steadily out of the door, and over to where Olimpia was lying in a deckchair on the grass with Edward protectively beside her.

Olimpia had eaten nothing, but had obediently drunk the brandy he had given her. Giulia appeared beside the chair very gently and solicitously. She said: 'Signora Montesanto!' in the most limpidly sweet of voices, and poured out a flood of Italian far too rapid and unemphatic for Edward to follow. He thought how kind and how brave it was of her to come straight to her fellow victim like this, and offer her sympathy in this childlike manner.

Olimpia looked up, startled for a moment, through her long, bright-gold lashes, and a faint smile touched her lips.

Edward could not tell what she answered. He felt the play of certain feminine undercurrents.

Giulia had a quaint, vindicated dignity now, something she would perhaps never lose again. Drawing back a step or two for departure, she looked at him for a moment. She smiled. She made some last soft remark to Olimpia, and turned, still smiling, and walked back towards the house.

Olimpia sat looking after the slight, upright figure. She said tranquilly: 'Giulia is very pretty, and quite sensible. She will not be a widow for long.'

He was trying to run to earth a word Giulia had used, and which he was almost sure he ought to remember.

He was still thinking warmly how good women could be to one another, when he went in to tidy himself for dinner. It was quite a shock to him, when he remembered and looked up the elusive word. He had heard it before, all right! A man in the market at Brescia had once said it in his hearing to a woman at one of the stalls, and it meant, quite simply, 'whore'.

It gave him a nasty jolt to think how mistaken he had been in Giulia, and for a few minutes he was filled with an illogical fury against her. Then he remembered Olimpia's compassionate forbearance, and recalled with shame the legacy of shock and grief under which the poor little woman was labouring.

Olimpia came down to dinner in the black silk skirt and another white blouse, against which her bronzed arms and throat glowed enriched and polished in the lamplight. She sat at her table alone, declining, though graciously, all offers of company, even Edward's; but for him she said, softening the brief banishment: 'Afterwards we will go for a walk. Please! Then we—'

She never completed whatever she had been about to say. Her eyes had a look of astonished discovery, as if even the pronoun had taken her by surprise.

He sustained the eager questions of the English party, not long returned from their day's climb to a mystery resolved, on the strength of that 'we'.

Afterwards Olimpia rose, and in leaving the room turned and looked at Edward from the doorway.

She came down buttoning a short woollen jacket, and hugging soft kid mittens under her arm. As soon as they were on, she slipped her hand into his arm, and they went out together, and turned towards the saddle of the pass.

Olimpia halted suddenly, and her gloved hand was drawing his head down to her, and her lips feeling softly, imperiously for his mouth.

She shut her long, strong arms round him wildly, arched against him into violent stillness.

'You saved my life,' she whispered. 'If I hadn't known you were there, close to me, I should have died of terror. Oh, Edward!' Feminine to the bone, she said self-reproachfully: 'What must you think of me, that I throw myself into your arms like this, after so short a time?'

'I think you love me – I know I love you. What has time got to do with it, when so much has happened to us?' Was it really Edward Stanier speaking? His face flamed for his own audacity, but as much with triumph as embarrassment. Her hair was soft, like live silk; it seemed to quiver as it stroked his face, and smelled of lemon-blossom. He was faint and tipsy with the sweetness of her mouth, and her eyes, whenever he opened his own, opened responsively to receive the close, unfocused gaze, a luminous haze of gold, rapt, placid and satisfied.

'A cigarette?'

'Light it for me, please.'

They stirred out of the trance slowly, and stood apart, smiling. He lit the cigarette, and transferred it from his lips to hers.

He watched her fondly, still a little drunk; and it was in the absorbed solemnity of drunkenness that he found himself dwelling upon the little elaborate glove in the glow of the cigarette. A pretty little mitt, the palm of black kid, the back of cherry-red, the wrist encircled with a thin black kid strap about eight inches long, two half-loops of chromium or steel making an unusual buckle in front.

For an instant the night was absolutely silent, with a silence which hammered his senses like the explosion of a gun. He held his breath, and his fingers felt instinctively at his inside pocket, where he had left something lying quite forgotten all day. He slid his gaze down, wincingly, reluctantly, towards her other hand, which at that very moment was rising innocently to touch his cold cheek. He felt the sweat break out along his hairline as chill as frost.

There was no little black kid strap on this wrist; only a few frayed threads of silk along the seam marked where it had once been.

When he closed the door of his room his legs gave under him, and he had to sit down quickly on the edge of the bed. Heat broke out through his body as intense as the first bitter cold. He wiped his face, and watched his hands trembling.

The taste of her love-making, terrifyingly sweet, was still on his lips.

So Giulia had known what she was talking about, after all. The rest might say that the Lion had pestered Olimpia without result, but Giulia knew better. There had been results, all right! Once, at any rate! Yes, probably only once, that was what had baffled the Lion. He couldn't realise that there could be a woman who lived just as he did, taking whatever she wanted wherever she found it, and then throwing it away.

She had been quite ready, perhaps, to jettison Tonino, but not for an easy creature like Paolo Leoni. And a man like that might easily become a serious nuisance to a woman who dared to tire of him before he tired of her. Maybe he only bored her. Maybe he threatened, in his baffled indignation, his offended maleness, to talk to her husband, since he couldn't talk sense into her. Either way, he got his one more meeting. And he was dead.

Edward thought of Olimpia as he had first seen her, pleased with her solitude, eased of her encumbrance, gambolling in the snow with all her heart and mind. The gun must have been in the pocket of her slacks then, the gun she had planted on Tonino this morning, when for five minutes she was left behind with his body.

And Edward knew the rest of it, too, the part Giulia didn't know. It wanted only one bit of the puzzle orientated correctly, and all the rest fell into place. The summons of her eyes pulling him after her to the mountain, the chosen witness – not only for his lovesick gullibility, but also as a sort of favour, because he had already been chosen for something more than a witness. Olimpia liked him.

She had persuaded him back to Sella in the first place as much because she liked him as to avoid the possibility of a premature discovery of the Lion's body. This time she even liked him enough to shrug off Tonino in his favour, it seemed, especially as Tonino was beginning to offend her a little with his tragic forbearance and his tedious unhappiness.

It had been childishly easy; he saw that now. The pitch of the climb carefully chosen, the husband unwarily leaning to give her a hand. A little jerk outward when he was least expecting it, and the iron hand-hold wrenched from its already precarious anchorage on the rock and tipped down after him. Yes, after him! Edward realised now more clearly the order of that fall. And then she had nothing to do but stand there huddled against the rock, screaming delightedly into her own shoulder, her eyes closed in the satisfaction of artistry, until the sweet besotted fool of an Englishman came panting to her rescue.

But who was going to believe it now? What was there to show for it all but a little black kid strap from a glove, and if it was what he said it was, and he'd found it where he said he had, why hadn't he handed it over to the police? And in any case, whose word was there for it but his?

He thought of what it would be like to come out with this accusation before Olimpia's wide, wounded eyes, and a fiery sweat broke out all over him. Even if he could do it, even if he had the courage, even if they believed him, it could never be made good against that invulnerable serenity of hers. She would have nothing to do but fold her hands, and endure the torrent of words, and make it clear in her lovely, resigned silence that he had attempted to extort for his services a reward she was not prepared to grant, and had taken this method of avenging his slighted masculinity. She wouldn't even have to say it; that was the kind of conclusion to which people leaped where Olimpia was concerned. And at the end of everything, with her wild, candid kisses still burning on his lips and cheeks, did he even want the truth at that price?

So when everything was said and done, there was only one course open to him. Only one! Ignominious but inevitable!

He packed his rucksack, and lay down fully dressed on his bed, and even slept a little. At dawn he washed and shaved, and crept down to the office to wait for the porter. They were used to people rising and paying bills at short notice, and the police were no longer interested. By seven o'clock he was striding down the valley towards Plan de Gralba, to catch the early bus over the Passo Gardena for Brunico and the north.

He went down the road as if the devils were after him for the first mile, and then inexplicably his feet began to drag. He could hardly feel proud of himself. He was turning his back on a duty, he was going to be haunted for years by uneasy speculations about all the other poor devils who were destined to blunder along after Paolo and Tonino, and come to the same sticky end. But what else could he do? He was astonished to find that his walk had slowed to a stubborn crawl and, at every panicky spurt he put on, his implacable conscience jammed on the brake. But they'd never believe him. Why should they?

It was at this point that it dawned upon him that he was afraid of her. He stopped in his tracks, digging his heels indignantly into the turf by the roadside. He could throw overboard all the arguments of chivalry, for do what he would, Olimpia needed no help to protect herself from him. He just hadn't the courage to face her.

The realisation fired his gentle heart into a totally unexpected anger. Not only had she made use of him as an assistant in disposing of her husband and her lover, and fooled him to the hilt, but she had brought him face to face with a mirror he had probably been avoiding all his life. He was afraid to tell the truth, because it was going to put him in a dubious position, and he might not be believed! As if that altered the fact that it was truth! So he was that kind of timorous soul, was he?

It confused him a little to find that he had turned, and was striding back up the white road as hard as he could go. He didn't pause to examine his motives too closely, and it was never at all clear to him whether the deprived ghosts of Paolo and Tonino had really had any hand in turning him, or whether his own galled self-esteem had done the job single-handed. He hoped it was his sense of duty to society, but he wasn't going to look too closely. He had more than enough on his mind.

The first climbers were out in front of the chalet when he reached the *rifugio*, and Professor Lacey was sniffing the air and measuring with his alert old eyes the day's possibilities. A terrifying air of normality had already settled over the house.

Before his courage could fail him, he approached the

Professor, with so abrupt and strained a note that the old man stared and bristled like a pointer.

'My dear chap, the porter said you'd left. Did you miss the bus?'

'Not exactly. I had to come back. Professor, would you mind coming and interpreting for me? I've got to talk to the police.'

'The police? Something new?' The blue eyes brightened with glee and widened with anticipation. 'Surely they'll have gone by this time? But, of course, anything I can do—' He abandoned his study of the weather and was through the door ahead of Edward, and panting at the office doorway in a moment.

The police were still there, clearing up their records at leisure. They received Edward with alert interest. He began abruptly: 'Tell them, will you, that I've got something to say about the case, and I should prefer to say it in the presence of Signora Montesanto, if they wouldn't mind asking her to come.' He owed her that much, at any rate; or perhaps the debt was to himself. At least he kept his story obstinately to himself until the door opened upon the morning vision of Olimpia, fresh as a flower, with a white ivory necklet round her bright bronze throat, and the innocence of spring in her serene and dewy smile.

That was his worst moment. When her eyes lit on him, and brightened, and she exclaimed: 'Why, Edward!' he felt like a murderer himself.

He had almost hoped that she would have got up early and asked for him, and finding him gone, suspected her immunity here, and slipped quietly away to new pastures. He ought to have known that Olimpia never ran away; it looked bad, and would have inconvenienced her, and besides, there is always a better way of dealing with any situation. Several better ways. She had only to pass her slender brown hand over the facts, and the appropriate arrangement would come to her fingers naturally.

'You sent for me?' she said, composing herself serenely in the chair they offered her. She looked at Edward again, and more softly, and knew what was happening; and when he raised his head and looked miserably into her eyes she gave him a sweet, tantalising smile. Good God, what chance did he have, when she even began by teasing him?

She wasn't angry or alarmed. She didn't feel guilty at all. She had only broken other people's rules, not her own, and to wind her way out of a contretemps of this kind was normal exercise for her. She might even repay him good for evil by turning the whole thing into a silly misunderstanding, and getting him out of it gracefully, into the bargain. If she did, he'd never be able to bear the sight of himself again.

Forcing himself to face her, he told his story, pausing to give the amazed Professor time to translate. With all those unbelieving eyes upon him, and Olimpia wide-eyed in silent horror, it was the hardest thing he'd ever had to do in his life, but he went through with it; and when the little black kid strap was on the table in front of the police, he turned his head, and looked despairingly at Olimpia again. 'I'm sorry! I couldn't do anything else.'

'But I don't understand. Of course that's mine, it's off

one of my gloves. I lost it two days ago, after we came back to lunch. If you had it, why didn't you give it to me?' Her lips were quivering with hurt and bewilderment, but her eyes laughed at him gently. 'I'm sorry if you didn't think I was appreciative enough after all your kindness to me – but I didn't think you'd try to make trouble like this – I didn't think you wanted to hurt me.'

The policeman questioned her in rapid Italian, and she answered as promptly and directly. The Professor, wild-eyed with excitement, translated breathlessly: 'She says she told the whole truth before; she doesn't want to change anything. She lost the strap, and she hasn't seen it since. She says Tonino must have picked it up somewhere, and put it in his pocket until he could give it to her. She – my dear chap, she hasn't said it – but they seem to have the impression that, for private reasons, you've – well, developed a grudge against her. Last night, apparently, she thinks you – rather expected more of her than she felt like giving.'

He had known how it would be!

No one could manipulate truth as expertly as she did, with such appropriate silences, such wounded reluctance to wound. She had an answer for everything; and, of course, what could be more probable than that her husband, observing something of his wife's shed along the road or in the hall, should pocket it until he could give it back to her? His one bit of evidence, and she blew it away delicately, like a bit of thistledown! Not a word too much, no counter-accusations against her accuser. She could not believe that Signor Stanier was insincere or malicious, it could only be that he was terribly mistaken. No, it was the police who suspected him of malice. Here they came, the long measuring looks he had expected, the crisp, polite questions, so devilishly hard to answer.

'If you found the strap on the scene of the murder, why did you not bring it to us at once?'

'Why did you leave the house this morning, and then come back to bring this charge?'

'Do you not agree that your attitude yesterday indicated rather more than an ordinary interest in Signora Montesanto?'

He discovered, in five horrible minutes, how like a clumsy lie the truth can sound, even in one's own ears. And there was always Olimpia, reproachful but gentle, holding him in the fixed and shining regard of her great eyes; and behind their bewilderment and hurt he caught the irresistible flash of amusement, and worse, of half-affectionate indulgence.

'Silly child,' she said to him clearly, without a word, 'to think you could ever drive me into a corner. Now see how much trouble and suspicion you've brought on yourself. And I could make it much worse for you, if I chose.'

She still liked him, there was no resentment in her at all. She would only scratch if he persisted, and then without malice. Her eyes reminded him of the previous night, of her mouth surrendered to him without reserve, of the stars drowned in her eyes.

'But there is no evidence to suggest that Signora Montesanto had more than a passing acquaintance with Leoni – none that she ever saw him alone.'

'I did not – ever. I have only spoken to him among other people, in the dining room or the hall—'

It was at that moment that the door opened quietly, and Giulia came in.

She had been crying again, though there was little to show it except the brightness of her eyes, and the slight unsteadiness of her lips. She gave one intense glance round at them all, sitting there tensed and wary in their chairs, and then she advanced towards the table, extending a slip of paper in her hand. Halfway across the room she wavered, and presented it instead to Professor Lacey. 'Please – read it first in English. It is best your friend should hear this.'

Charming as she was, it had never occurred to Edward until then how much delight and satisfaction there could be in looking at Giulia. A fine little woman – straight! She called a *bagascia* a *bagascia*, and to her face, too, not behind her back. A man would be safe with Giulia. Paolo had been safe with her, if only he'd had the sense to appreciate his luck.

'I find it,' said Giulia, her large eyes resting gently upon Edward's face, 'in my husband's card-case, in the coat he wears the last morning he lives. At lunch he changes his clothes. Now I am packing his things, and I find this.' She looked at Olimpia, who had drawn herself back into her chair, and was as still as stone, her eyes flaring greenly in her taut golden face.

'Paolo is not a good husband,' said Giulia simply, 'and it is not easy to live with him. A long time now I am not in love with him, but I love him like a troublesome child, and I do not let my child be killed.'

Professor Lacey read, translating reverently in the midst of a deep and foreboding hush:

> Very well, then, at six, but be a little sensible about it. Wait for me well down the slope, and out of sight of the path. If I can get rid of Tonino, I will be earlier, but you know what he is. Be sure no one follows, or knows where you are going, and take care to burn this. You are a fool, but nice. Olimpia.

Olimpia's eyes were lowered, but her face was serene again. She had begun to reassemble her powers already. By the time she looked up she would be ready with her parry, and it would be tireless and ingenious, and she would take delight in it still. Silly children, to think they could ever drive her into a corner! But, the world was narrowing.

Limp with relief, Edward was not thinking of her, and that in itself was remarkable. He was thinking first and foremost of his own self-esteem, which had been so unexpectedly reprieved, but close upon that preoccupation pressed the thought of Giulia. She lifted her fine, dark eyes, and gave him a kind, regretful, partisan look. She did not like her children hurt, and any man in trouble had acquired a sort of kinship with Giulia.

'She is very sure of her power with men, you see,' she said simply. 'But these are the only words Paolo has from her, he cannot bear to burn them. It is perhaps the only thing in the world she can ask of him,' said Giulia very softly, 'that he will not do for her. But this time she asks too much.'

Credits

'Achilles Heel' by Ruth Rendell from the collection *Means of Evil* © Kingsmarkham Enterprises Ltd, 1977, is reprinted with permission from United Agents.

'The Unsolved Puzzle of the Man with No Face' by Dorothy L. Sayers, from *Lord Peter Views the Body*, reprinted by permission of David Higham Ltd.

'The House in Goblin Wood' by Carter Dickson, from *The Third Bullet*, reprinted by permission of David Higham Ltd.

'The Villa Marie Celeste' by Margery Allingham, reprinted by permission of Peters, Fraser & Dunlop (www.petersfraserdunlop.com) on behalf of the Estate of Margery Allingham.

'The Exploding Battleship' by Michael Innes, reprinted by permission of Peters, Fraser & Dunlop (www.petersfraserdunlop.com) on behalf of the Estate of Michael Innes.